The Salt-Stained Book & A Rav

'This is *Swallows and Amazons* for
twist. It really is a very special b⌐
family especially those who have any experience of sailing or who love
adventure and mystery.'

— Louise Weir *LoveReading4Kids*

'It is in short terrific; wonderfully written both tough and charming, a
rare combination […] People ask if *The Salt-Stained Book* is for children
or grown-ups. In a sense it is both. It is one of those singularly English
novels that anyone from 10 to 100 can happily read.'

–Reggie Nadelson *The Lady*

'This adventure story is a gripping read where you really care what
happens to the hero.'

— Jack Parker *The Outlaw*

'*The Salt-Stained Book* is a multi-layered novel that sweeps readers along
on an exciting adventure, but which addresses many far deeper issues.'
— Bridget Carrington *IBBYlink*

'This is a story full of adventure which saves its most satisfying
revelations for the end.'

— Charlie Swinbourne *Action on Hearing Loss Magazine*

'An adventure of the type which you'd despaired of ever finding again
– with an elegant nod to *Swallows and Amazons* and a story which is
bang up to date and completely timeless.'

— Sue Magee *The Bookbag*

'It is an intense, absorbing read featuring iPods, swipe cards, Googling
and Jimmy Choo shoes. Get on board for a very modern adventure.'

— Gideon Spanier *Evening Standard*

'It's pure yachtie goodness.'
— Peter Dowden *Otago Daily Times*, New Zealand

'Both shocking and funny the book is a triumph; allowing a child to engage with a confusing world and feel they are not alone and an adult to reflect upon the world we foist on children… Central Ransome themes such as the banding together of children in the face of the alien adult world, a sense of freedom, excitement, responsibility and fear are all here in *The Salt-Stained Book* but in a contemporary and classless package that will make this book appealing to a wide range of readers.'
— Cally Phillips *indie e-book* review

'The plot has plenty of excellent and unexpected twists. Layering a quirky take on political correctness on top of the age-old battle between good and bad gives these first two volumes an unexpected richness.'
— Rosie Boycott *The Oldie*

'With Donny and Anna's grit and determination and some unlikely new allies [...]wrapped up in ingenious plotting, suspense-filled writing and a rare warmth towards its characters, it delivers its rewards."
— Peter Willis *The Marine Quarterly*

'Duffers will hate it' — Amanda Craig *The Times*

'I loved it' — Griff Rhys Jones

'The characters feel very real and the story gets more and more exciting. I can't wait for the final resolution in Volume Three.'
— Jan Needle *Watercraft*

Ghosting Home

Ghost, ghosting (v): sailing quietly and gently in light airs
(source: Sea Talk Nautical Dictionary)

This book is dedicated to my mother, June Jones, who was born in the same year as Great Aunt Ellen.

This photograph was taken by my late father, George Jones, on passage from Flushing in Barnacle Goose, a yacht that was borrowed the following year by Arthur and Evgenia Ransome for their final East Coast holiday.

I also dedicate this book to my brother Ned and my niece Ruth who come adventuring with me in Peter Duck.

Ghosting Home

Julia Jones

VOLUME THREE
OF THE *Strong Winds* TRILOGY

Illustrated by Claudia Myatt

GOLDEN DUCK

First published in 2012 by Golden Duck (UK) Ltd.,
Sokens,
Green Street,
Pleshey, near Chelmsford,
Essex.
CM3 1HT
www.golden-duck.co.uk

ISBN 978-1-899262-06-9

All illustrations © Claudia Myatt 2012
www.claudiamyatt.co.uk

Design by Megan Trudell
www.emdash.me.uk

e-book conversion by Matti Gardner
matti@grammaticus.co.uk

Printed and bound in the UK
by the MPG Books Group Bodmin and King's Lynn.

Contents

People you may have met already…

From *The Salt-Stained Book*

Greg and Ned Palmer	two brothers who have died during WWII.
Donny Walker	christened John by his Granny, nicknamed Sinbad by his great-aunt.
Skye Walker	Donny's mother, nicknamed Nimblefingers.
Edith Walker	(formerly Palmer) Donny's assumed Granny, aka Old Nokomis.
Ellen Walker	(formerly Palmer) Donny's great-aunt, aka Gold Dragon or Polly Lee.
Inspector Jake Flint	the fat policeman. Not a nice person.
Denise 'Toxic' Tune	supposed to do Welfare, actually it's Mal-fare. She makes bad worse.
Rev Wendy	vicar of six parishes, foster-carer.
Gerald	Rev Wendy's husband, foster-carer.
Anna Livesey	being looked after by Wendy and Gerald at Erewhon Parva vicarage. In year 9 at Gallister High School.
Luke and Liam Whiting	Anna's stepbrothers, being looked after by Wendy and Gerald at Erewhon Parva vicarage.
Vicky Whiting	child of Anna's mother and Luke and Liam's father, being looked after by Wendy and Gerald.
Mr McMullen	Design Technology teacher at Gallister High School and Donny's form tutor
Joshua, June, Xanthe and Maggi Ribiero	a neurosurgeon, a magistrate and their two daughters. Both at Gallister High School.
Sandra	a social worker.
Mrs Everson	lives in Swallow's End, a cottage down river from Pin Mill.
Mrs Everson's daughter	owns a rowing dinghy called the *Margery*.

From *A Ravelled Flag*

All the characters from *The Salt-Stained Book* plus:

The Tiger	a mysterious and violent character, frequently disguised.
Creepy Tony	a Social Services line-manager.
Hawkins	a canary.
Ai Qin	owner of a Chinese restaurant in Lowestoft, the Floating Lotus.
Hoi Fung	chef at the Floating Lotus.
Eirene Walker	(formerly Palmer) Skye's mother, aka beautiful Wenonah. Sister of Edith and Ellen, Greg and Ned.
Henry Wadsworth	an Ojibwa *sachem* (leader), aka Mudjekewis. Served with Canadian forces in World War II, married to Eirene, father of Skye.
Seraphina Spinks	deputy head teacher at Gallister High School.
A Chinese Cleaner	
Professor Callum Reif	aka Oboe. Distinguished wartime scientist and inventor. Anna's great-uncle. Childhood friends with the Palmer family. Could have loved Ellen.
Theodora Thorrington	Cal Reif's sister. A successful novelist. Died rich.
Bill Whiting	father of Luke, Liam and Vicky. Currently in prison.
Edward	a lawyer from Cambridge.
Ben Gunn	a crazy black terrier.
Lottie Livesey	Anna and Vicky's mother.

Boats you may have met already…

Lively Lady
Mirror dinghy loaned to Donny by
the Ribiero family.

The shark-boat
Inspector Flint's expensive
power-boat. As much a bully as he is.

Margery
Sturdily built wooden rowing dinghy
owned by Mrs Everson's daughter.

The 'Hispaniola'
Not her real name. Inhabited by the Tiger.

Snow Goose
Classic 1920s yawl belonging to the Ribiero
family. Described by Joshua Ribiero as
'designed by the hand of God'.

Spray and *Kingfisher*
Two laser dinghies belonging to
Xanthe and Maggi Ribiero and named
after yachts sailed round the world by
Joshua Slocum and Ellen MacArthur.

The *Houdalinqua*
Sea-going canoe built by Henry Wadsworth,
Donny's unknown grandfather. Her name
means rushing water.

Strong Winds
Built for Gold Dragon in Bias Bay,
China.

Vexilla
A 16' day boat bought by Great Aunt Ellen.
Her name means flag or standard.

My father left when I was a baby. He went to the city to work for us and my mother stayed to care for me and work with my grandparents in the fields. We are rural people; we have no rights in cities. It is the classification system, the hukou.

When I was born my father wanted the best for me. I am the only child. If he went away and worked in the new factories and lived in one room and saved all that he earned, then there would be better food for all of us and extra lessons for me. English lessons. Then one day I could take the gao-kao and go to university, if I passed. Then my hukou would change and all my family would have a better life.

My father died when I was three years old. My grandfather and my mother went to the city to find out what had happened but no-one was able to explain. He was just another rural worker. He had been strong and healthy when he left this village but he had collapsed. A heart attack, they thought. He didn't have rights to a pension so they didn't give my mother anything, except his ashes to bring home. The factory owner offered my mother a job but she said no. She would stay in the village and help my grandparents and when I was older I would help them too. It had been a mistake to try to change our lives, she thought then.

There were no men in our village when I was growing up. There were the old, the young and the women. That's how it got its nickname – the Village of Living Widows.

Then the women began to go.

Families are very important in China. My mother was unhappy that she could not do more for my grandparents and for me. She worked so hard but farming was changing. My mother and my grandfather began to think that my father had been right. If there was a chance for me to make a good life in this new world she would have to go away. She would earn more and it would help us all.

She went when I was seven. But she didn't go to the city, she went across the sea to England, where the ghosts, the gweilao, live. My grandfather gave her all his savings and they borrowed the rest from a moneylender. Then they paid a she-tou, a snakehead, for her journey. It was a long way and very expensive but the she-tou said she would do well in England. Other women had gone. As soon as they'd paid the travel debt they were sending money home to their families. He told her that she'd made a good decision.

It was early in the morning when she left. My grandmother marinated eggs in tea for her to eat on the journey. She packed some rice balls too and small sweet biscuits. No-one said much when she'd gone. My grandparents went to work as usual and I went to school. I promised I would study hard to be ready for our new good life.

I am fourteen now. My mother doesn't ring us any more. I know that she's still in England but she says that phoning will put us at risk. She has had to borrow more money. There is a new gong-tou, a gang-master. I think she's frightened.

My grandfather is dead and my grandmother will live with her cousin. I have made up my mind. I am leaving the Village of Living Widows and I am going to find my mother in the Country of the Ghosts.

CHAPTER ONE

Homework

River Stour, Suffolk, Friday 13 April 2007

"Your homework this week …is to draw your dad." The art teacher at Gallister High School looked round encouragingly at her Year 9 group. "Try and catch him when he's quite relaxed, maybe watching TV or something. You'll need a selection of your softer pencils or you could even use charcoal. Men's faces can display a fascinating range of textures. Sweaty if he's been working out or jogging. Stubbly at the end of the day or maybe bags under his eyes from a heavy night."

She paused. Perhaps she noticed how many of the class had shoved their planners back into their bags unopened.

"Oh," she said. "Maybe not everyone's dad is there for them right now. Step-dads are fine, uncles, granddads, older brothers. Everyone's got someone, surely?"

People stood up, put their folders away in the wide, flat drawers, pushed their chairs under the high benches or left them as they were. They shrugged their bags onto their shoulders and turned to leave. She knew she'd made a mistake.

"Look," she tried again, "If you're really stuck, find me and we'll talk it through. I might rent out one of my colleagues – the department could use some extra funding!"

The bell had gone. They ignored her and left.

"And if anyone doesn't hand it in on time – anyone

at all – I'm setting detentions!" she screeched.

Donny Walker was out of his seat and heading for the door with the rest. Donny liked art. He'd put it on his list for GCSE options. But this was one homework he wouldn't be doing. Stuff detentions.

"Everyone's got someone, sure-ly?" That's what the teacher had said. Tum-ti, tum-ti tum tum, ta ta. Yup, he was a lucky one. He had his family and he had his friends. It was just that none of them happened to be male.

Donny had to work to a Care Plan. It said he must never miss a day of school, must never be late, must always hand his homework in on time and must achieve 'challenging' academic targets. Or he risked being taken away from his home.

All the same, as of today, stuff detentions!

This was Friday afternoon. The art department was on the top floor of one of the school's collection of greyish flat-roofed blocks and, as Donny started down the first of the concrete stairways, he was soon caught up in a stream of chattering, barging students heading out for the weekend.

Donny's home was *Strong Winds*, a Chinese junk anchored on the Suffolk side of the River Stour. The River Stour was completely beautiful but it did present problems for a boy who absolutely had to arrive for registration at the same time as everyone else – when a west or south-westerly gale was ripping down it, for instance, or when the tide was out, emptying the creeks and leaving flat gleaming expanses of soft mud on either side.

There was no way Donny could explain the school to the river or the river to the school. So he kept an alternative timetable – the one with tide times and weather conditions – running on auto in his head and sorted his own complex arrangements for fitting it to school time.

If he hadn't got so irritated with that art teacher he wouldn't be rushing now. The tide had been kind to him that morning. It had been a nine am high water so he and *Lively Lady* had come flooding into Gallister Creek at eight with plenty of depth and plenty of time to step ashore, collect his bike, and arrive clean and correct with the rest of his tutor group.

Getting home wasn't going to be so easy. A three pm low water would by now have emptied the twisting channel. Donny could either hang around for a couple of hours until the water returned or he could push the dinghy across the metres of mud that separated him from his floating home, sticking and squelching. He'd get yelled at by Gold Dragon if he brought any of the gluey gunk onto her immaculately clean ship. Maybe he'd alter course and head for the DT block where his tutor, Mr McMullen, would be ending the week in a more leisurely style.

Mr Mac had a snowy beard and beetling white eyebrows. No shortage of texture, Donny thought. Okay, so he wasn't a relation, or exactly a friend but … he was his tutor, the one adult in this school that Donny trusted. He wouldn't use charcoal; maybe crayon on a tinted paper? He could do a sketch in a DT open department evening. Especially when afternoon tides were getting later …

"Donald!"

They'd reached the ground floor. Donny took no notice. He put his head down and got ready for the final crush as the students surged through the exit doors to freedom.

"Donald! Donald Walker, over here please!"

Donny cursed. He knew that voice. Ms Spinks, one of the school deputy heads, could never be bothered to get his name right. His given name was John, not Donald. It was to do with his great-uncle Gregory who'd wanted to be a character from *Swallows and Amazons*. Donny had never known either of his great-uncles. They'd died in the war. He'd read some of the books though. He had one in his backpack now, *We Didn't Mean to Go To Sea*. He thought it was probably his favourite.

"Donald! Oh, all right, Donny then, Donny Walker. I can see you perfectly well and you're to come here at once. Or it's detention on Monday. And a letter home."

"Ai'm afraid that doesn't hold quaite the terrors that it ought," cooed a sugar-substitute voice that bought shame on little white pills. "Literacy isn't a strong feature of John's family background, is it, de-ah?"

Denise 'Toxic' Tune, the person Donny hated most in the entire world (except for her colleague, the fat policeman, Inspector Jake Flint) was grinning with her tombstone teeth and dripping pink gums. She never missed a chance to have a go at his family, usually at his mother, Skye.

Donny's mum was deaf. Her mum had had rubella when she was just a few weeks pregnant and the baby had suffered brain damage. The birth had been bad too. Skye couldn't read printed books or speak with her mouth like most people. Instead she spoke with her hands. Donny thought she was poetic but other people didn't see it.

"Severe Learning Difficulties on the mother's saide and the

Capacity Challenges of Extreme Old Age," Toxic smiled at Ms Spinks. "Ai've been Monitoring, of course, in my Professional capacity. Assessing, but there's no co-operation. No Recognition of the Need for Change."

So she was getting at Gold Dragon too. Donny's Great Aunt Ellen was over eighty and had a hook instead of one hand but no-one who'd ever seen her at the helm of her beloved *Strong Winds* would dare to speak about Capacity Challenges..

"Donny's bi-lingual at home. He speaks BSL as well as English. Aren't we meant to be celebrating that sort of thing? Donny's tutor says it's all part of diversity. I think it's brilliant."

Anna Livesey had elbowed her way out of the crowd. When Donny had first met Anna, she'd spent most of her time merging into it, risking nothing that might get her noticed. That had all changed now her mum was back.

"And who is this tutor, de-ah?" asked Toxic.

"Mr McMullen. He's one of the senior teachers – the ones people really listen to," said Anna, dimpling innocently at Ms Spinks.

Donny didn't know whether to chuckle or puke. He knew Anna totally despised the deputy head. Not only because she was a slippery liar but because Anna had once heard her say that she didn't think dates were all that important to the study of history!

"It was during citizenship week. We were being helped to re-think the concept of disability. Wasn't it something to do with the Government?"

Ms Spinks was looking uncertain but Toxic's expensively reconstructed smile glared on.

"Mr Mac …whatsit," she said, as if she'd got mouthwash under her tongue. "So you expect he'll be missed when he's gone? How quaint! Adolescent Insecurity, of course. Ai'm always remainding mai team to Be Aware."

"What do you mean, gone?"

Apart from Anna and his Allies – Maggi and Xanthe Ribiero – Mr McMullen was the mainstay of Donny's life at Gallister High.

"Oh de-ah! You didn't know? Well, if your tutor hasn't bothered to mention it, Ai mustn't say another word! Now, if you'll excuse us, Seraphina, Ai need some S & M with this young man."

Toxic shoved Donny into a nearby classroom, smirked at Ms Spinks and blanked Anna. He was doomed.

"Support and Monitoring, Friday April 13th 2007, Denise Tune, Statutory Services, Chief Welfare Executive, Entire Area, with John Walker, age 12, no fixed abode."

Toxic had got her digital recorder out. He knew she could edit whatever he said.

"I'm fourteen, not twelve, and I live on *Strong Winds*." He said it anyway.

"But Auntie's boat isn't a fixed abode is it, de-ah? Which remainds me … time to give the old junk a Health and Safety check. Tell Auntie Ai'll be sending some of mai team round tomorrow. They'll arrive whenever it's convenient. To them. Ai don't suppose Auntie's going anywhere."

"She often does. She and Mum go sailing in *Vexilla*. You can't stop them. Anyway, I thought you were meant to contact

Edward, her lawyer, if you wanted permission to come on board."

Toxic was perched on the edge of a table. Her skirt was hitched up and one leg was sort of waving out in front of her.

She hadn't asked Donny to sit down. He was standing between her and the door with this leg in its shiny flesh-coloured stocking poking towards him like a proboscis.

She gazed at her own ankle, admiringly. Tipped her head on one side. Twiddled her pointed foot and smirked. Her shoe was bizarre. He supposed that meant it was expensive.

"Such a shaime – Auntie's lawyer-friend's away. Fishing. Always does, this taime of ye-ah. Baltic, somewhere. Northern paike. Impossible to contact and no-one else in his office wants to bother. Ai'll remaind mai team to fumigate. The old junk's sure to be mouldy."

Donny began counting to ten. Couldn't get past two. Had to keep his temper somehow. Tried breathing deeply but got a nose-full of her perfume.

"Now," said Toxic, pulling out a clipboard and ticking boxes. "How about you? Saime as usual, Ai expect. Unstable background. Lack of Boundaries. No age-appropriate socio-gendered networking – you haven't made friends with any of the boys here, have you? No, Ai thought not."

Donny planned to go camping with Anna's young brothers this weekend. He wasn't going to tell her that.

"Laife-taime absence of male role model." She completed her form, signed it and made Donny sign too. He'd do anything to get away.

"Oh, good news – er, John." Her long fingers were busy smoothing the creases from her skin-tight outfit as she teetered to her feet. "Inspector Flint's offering a New Initiative for the Fatherless. It's a boxing club. Ai'm sending some of mai special lads along. Ai'll tell him you've saigned up."

"But I haven't," said Donny. He knew her 'special lads'. They'd cornered him in school often enough. He wouldn't mind learning some basic self-defence but he wasn't going to set himself up as fat Flint's punch-bag every week.

"You just did!" smirked the Welfare Office. She pushed the signed paper and digi-corder into her alligator-skin briefcase and shut it with a happy snap. "Our Initiative starts Monday. Your attendance is compulsory. Ai've made it an additional part of your Care Plan – which you've saigned. Unless you've some suitable alternative? No, I thought not. Research agrees: young boys need Father Figures and mai colleague's delaighted to be on your case!"

Then she was gone, leaving her sick smell behind.

Anna would have left by now. She still caught the school bus to Erewhon Parva vicarage, though she wouldn't for much longer. As soon as she'd inherited all that money from her grandmother, she'd announced that she was going to take some scary scholarship exam to a top girls' boarding school. She'd be moving house as well. All her family were going to live in Bawdsey Manor. It looked well posh. And Xanthe was taking her GCSEs and wasn't sure about sixth form. Said she might change schools to do the IB. So there'd only be him and Maggi left.

He didn't have the heart to call in at the DT block to ask Mr Mac if it was true that he was leaving. Toxic had been so sure and Spinksy hadn't denied it. He supposed it wasn't any of his business. Mr Mac had made him feel that he mattered. Obviously he didn't.

Donny crammed his bike into the slot behind the Water Board hut at the top of Gallister Creek. He couldn't go to Flint's Boxing for the Fatherless. He just couldn't. And Edward was going to be away for three weeks! They must have known that. Three weeks of abuse by the fat policeman and his goons. Starting on Monday. Only three days away. Would Luke and Liam have to go? Their dad was in gaol. Did he still count?

No water in the creek yet.

Donny didn't usually find it too much of a hardship to wait for the tide. There was a big old curlew who stalked the mud getting irritable and a pair of oystercatchers who didn't even bother flying up when the Mirror dinghy *Lively Lady* grounded near their marshy nest. They were domestic and devoted and funny. Donny plonked himself on a hump of salting. He wondered whether to chuck a stone at them.

Everyone had to have a Father Figure, did they? Well, where was his? He knew as much about his dad as if he'd been fertilised by a fish. One final underwater spasm in the sun-warmed shallows and there was his dad, swimming away. A bit flushed around the gills, probably.

Donny tugged on his mud-shoes and began shoving *Lively Lady* an unnecessarily long way back towards the river, getting grubbier and crosser as he went. It was time his mother answered some questions. She was good at telling him stories but now he wanted facts.

Contact details would be better.

Then he'd put in some practice at Flint's club, go find his dad … and punch him.

CHAPTER TWO

A New Year's Luck

Rural Fujian, China, February 2007

In the last days of the old year Min's grandmother cleaned the house more thoroughly than ever before. It didn't matter that neither of them would be living there more than a few weeks longer; she was determined that every last mite of bad luck was going to be chased out of the small rooms where they had once been a family. She opened the front door and all the windows and mopped and swept and shook the cloths again and again as invisible traces of misfortune lifted away on the breeze.

"If I don't do it now," she said, "who knows what might cling to the shoes that you will wear to make your journey. You should have new shoes, new clothes – everything fresh for the Year of the Pig."

"We can't afford new clothes. My shoes are fine. You've washed everything."

"If the Lion Dance comes through our house, the evil spirits will certainly leave."

"We'd have to pay the dancers …"

"When all the families are home, someone will help us. Your cousin, Chen Kai, is coming from Xiamen. He will know what to do."

Then she hurried off to fuss over her New Year cake.

Min wondered whether he should use this time to study. The village would soon be overflowing as the workers came home from the cities. It didn't matter that he and his grandmother had no-one special anymore. People would drop in. They might stay even though the house was small and old and hadn't got a television. There would be long games of Mah-Jong. He would probably have to share his bed with people whose houses were full.

Some of his friends would be back. The ones who'd left school already and gone to work in the factories. They'd be showing off their mobile phones and new clothes, telling him that there was no point staying any longer. He should come with them after the holiday and they'd find him work. The village was home but it was boring. The cities were where the future was.

He wouldn't tell them what he was planning to do.

He hadn't told the school that he was leaving. When he didn't come back they'd think it was because of the fees. It was, of course, but not the way they thought. If education wasn't so expensive, if it didn't matter so much, his mother wouldn't have gone away. And he wouldn't have to leave to go and find her.

It was an ordinary rural middle school. Students were always dropping out because they had to go to work. Their families needed the money. He was one of the best students, mainly because he tried so hard. His grandmother kept all the certificates he had won. She had been planning to show them to his mother when she came home.

It felt odd to have free time and not be studying.

"We should have fresh red paint around the doorway." She'd hurried in again. "And some poems for decoration. All our favourites. Perhaps Xiao Ling will surprise us with a phone call and you can tell her which ones you chose."

She had always been like this. Always busy and full of hope. Always assuming that he was still the trusting child he'd been when his mother went away.

Min's grandmother gave two red envelopes this year: one to him and the other to his cousin, Chen Kai. Both of them were full of money, all in crisp new notes. He didn't think she'd kept anything for herself. She packed tea-marinated eggs and rice balls for their journey – just as she had done for his mother – and gave them both a big bag of mandarin oranges and the last slices of the niangao, her special New Year cake.

On the evening of the last night he went to fetch some more coal but there wasn't any left. Just a few chippings and the dust. She said it didn't matter as she would be moving to her cousin soon. "Please ask Xaio Ling to call me when you have arrived. I am not afraid of the money-lender. I have nothing more to lose. You are a good boy and I know you are going to have a good life in your new country. This New Year's luck will travel with you."

"The village will always be my home, Grandmother."

"And I will always be here. With your father and your grandfather. Always."

They had climbed the mountain together on the eve of the New Year. Carried offerings to the family graves in a small clearing surrounded by trees and bushes. Min knew what she meant.

"Don't worry," he said. "I'm sure to find my mother soon. I can help her pay off anything that is left and then we'll come back. Perhaps we'll bring you a big coat to keep you warm next winter."

"I have had good fortune in my life," she told him. "I have never made long journeys."

CHAPTER THREE

Muddy Trousers

River Stour, Suffolk, Friday 13 April 2007

Skye was weaving. Donny had made her a wooden frame for Christmas and she always had some piece of work under construction. Her latest project was shredding his outgrown clothes and ravelling them up again into an extra bed cover.

"Doh," she said with a glowing smile. Then she signed to ask him how his trousers had got so wet?

Great Aunt Ellen was there too, not at all pleased at the dirt he was bringing in.

"To the scuppers with you, Sinbad. At the double. Tea'll be ready when you're sluiced down."

She stood up as she spoke. She wasn't a tall woman. Donny backed away and went up on deck to begin cleaning himself. Whatever your state of emotional meltdown you didn't argue with Gold Dragon when you'd tramped mud down her companionway.

Skye followed him. She brought a clean pair of jeans and a bucket. There was a thin rope tied to the bucket's handle. She swung it confidently over the junk's high side then let it trail in the river until it filled with saltwater. She could get the worst of the dirt off that way before she or her aunt sailed the week's washing down to the marina laundrette.

"Doh?"

"I have to draw my father for Art homework," he signed, grumpily. "So I need to know who he is. And don't tell me he's Kwasind, the North Wind, or anyone like that because my drawing skills aren't up to it. I'm old enough now. I want facts, not stories."

The lanyard dropped from her hand and Donny had to grab a boat hook to retrieve the bucket before it filled completely and sunk.

"Father?" she signed.

He had to put the bucket down and disengage the boat hook before he could sign back. It wasn't like he'd been a virgin birth for god's sake. Maybe she'd been drunk.

"My other half. The fifty percent of me that I don't have a name for. The person I possibly even resemble? Because – love you, Mum – but nobody would guess that I was your child from looking at us, would they?"

She had dark hair and a coppery skin: he was sandy-haired, grey-eyed, pale. She was big-built: he was wiry.

How could he have said that? He hadn't even known that it was what he thought. He didn't think it. Couldn't. His anger was completely gone, replaced by tears that hurt him to cry. He was in Skye's arms, clinging to her.

"Mum," he wanted to say, "I didn't mean it. I'm so sorry."

But he couldn't. He couldn't use his hands to sign because he was holding his mother's solid, utterly familiar and beloved body as if he were a drowning person.

Skye hugged him back. Then, very carefully, still holding him close, she sat them both down on the cabin roof. She pulled her head back, breathed deeply.

"Er-mann," she articulated, as if from way down buried and dark. "Er-mann."

A man? Her man?

That was the one bit he could probably have figured out for himself! Poor Mum. She hadn't been to normal school. Maybe she'd never had Sex Ed? Maybe Granny Edith hadn't got round to telling her the facts … and someone had like … well … forced her? He wished again that he hadn't asked.

His mum existed every day like a flightless eagle on a ledge. Poised above chasms of panic and darkness. She was different. She was an artist. She loved him. He loved her. He couldn't bear to think …

" 'S okay, mum. We're okay. Who needs dads? I'll find someone else for homework."

He wouldn't tell her about Flint's Initiative for the Fatherless. That was Monday: this was Friday evening.

Skye had stopped embracing him; stopped trying to speak words. Instead she was signing directly into his muddy hand – in the complicated private way that they'd developed when he was very small.

"His name was Hermann. But I lost him. Old Nokomis never saw … she didn't know. And then it was too late."

"Huh?"

He pulled back so he could stare as well as sign. This wasn't one of her stories.

"Hermann?" he repeated. "My father's name is Hermann. A real name. Hermann who? Where did you meet him? Why didn't he stay?"

Facts, questions, real names.

"I lost him," she repeated. "Then it was too late."

There was desolation in the shape of her brown hands, every bit as eloquent as the quiver of a speaking voice.

"We travelled home with you inside. Smallest of the sprouting seeds. I didn't know. But then we loved you, Doh. How we loved you! And Hermann … would have loved you."

"Except he didn't the chance because he didn't know I'd been conceived."

So, that was it. He was an unplanned souvenir from a holiday romance. But the way she lingered over his father's name sounded … as if she'd really liked him.

He couldn't remember Skye and Granny having holidays. Not the sort where you met people. They used to go off in the camper van and park by woods and look at stately homes and things. Walk up hills. If they'd gone back … to wherever it was … couldn't there maybe have been a chance that they'd have met the guy again?

Not 'the guy'. This was – Hermann – his father!

"They tried to take you, Doh. As soon as you were fluttering, the invaders came. They said I couldn't be your mother. Old Nokomis was your champion. All her fight and all her money. Then there was nothing left but us, still together."

Skye didn't do lying. Donny remembered when he'd overheard Rev. Wendy telling Gerald what a pain Granny Edith had been, spending everything she had on lawyers, refusing to let Leeds SS take him as a baby. No wonder there'd been no wild goose chases trying to re-trace the holiday, re-discover Hermann, tell him …

"We were dancing in long lines. The chain was broken by

shields and truncheons. Angry men with boots and helmets. Then Hermann was gone."

"Where were you?"

"We were in the Northlands. With the people who were free. Hermann was … free."

Her hands were telling their own story. She had loved this unknown bloke. Losing him had been one more tragedy in her unlucky life.

"You're tired, Mum. So'm I. But thanks for letting me know. About my dad. About … Hermann." He kept trying out the name. "I bet he was a really great guy!"

"Hermann was a sailor. Like you, Doh."

Skye put her arms round him once more and he hugged her back. A sailor. That was good.

Gold Dragon had set out the big brown teapot and a pile of bread and jam. The mud on Donny's trousers had dried now – which was lucky as he and Skye had both forgotten what it was that they'd gone up on deck to do.

"I had a problem with my homework. I needed to ask Mum."

This sounded a bit inadequate.

"To do with not having a dad. I needed one for Art."

His great-aunt laughed like a barking seal. "That must be the reason why I've never learned to draw! My father was away for years. You were if you were in the Navy then. And there was boarding school. Did I ever tell you about the only week we were all going to take a holiday together – both parents and all five children? He got recalled by the Admiralty before we'd even begun storing the ship."

"So what happened?"

"Oh, he and Mother marooned the lot of us and sailed off into the sunset while we stood waving on a desolate shore."

Donny felt better now.

"Is it still okay if I go to the vicarage tomorrow? Anna gave Luke and Liam a tent for Luke's birthday but they're too scared to sleep out in it. I thought I could maybe help them pitch it in the garden and we could have a sleepover."

"Borrow *Vexilla* if you're going adventuring. The forecast's north-easterly, fresh to moderate. You'll have a stiff beat most of the way, but if you can bear to stay skulking in your bunk a bit later than usual, you'll have the tide with you as far as Shotley."

"You don't mind if I'm away for a night? How about you, Mum?"

Skye looked uncertain but Great Aunt Ellen was full of jollity. She fetched a chart from the locker and spread it in front of her niece, tapping it significantly. She still couldn't sign – the fact that her left hand was a hook made this almost impossible – but living and sailing together had brought the two of them onto the same wavelength.

Skye nodded. Donny had the impression that this was something they'd been planning for a while. He felt left out.

"Twenty-four hours shore leave for you, Sinbad – thirty-six if you want it. Nimblefingers and I are going to take this old lady for a turn around the bay. Batteries need recharging."

Skye's dark plaits swung forward as she leant over the chart, her look of uncertainty replaced by a gleam of interest. Gold Dragon was enthusiastic.

"There's a spot of reconnaissance we've been waiting to do and if you're not with us the SS bureau-rats won't have any reason to complain. I'll get the dinghy up in davits before we turn in."

"Where're you going?"

"The Desolate Shores," she replied, tucking the chart away. "Now cut along and scrub those ducks of yours and I'll give you the lat and long after supper."

She was looking at his trousers again. These were school trousers. They'd got to be clean by Monday morning and no-one wanted to waste this weekend taking trips to the laundrette.

"Aye, aye sir!" he said, saluting smartly.

"Back of the hand, Sinbad, back of the hand. You're not in the Army here. We don't want to see your tarry palm."

The blackness on his hands wasn't tar, of course. It was more black mud, cracking across his lifeline between fingers and thumb where his hand had been curled round the mug of tea. Donny retreated hastily.

CHAPTER FOUR

Scouting

River Orwell, Suffolk, Saturday 14 April 2007

It wasn't warm next day when Donny set out to sail *Vexilla* down the River Stour and up the Orwell to Pin Mill. The sun was out, making the waves jump and glitter, but the wind had the biting freshness that he'd come to associate with a north-easterly. The water would be cold and he'd have to wade a bit if he wanted to leave *Vexilla* far down the Hard for later.

He'd squeezed into an old wetsuit of Xanthe's so he could get himself and all his stuff ashore without getting totally frozen. *Vexilla* was an open boat, more than five metres long. She was shallow draught but heavy. You couldn't push her up and down the mud as easily as *Lively Lady*. Xanthe and Maggi were away with their parents, racing.

He wondered where the boys would like to go. Anna had bought an outboard motor so they didn't risk being late for vicarage meals. Gerald and Wendy hadn't really caught on to the idea of alternative wind-and-tide timetables.

He could hear *Strong Winds*' diesel engine beginning its powerful tgg-tgg-tggg behind him. His mum and Gold Dragon would be winching up the first of her two anchors. It wouldn't be long before they passed him, heading down the river, then out to sea. He guessed they'd motor this first stretch dead into the wind. It wasn't the junk's favourite point of sailing and his great-aunt was edgy this morning, eager to press on.

She and Skye were planning to spend the next two complete tides somewhere near the camping place that she remembered from her childhood, the place her parents had marooned them. How much would it have changed? The map looked much the same – a half dozen marshy islands surrounded by saltings, a maze of drying creeks and a handful of disused quays and farm landings only accessible at high water.

She'd probably take a long board out to sea first, get some air into her lungs. He knew that she found their river life stifling, longed for blue water and nights far away from the sight or smell of the land. She was still Polly Lee at heart, single-handed, round-the-world sailor.

All the same, he was glad his mum was with her. Great Aunt Ellen was skilful and intrepid but he had noticed her getting a bit tired in the last couple of months – a bit pale beneath the wrinkles. *Strong Winds* was getting older too and she hadn't been built for a North Sea winter. Her woods swelled or contracted as the weather varied: pulleys or hatches stuck and needed a good biff to free them. Skye was quick with her hands and she was strong too.

He realised he'd completely forgotten to tell his great-aunt about Toxic's threat to send out a fumigation team. They'd have a wasted journey. Good.

Donny waved as *Strong Winds* came past. For a moment, ridiculously, he wanted to cheer.

The junk looked stately and splendid in the morning sun. Her black silk dragon pennant streamed behind her; touches of colour and ornamental gold leaf glistened against her white upper works and black hull. Even without her sails up, she was an exotic and somehow gallant sight as she drew away into the distance down the slate-blue English river.

Vexilla was sailing close-hauled, her high bow slicing keenly through the waves. She'd been a dull white plastic when they'd first discovered her, half hidden in the nettles on the forgotten fringes of a boat-builder's yard. Luke and Skye had persuaded each other to paint her navy and crimson, with hawk's eyes staring on either side of her prow.

Time to bear away. There was the red-and-white three-masted schooner moored close to Bloody Point, at the end of the Shotley Peninsula. At first he'd thought she was as exciting as a vessel from a classic story – he imagined her as the *Hispaniola* from *Treasure Island*. Now he knew he'd got the wrong book.

His skin between his shoulder-blades prickled with wariness and he felt a bit chilly under his armpits. This *Hispaniola* wasn't a sailing ship at all. Gold Dragon had identified her as a former Royal Navy gunboat but she couldn't remember what she'd been called then. Or she said she couldn't. He didn't know whether it mattered.

Sometimes he worried that it might.

The identification couldn't be wrong. Ellen had been the youngest of five children in a naval family and had learned to tell her frigates from her freighters almost before she'd learned to talk. When her older brothers and sisters had been away at boarding school or on long summer holidays with their friends, Ellen and her mother had snatched moments with their father in Shotley and Dartmouth, Malta and Singapore.

Much later she had chosen to become an Australian citizen and later still she'd settled in Shanghai but her true home, if she had one, other than *Strong Winds*, was somewhere hidden amongst the remote islands of the South China Sea. Somewhere at the top end of the Java Strait.

If Gold Dragon said she'd seen the *Hispaniola* in those waters it was beyond dispute. Donny had the oddest feeling that there was something more. More than just seeing. But no amount of clever conversational manoeuvring had brought him any closer to finding out. Gold Dragon either couldn't remember or didn't want to.

And now the mystery ship was here. Perfectly positioned to keep watch on the comings and goings of two rivers, two major ports and the Harwich harbour entrance. She looked as lifeless as she always did. That was because all her lights and portholes had been painted over, her doors were padlocked and her deck was daubed with notices warning people to keep away.

Donny hoped that they had. If there was anyone on board today – such as the small and violent man they called the Tiger – they'd have seen *Strong Winds*, turning south, setting her creamy sails and heading gaily out to sea.

No-one was doing anything they shouldn't. He was going to his former foster home: his great-aunt was hoping to rediscover some childhood memories. It was even okay with the Care Plan, probably.

There was no visible movement on the schooner. No tender lay alongside. She flew no flags. Donny kept to the far side of the harbour for as long as he could. He hoped that his mother and great-aunt had slipped past unobserved.

As Donny rounded Shotley Spit and set his course up the River Orwell, he found that he and *Vexilla* had a struggle on their hands. Several times he was tempted to give up, take down his sails and switch on the outboard motor. Each long up-river tack was followed by depressing boards across the current where *Vexilla* was swept sideways almost faster than she could forge ahead.

They plugged on together, he didn't quite know why, until at last they rounded Collimer Point and he had to perch himself high on her gunwale as she heeled over and tore along, water foaming against her bows, the sail almost heavier than he could hold. When Donny had finally completed the business of landing his belongings, anchoring off the end of Pin Mill Hard and wading ashore to tramp up the lane to the vicarage, he felt breathless, satisfied – and ravenous.

Lunch at the vicarage was long cleared and the kitchen wiped to its usual state of hygienic barrenness. Lottie, Vicky and Anna had gone to Ipswich; Rev. Wendy was in her study and Gerald was hunched uncomfortably on the sofa trying to do the crossword.

Luke and Liam were scowling at one another, shoulders hunched, bottom lips stuck out. Donny's heart sank. They couldn't stay safe in the same room when they were like this and they couldn't leave one another alone. He made Gerald a herbal tea while both of the younger boys tried to tell him what the other had done wrong. Then they both got angry all over again and started shoving each other.

Donny took the boys into the kitchen and made hot Ribena, the kind that's seriously bad for your teeth. He dished out biscuits and asked again what had happened – though he could have guessed. Luke had been trying to pitch his new tent on his own when Liam had kicked his football into it. The football had been muddy and the tent had collapsed. There'd been swear words and a fight, then Rev. Wendy had lost her temper and banned them from going outside at all until they could be trusted to behave sensibly.

Donny wished he was back on *Strong Winds*.

"Tell you what," he said, after all his sailing suggestions had been rejected, "we need a bigger challenge than a night in the garden. I'm going to brave Rev. Wendy in her den and see whether she can't fix for us to camp somewhere else. Somewhere not in a garden. She's the vicar of six parishes. She should know."

Rev. Wendy, taken by surprise in the midst of composing a sermon on the Importance of Faith and Saying Yes to God, suggested somewhere immediately.

At the downstream end of the Pin Mill anchorage was a little beach where Donny had sometimes landed in *Lively Lady*. Behind it was a long tussocky field that sloped down to the dyke and the seawall and a plain white cottage called Swallow's End. This was the home of Mrs Everson. She was a small, round lady who wore an olive-green felt beret and had the most extraordinary habit of popping up exactly when you needed her.

Mrs Everson owned the field as well as the cottage. It would be perfect.

Rev. Wendy began to worry. What if it rained? What would

they eat? A fire would be dangerous. Who would look after them?

"We wanted to look after ourselves," said Donny. "That was sort of the point."

Wendy went through to the living room to consult Gerald.

"What is it now?" he grumbled. "I did hope I'd be allowed a little peace this afternoon. It's the *Guardian* Prize Crossword."

"Yes, dear. And I have three sermons to write – well, three versions of the same sermon. What suits Erwarton will never quite do for Harkstead and will certainly cause offence in Shotleygate. Then there's a churchwardens' meeting at Collimer and not enough foliage for the flower arrangers at Freston. The boys want to camp for the night in Mrs Everson's field."

"They'll have to wait until their stepmother comes home, won't they. They're not our responsibility anymore."

Luke gave a gasp and went running upstairs. Wendy hurried back to her sermon but, if Gerald thought that had ended the discussion, he was wrong.

Luke was back, holding out a mobile phone.

"Let's get on and ring 'em. Lottie's got her phone with her so Anna said we could borrow hers. And she showed me how to text."

"Oh really … you'd better use the land-line. If you must. I don't like those things – too many micro-waves."

"Lottie'll be cool. I know she will."

Gerald looked back at his newspaper. Sighed. Then he stood up.

"When you've spoken to your stepmother," he said, walking over to the telephone, "perhaps you could pass me to young

Anna. There's a clue here that I can't quite get …"

"Maybe you oughter try texting. Them micro-waves won't hurt you."

" 'Cos you're too old!" put in Liam. It was rude but sort of friendly.

"I can't text. I don't know how. I only want to speak to her."

The brothers grinned at each other.

"As long as we get to talk to Lottie first."

Lottie said yes at once. Then she asked if she could speak to Rev. Wendy, to thank her for arranging the expedition.

Lottie was clever.

They fetched Wendy from her study again. Watched her change from annoyed to surprised and then rather pleased. After all, it had been her idea.

If Mrs Everson agreed, said Lottie, the boys should collect their gear and set out immediately. There was no need for them to put Gerald and Wendy to any trouble at all – if perhaps they could borrow the wheelbarrow? She'd already bought a single use barbecue which she would take down to the field for their supper and she'd call at the farm shop on her way home from Ipswich and buy enough burgers, sausages and baps for everyone.

"I'll make everyone's supper out of doors – we'll invite Mrs Everson as well. What an inspiration, Wendy! Oh, and Anna and I noticed some spectacular pollinated catkins at the top of the lane so we picked two armfuls and delivered them directly to Freston. They said to thank you very much."

Then Anna came to the phone and Gerald read out the clue.

"OLD SCOUTMASTER'S ILL THEN HEALTHY AFTER OPEN SURGERY (5,6) Second letter's A, last letter's L. Frightfully hard. I don't suppose you've got any ideas? Just thought I'd ask."

"Even you can get this one, Gerald," he heard her say. He could tell she was trying not to laugh. "Think about it … It's so obvious. 'Old Scoutmaster' – that's the definition. Then try some other words for 'ill' – BAD, maybe? And you could have WELL instead of 'healthy' – ?"

Gerald was looking down at the newspaper.

"Then all you've got to do is perform surgery on 'open' – you know, swap the letters about – and then the word 'after' tells you what order the clue goes in. Simple isn't it?"

He was fumbling for his dictionary.

"Hello, Gerald? Come on! You can get it – even you … THINK … whose centenary is it?"

"Pick me, pick me!!" yelled Liam.

"It's SCOUTS!" Luke couldn't wait. "We had an assembly. They've been a hundred years. Sounds wicked."

Slowly Gerald fitted the letters into their squares.

"B-A-D-E-N-P-O-W-E-L-L. Er, thanks Anna."

He put the phone down and returned to his sofa. Anna was too quick sometimes.

Rev. Wendy closed the study door as if she was finished for the day.

"You know I've never have been able to do crosswords, dear. But I do like having them explained. How did you get, um, this one, here, for instance?"

She sat down next to her husband then leaned forward and sort of snuggled up alongside him. Gerald looked at her, blinked a bit and then smiled. He spread the paper over both their knees and put his arm round her. "Well," he said, "Miss Snufflebeam. If I were Wizard Whimstaff …"

This was obviously a private joke. The boys stared; they'd never seen their former foster-carers behaving like this. Gerald brushed a lock of Rev. Wendy's grey-flecked hair away from her lined forehead and pulled her closer.

"Help!" thought Donny, "He's about to kiss her!"

After a single horrified glance, the three boys turned and legged it.

CHAPTER FIVE

Tiger on the Prowl

River Orwell, Sunday 15 April 2007

They woke very early. So early that it wasn't light outside the tent. It wasn't dark either. It was as if both light and dark had gone absent without leave. Night had finished its shift before day was ready to start. It was a strange sort of nothing time.

Donny guessed that it must be about four in the morning. The tide would be flooding again now and it felt as if the wind had changed. He suggested that they should put on their trainers and fleeces and go down to the seawall to take a look.

The tent had only been meant for two people so they'd slept close together. It had been cold too. When each one woke, he'd tried to lie extra still so's not to disturb the others. When they were truly asleep they'd muttered, snored and wriggled.

It had been fun when Lottie and others came for supper. Gerald and Wendy had stayed behind at the vicarage to spend time on their own – but Mrs Everson had come stomping across to supper on two stout metal sticks. She'd cheered Liam loudly when he'd demonstrated the Ronaldo Seven: left foot, right foot, left knee, right knee, left shoulder, right shoulder … HEAD! It was the sequence that he'd been practising earlier when he'd knocked down Luke's tent.

Most times the ball bounced away into the twilit field or scraped past the glowing barbecue but Liam succeeded more than once. Mrs Everson had glared at the first person who suggested he should give up and sit down.

"He's very good," she announced.

Liam stopped kicking for a moment.

"He wants to be best player in the world. He was signed for Man U in 2004 and he's won loads of awards already."

"He was FPA Young Player of the Year," she agreed. "But I didn't mean Cristiano Ronaldo, I meant you. You're very good."

"Do you support Man U? Did you see 'em in the UEFA cup last week? I wasn't allowed but they beat Barca 3-0! They were against Chelsea today. I reckon you could catch the highlights if you stay up."

"I often sit up late. Or wake early. I'm an old trout and I like to know which way the stream is flowing."

Donny glanced across the field as he and the boys crawled out into the pre-dawn greyness. There were no lights in the cottage but that didn't mean there were no eyes open. You could never be sure with Mrs Everson.

It was okay. They weren't doing anything wrong. They'd said that they were planning to get up early.

They kept close together as they crept down the field and found the plank-bridge across the dyke. Then they scrambled straight over the river wall and headed for the patch of beach.

It was lighter here but in odd ways. The contrasts seemed different. There was no colour anywhere but, further up in the anchorage, boats with white hulls stood out with startling clarity while others were no more than deeper shades of charcoal. Rather like a negative.

The younger boys weren't saying much – except for the occasional "Spooky!" or "Wicked!" Donny didn't think they were scared. They were concentrating.

"Do you reckon we're the only ones awake in the world?" Liam breathed.

" 'Course not," Luke whispered back. "There'll be evil spirits creeping home to their tombs and vampires winging it to hang upside-down in the old church tower, their fangs dripping warm with blood."

The moon was still up, shapeless and hazy behind moving clouds. A harder outline in the east showed that the sun was also on its way. When you really listened you could hear the rustle of wind over water and occasional cries from shorebirds. There was an owl hunting somewhere in the Pin Mill woods and there were sudden snatches of daytime song, cheerful trills and chirrups that stopped as abruptly as they'd started.

Then, from downstream, Donny heard a boat engine. It didn't sound like a cargo ship heading up river for Ipswich, but it didn't sound yachty either. There was a growl to it.

He motioned Luke and Liam to crouch down. There was no reason why they shouldn't be there. He knew that. He also knew he didn't want anyone to spot their early-morning silhouettes, dark against the not-dark sky.

"Dirty your faces," he whispered. "Or keep your heads bent. Pale and vertical reflects."

Between the beach and the wall they were camouflaged by scrub and tall grasses that merged indistinguishably in the absence of light. The tide was out and river was far away, held at a distance by the long soft slope of mud.

Nevertheless, when Donny saw which boat it was, slipping stealthily up river in this dead hour between night and day, he crouched lower and motioned the others to do the same. Then he lay completely flat.

No precaution could be too extreme. The *Hispaniola* had left her mooring.

The tips of her three tall masts were only partially visible above the high woods of the opposite shore but the white band of her red-and-white-painted hull was weirdly luminous in the surrounding grey.

She showed no other lights at all: no mast-head steaming light, no low red light to confirm that she was port-side on, and, once she had passed them, there was no white stern light as she followed the curve of the marked channel through the anchorage and disappeared from view. The muffled sound of her engines lingered but the wind was picking up again and had blown it out of hearing before she could even have reached Woolverstone.

This new wind was from the south-west – a 180 degree change. He and *Vexilla* would have another beat on their hands when they tried to return to the Stour.

"The Tiger's on the prowl," he whispered. "When it's properly morning we'll explore up river and track him to his lair.

Anna'll be on for it. Time spent on reconnaissance is seldom wasted, as Gold Dragon always says."

"An' he won't know we've spotted him. Not if he was trying to do a dodge and get past while he thought we weren't looking."

There was a reverberation from those engines – yes, engines, he was sure now that the *Hispaniola* had more than one – that was ruffling up memories that weren't directly his. Great Uncle Greg had been in the Navy and now Donny had heard that muffled, throaty purr, he knew that Great Aunt Ellen had been right. Whatever the *Hispaniola* looked like on the outside, deep down she was still a gunboat. What was her story?

"Let's get a bit more kip. Anna said she'd meet us at the Hard between half eight and nine. Gives us plenty of time to get up again, strike camp and thank Mrs Everson. We might even manage some breakfast."

They'd only been out of bed for maybe half, three quarters of an hour. Already there was colour creeping back across the landscape and the distant birdsong was getting stronger. They stood outside Luke's tent a last few seconds.

Donny was just thinking that this was why people went on about the loveliness of dawn when there was a sudden, terrified squealing.

"No!" said Liam, pointing.

"Drop it!" yelled Luke, running forward.

Two small, prick-eared fox cubs were hurtling towards them. The first cub had a baby rabbit in its mouth and the second one wanted it.

The rabbit was only tiny but it must have been quite a weight for the running cub to carry. And it was making such a noise! You'd never have thought that anything so small could shriek so loudly or continuously.

Not unless you'd grown up with Vicky for your baby sister, as Luke said afterwards.

That was much later, when he was feeling better enough to joke about it.

"Drop it!" he yelled, running at the cubs. "Leave it alone. Drop it right now. I'm telling ya!"

He'd picked up a bit of stick down by the foreshore and he chucked wildly. Amazingly it connected. The leading cub was almost knocked down. It hesitated.

Luke didn't. He was rushing forward, yelling like a maniac. The fox-cub saw him and opened its mouth, dropping the rabbit.

Then the second cub saw its chance, seized the trophy and dashed on towards the woods. The first one chasing after.

The rabbit's screams continued on and on. Then stopped.

Luke was almost in tears as he crawled back into the tent.

"Poor little feller," he kept saying, "poor little feller."

Donny didn't know what to say. The two cubs had been so jaunty, so delighted. He'd admired their energy, their neat small size, the hint of fluffiness that gave away their youth. Luke made him realise that he'd been callous.

Liam reached out a consoling hand.

"Foxes gotta eat, Lukey."

Luke nodded but ignored the hand. He sniffed a bit then got

into his sleeping bag and pulled the top over his head. Donny and Liam looked at one another, shrugged and did the same.

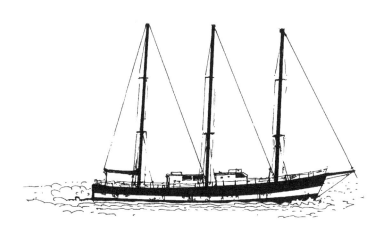

CHAPTER SIX

An Empty Lair

River Orwell, Sunday 15 April 2007

They slept late and woke uncomfortable. Striking camp wasn't fun. In the end they bundled everything up and put it in the wheelbarrow. Pushed it with them to Swallow's End to thank Mrs Everson.

"Um, sorry if we made a bit of a rabbit last night," Donny mumbled. He felt thick-headed. The younger boys were looking at him.

"I meant racket. There was a rabbit, you see … and foxes."

"It screamed," said Luke. He was pale and had grey shadows under his eyes.

"They do," she said. "Why shouldn't they? They've got a place in the food chain but they don't have to like it. I don't expect you'll come again. Goodbye."

She turned and stomped back into her cottage, shutting the door.

The boys didn't want to go through the woods. They took turns shoving the barrow along the foreshore and met Anna who was getting fed up waiting for them at the Hard. They used the public toilets then loaded most things into *Vexilla* and set off up river to Ipswich.

The breeze was fresh and favourable. Anna'd brought generous supplies of food. But they couldn't find the *Hispaniola* anywhere. Began to wonder whether they'd dreamed her passing at that dead hour.

There was a marina on the west bank of the river. They landed scouting parties to run round it in all directions until they met again. She was too big for the New Cut. The most likely place was Ipswich Haven, a wide renovated space entered through lock gates. The Customs and Excise launch, HMRC *Valiant*, was there, festooned with whippy aerials and radar receivers and with what was unmistakably a gun on her foredeck. She was open to the public but the children didn't have any money. They hung back and stared from a distance.

"What's that gun for?" asked Liam.

"Smugglers," said Anna. "You know, people bringing in drugs and stuff. I expect it makes them stop when they're told to. So the excise men can go on board and search for … whatever."

She looked at Donny. The gun was shocking.

Luke and Liam had cheered up a lot.

"Stand and deliver!" they yelled.

"Your money or your life!"

Their Ipswich Haven search was thorough. They even sneaked round the sheds where power cruisers like Flint's shark-boat were built. They couldn't believe the prices on the sales board. No wonder Xanthe had suspected him from the start.

But there was no *Hispaniola*.

"She must be somewhere on the East Side," said Donny. "Cliff Quay. Where the grain ships go."

"And where we're so not allowed," said Anna, checking the No Mooring notices and 24-hour security signs.

"No harm in drifting casually past having a good stare

though, is there?" Donny suggested. "There won't be anything else with masts like hers."

"S'pose not."

Putting the mainsail up was a mistake. The tide had turned and the wind had freshened even further. Drifting was not on *Vexilla*'s agenda. She went plunging down-river, heeling at such an angle that it took all their weight to steady her. They hardly had time to glimpse the leeward bank, let alone scan it for masts.

Luke and Liam had gone into white-knuckle mode, gasping with delight every time a fresh gust threatened to lay her over. They grumbled when Donny turned the day-boat into the wind, took down her mainsail and motored back the way they'd come, painstakingly checking every inch of quayside and even the smallest sluice gate.

"It's getting incredibly late," said Anna. "I've got loads of work and you've got to get all the way back to Gallister Bay."

"I know," said Donny shortly. These semi-derelict warehouses, these underused docks, the security fences and warning signs – prime territory, surely, for the Tiger?

"Are you certain that you saw her? You said the light was pretty strange. Maybe it was some other boat with tall masts. A sail training ship or something?"

The sound of those engines had run right through him.

"'Course Donny saw her," said Liam. "We knew it was the Tiger because we all dived down and hid. Then we put mud on our faces and I shut my eyes."

Anna rolled hers.

"Okay, okay, I give up. Let's all go home. But first we're going to put a reef in that mainsail. Even Anna can't do six GCSE maths papers before bed if she's been tipped overboard in the path of a freighter."

"Actually, it's GCSE French papers that I need to work at. That's the scholarship level. They say they'll give me an exemption for the Latin because I'm taking it from a comprehensive school. But I'm still going to have a go."

"You're seriously planning to leave? Go to some posh place where they wear all-wool kilts and dry-clean-only blazers? Just because you've got rich?"

Anna's face went a bit rigid.

"What I'd like, for once in my life, are some choices. Then I'll make my own decision in my own time. If that's okay by you, of course."

They didn't say a lot after that.

The ebb was sluicing down the river so he landed them as far along the Hard as he could, then pushed off quickly, before *Vexilla* could get stuck. He could see Lottie and Vicky already waiting on the bench near the pub. Rev. Wendy's little car was there too so they'd have plenty of help getting back to the vicarage. They'd even fit the barrow in, probably.

He saw Lottie stand up. She looked as if she was going to come right down the Hard. Then he saw Vicky trip over. Lottie had to scoop her up, cuddle her.

She might have been calling but the wind blew her words up and away. She made big arm movements with her Vicky-free hand. Possibly she was waving some papers?

Donny set sail hastily. Maybe she was going to yell at him about making Anna late for her pluperfect prep. Anyway he had a home of his own to get to and a mother who would be won-dering where he was, even if she couldn't shout across the mud at him. *Vexilla* surged down river to Harwich harbour.

The *Hispaniola* hadn't gone back to her Shotley mooring. Donny knew he had been right. He was certain she was up in Ipswich. He didn't know why. Or how they'd managed to miss her.

He didn't have any time to think about that now. Wind and tide were hard against him and he was longing to be back to the comfort of the junk's main cabin and one of Skye's warm suppers. Even a pile of spaghetti or two tins of beans would do as long as he could just shovel it in and keep on eating until he was full.

Strong Winds wasn't in Gallister Bay.

He'd used the outboard to get round the low headland of Erwarton Ness, keeping close to the northern shore. Then the motor had begun to splutter and he realised he was low on fuel. So it was up again with the sails and bearing right away across the river. The Copperas Bay mudflats were uncovered but he'd stood in as far as he could before bringing *Vexilla*'s head around in the happy conviction that he'd be able to make his home anchorage in a single close-hauled tack.

Gallister Bay was empty. Not even a single Sunday fisherman. Had Gold Dragon brought up on the Essex side of the river to take shelter under the Wrabness Cliffs?

No.

Donny struggled to rationalise.

Skye and Gold Dragon must have enjoyed themselves so much

that they'd stayed an extra tide. Then, once the wind had shifted, they'd thought it best to wait and come back with the first of the flood. Or maybe they'd had engine trouble. Or run aground.

Or something.

There was no reason to think that the non-appearance of *Strong Winds* and the disappearance of the *Hispaniola* had any connection with each other. There was nothing to worry about except his empty stomach.

He found a mooring under the lee of the cliffs on the Essex side and scoured *Vexilla* for any remnants of lunch. Two mini scotch-eggs and an apple. He wished he hadn't let Liam throw his crusts to the gulls. There was some fresh water but nothing else, except the emergency chocolate and handful of boiled sweets. Donny took a green one then reached in his rucksack for the book.

He got cold after a while so he rearranged the mainsail. If he loosed its tires and pulled it down from the boom into the bottom of the boat, it would give him shelter and something to lie on. He allowed himself another sweet and got into his sleeping bag. *Vexilla*'s hull was so much roomier that *Lively Lady*'s. Donny imagined himself as a mountaineer bivouacking for the night between rocks.

Except he wasn't going to be there all night. It was near the top of the tide and getting dark. They knew he had school tomorrow. His books and uniform were on board. There was no chance of finishing the weekend's homework. Monday tomorrow. They'd have to be back soon.

Donny read. And then he slept.

It was quite dark when he woke. He bumped his head on the

boom as he sat up expecting to see *Strong Winds'* anchor light across the water on the Suffolk side.

Nothing.

If they'd run aground the tide would have floated them off by now. If they'd had engine trouble Gold Dragon would have sailed home. If there were something the matter with the sails, she'd have used the engine.

There must have been an accident. They should never have split up. It wasn't safe. Should he be calling the coastguard? What would he say? He hadn't got a phone anyway. Or a portable VHF. He hadn't any fuel for his engine and no friends nearby. Should he sail back to Shotley and ask the people in the marina office if they could help? They were open twenty-four hours. But then he might miss *Strong Winds* if she did come back.

He was so tired: he couldn't decide. He ate the emergency chocolate and lay down again to think.

River Stour, Monday 16 April 2007
The next thing Donny knew was that he'd been invaded. Xanthe Ribiero was scrambling on board, calling out cheerfully to him to show a leg and she'd check it was a hairy one.

It was grey pre-dawn.

Again!

He'd thought there was an emergency. And Xanthe was making jokes …? Donny tried to sit up and got into a complete tangle with the mainsail.

"Tucked up tight as a hermit in a whelk shell. Anna and the tribe came hollering for you hours ago but they were on the wrong side of the river and they hadn't got a boat. Up Gallister

Creek without a paddle – literally! So they called in the marines. And here I am in my war canoe."

He disentangled himself and looked over *Vexilla*'s gunwale.

Xanthe'd arrived in an inflatable rubber dinghy with a couple of lightweight oars pushed through plastic rings on either side. She was already re-stowing his unfurled mainsail and shoving his shoes and rucksack at him.

"I thought you were at Weymouth."

"All good things come to an end, Donny-man."

"My mum? Gold Dragon? Are they … dead?"

Now it was Xanthe who was brought up short.

"No way! They're hove-to off the Long Sand Head. Outside territorial waters. They got done over by the bureau-rats – as Gold Dragon calls them. Some no-brainer of a paperwork problem. I didn't really get it. Dad said it was a good thing you're not allowed to swear in a VHF transmission or she'd have blasted them broadside."

"You've spoken to her?"

"Dad has. Come on, Donny. Pipe to quarters! You and I are off to sea."

She'd secured the mainsail, checked *Vexilla*'s mooring rope and was climbing back into her inflatable. Donny shoved his sleeping bag into the rucksack with his book and charts and scrambled after her.

He knew the Long Sand Head. It marked a shoal about fifteen miles off the coast beyond the Black Deep. Beyond the Cork Sand, the Gunfleet, the Shipwash and the Sunk. You could send yourself to sleep counting the wreck symbols in that area, thicker than flocks of sheep. Except they'd give you nightmares.

It was a good thing that the wind had dropped if they were going all that way in Xanthe's rubber dinghy.

They weren't, of course. The yawl, *Snow Goose*, was standing by, her engine running silky-soft to hold her in position as she breasted the dark ebb tide.

June smiled as Donny arrived on deck and Joshua touched him welcomingly on the shoulder. Then he and Xanthe were lifting the inflatable onto the cabin top, while June pushed the throttle forward and turned the yacht in her own length until she was slipping swiftly back down river.

Donny waited for someone to tell him what was meant to happen next.

CHAPTER SEVEN

City Lights

Xiamen, coastal Fujian, March 2007

Min hoped that his cousin would stay for the whole of the New Year holiday. He imagined saying goodbye to the village on the fifteenth night when the last of the glowing lanterns was drifting skywards. Perhaps they would take the familiar country bus down the winding roads to the market town the next morning, just as if he was starting a new school week. After that the adventure would begin.

But Chen Kai became restless as the days of festivity passed.

"You don't know what it was like getting here," he said. "More people are travelling by road this year because the trains are so crowded. So the traffic's terrible and half the buses break down. We need to go soon. It's going to be a problem getting you a ticket. Even from a scalper."

Their journey south took sixteen hours. Twice as long as it should have done. There were three people to every double seat and people crushed into the aisles as well. No-one got off when the bus stopped – they couldn't be sure they'd ever get on again. Kai had warned Min he'd need a bottle to pee into. Some people on the long train journeys bought adult nappies, he said.

"We all want to come home to have a holiday and see our families and then we all need to get back to the cities where we work. *Chunyun* – it's the biggest migration of people on earth."

It felt like the loneliest as well. There were so many things Min wanted to ask but he and Kai got separated. He was pushed further down the bus until all that he could see was the back of his cousin's head. He couldn't see out of the window either. He was surrounded by people sleeping, people texting, people gossiping or swapping information about different jobs. There were people snacking and people being sick in plastic bags. Some older ones were sitting quietly and looking sad. Perhaps they'd left a child behind.

Min remembered his mother waving from behind the scuffed window of her bus. They'd made a special trip to town the previous week to buy a hard shell suitcase. So many hopes had been shut into that case and carried away.

He'd packed his own things in a rice sack. Just clothes, a small quilt, washing materials, pens and paper. He'd put his English textbook in but then he'd taken it out again. He wasn't a schoolchild any more. He was a traveller.

It was night when they finally arrived in Xiamen and he so nearly lost Kai in the confusion of the bus terminal. When they came out into the city, it was as if they'd stepped into the middle of a spectacle. Buildings, taller than anything Min had ever seen, were patterned with colour: mauve and jade and scarlet and gold. A pair of searchlights sprayed yet more light into the fluorescent sky. A hotel had giant orange letters on its roof. Advertising signs hung from every other building: sky blue and acid pink, flashing silver, throbbing red and gold. It had been raining; reflected light blurred in the puddles. There were people wandering around, eating, drinking in the street. Min felt giddy.

"Is it still festival?"

"It's tourist area and shopping streets. Lights stay on all night. Very expensive. Maybe we'll come again and have a look. Or maybe not. Now we need to get out to Haicang."

"That's where you live?"

"And where I work."

They caught a city bus across a bridge. It was long and graceful, shining. Min felt as if he was being carried across a mysterious void. Flecks of light far below.

"Mouth of Jiulong River and the deep sea port. We're crossing between islands. Those are ships."

Ships?

The city bus didn't go far the other side of the bridge. There were only a few passengers left when it stopped and they were told to get off. They walked for a while along the edge of a highway then into a factory area. Most of the buildings were dark and quiet but there was faint bluish light from some of the windows.

"Opened already," muttered Kai. He sounded anxious. "I have to leave you in the morning, little cousin. I need to get my job back."

"Your job?"

Kai had been telling them in the village how well he was doing at work. Not stuck on the assembly line any more. He was repairing the machines. A technician now. His new factory made moulded plastic for sports equipment. All sold abroad. They were doing good business.

"Everyone got laid off before the holiday. That way the boss doesn't have to pay us when we're not at work. No money this month. And when we apply for our jobs again he doesn't have to take on so many if we're not productive."

"Oh."

"I don't tell them everything at home. They don't understand city life."

Kai left school when he was fourteen. He said he couldn't see the point of staying any longer. First he helped his mother on the farm and then, when he was sixteen, he moved to the city. Now his parents' house was warm in winter and they could have medicine whenever they were ill.

They were past the factories now and into an area of apartments. These buildings were so close together that Min couldn't see the tops. As Kai led them up a path between two blocks the lights went out.

"A power cut, that's all we need. Looks like we'll be finishing Grandmother's New Year cake and eating oranges for supper."

Min was too tired to eat. By the time they'd felt their way up twelve flights of stairs and into Kai's apartment all he wanted to do was sleep. A Gaz light showed that there were other workers there. Kai pulled out a spare mattress. Min put his head on his sack of clothes and didn't ask anything more.

His cousin was gone in the morning. One of the other men was there, still in his vest and eating reconstituted rice porridge from a plastic container. He offered Min some hot water with sugar in it.

"Chen Kai has gone to ask for his job back. If the boss says yes he'll start at once. He works a twelve-hour shift so he won't be in until this evening. He says please try not to get lost. I can show you how to let yourself in and out. You're on your own after that. I've been at work all night."

Min didn't like to ask whether there was anything in the apartment that he could eat. Instead he ate two of Grandmother's tea-marinated eggs and tried not to mind that Kai had finished the cake. There were still some of the oranges and rice-balls left and the *ang pao*, his red envelope of money, was in a belt round his waist, comfortingly close to his skin.

"Which way to the bridge?" he asked when Kai's flatmate had taken him down to the ground floor and shown him how to manage the entry system. The bridge was the only feature he could remember from last night. That, and the wonderful lights in the shopping streets on the far side of the river.

"Half an hour over there," said the tired worker with a large vague gesture. Then he set off up the stairs again. The electricity was back on this morning but the lifts still weren't working.

Min stood with his back to the high-rise concrete block. He couldn't see out. He was surrounded by tall apartment blocks. They all looked alike. His home in the village was made of wood and woven bamboo and the windows were translucent paper. It was very old fashioned. Some other houses in the village had bricks and tiles and glass but that was when there were outside wages coming home. Every spare yuan in Min's family had been spent on his education. He had learned poems and how to write them in beautiful calligraphy. He had used them to decorate the entrance to their house, painted messages of good fortune, welcoming their neighbours and the New Year's visitors.

There were no greetings pasted on this bleak doorway. If he moved away from it, how would he find his way back? If he didn't move away, how would he begin the next stage of the journey that was going to lead him to the Country of the Ghosts?

CHAPTER EIGHT

Man Overboard

Thames Estuary, Monday 16 April 2007

Snow Goose hurried down the Stour and out of Harwich Harbour. They'd passed between Landguard and the Pye End buoys before the flood began helping them on their way and Joshua finally convinced Xanthe and her mother to go below and catch a couple of hours sleep.

Maggi was staying at the vicarage with Anna but the others had come straight to the yacht as soon as they'd arrived home from Weymouth. Yesterday had been a long day and there was a longer one ahead. As soon as *Snow Goose* had reached *Strong Winds* Gold Dragon was heading across the North Sea to Rotterdam and June was going with her.

Donny wrapped his hands gratefully round a mug of hot chocolate and struggled to shake the sleep out of his head as the Ribieros tried to explain.

There had been problems with the *Strong Winds*' papers. Someone, somewhere, had noticed (or been tipped off) that the junk had been in England for longer than six months. Her right to remain had been challenged. Great Aunt Ellen needed to go to Rotterdam to deal with the problem as that had been her port of entry into the EU.

"Otherwise she has to go to Norway!" said Xanthe, excitedly. "As the nearest non-EU country. Horned helmets ahoy and light the beacon fires!"

Skye was going with her and needed her passport. That was what Lottie had been waving at Donny from the Pin Mill Hard.

Skye also needed to say goodbye to Donny.

"What about me? Why can't I go? I'm a good crew – and they're my family. *Strong Winds* is my home."

"You haven't got a passport. Or if you have, Lottie couldn't find it. She said she turned the camper van inside out, searching. Have you got one?"

Probably not. Coming to Suffolk from Yorkshire was the longest journey he'd made in his life – since he'd been carried back in Skye's womb from the Northlands, wherever that was.

"There's also the small matter of school. June's coming back to England as soon as they reach Rotterdam but your great aunt may need to stay there until she can get legal advice from Edward. He's somewhere in the Baltic, pike-fishing. And you know your Care Plan says that you mustn't miss a day."

"Midshipmen in Nelson's navy did very well without school," Xanthe grumbled. "Anyway I'm about to be on GCSE study leave. If I miss a day or two no-one's going to mind much."

This was clearly a row that had been running for some hours. Joshua muttered something rather firm about the discipline in Nelson's navy being a bit of an advance on Gallister High and June reminded her daughter that she'd only been allowed on board *Snow Goose* on the condition that she went to sleep as soon as they'd collected Donny.

"You are going to school later this morning whether you like it or not. One more word and I'll radio the harbour pilots to take you in custody as a stowaway."

"Or an Excessive Baggage," added her father.

Sighing, Xanthe followed her mother down the companion-way and closed the varnished doors behind them.

"What about you?" Joshua asked Donny. "There's Maggi's berth if you'd like to get your head down. Our course from here is straightforward: 137 degrees or thereabouts to the South Cork, then north five or ten degrees to counteract the tide. June drove back from Dorset last night so I took some time out then. I'll call you if I need a hand."

"I'm okay. Really. I slept hours on *Vexilla*."

He'd have to be a narcoleptic zombie not to want to go sea in the early hours of a Monday morning, when most shore-dwellers were still unconscious in their darkened bedrooms.

"I still don't understand what happened to *Strong Winds*."

"They were ambushed," said Joshua, checking the compass course and settling himself comfortably into the windward corner of the cockpit. "That's what my daughters would say and, for once, I don't think they'd be over-dramatising. A Maritime Authority launch stopped them on their way back to the Stour and asked to see their Passage Plan. Everyone knows you don't need a written plan if you're staying within the harbour – which technically they were. But someone had been watching them on Saturday, apparently, and had seen *Strong Winds* go straight out to sea."

"That would have been Gold Dragon stretching her wings. She gets so fed up having to sit around on the mooring the whole time because of me and SS and the Care Plan."

"Naturally. However, the officers decided to make an issue of it. I can't imagine what had got into them. They demanded the

Ship's Papers and discovered that the import licence had only been valid for six months. Oh, and your great-aunt had no proof of *Strong Winds'* VAT status."

"VAT? But *Strong Winds* was built in China – ages ago. I don't think they had VAT then."

Donny's brain hurt. It was a bit like the day he and his family had got trapped in a meeting with Flint and Toxic and Creepy Tony who kept slinging regulations at them as if he was counsel for the prosecution instead of someone who was meant to be protecting children.

"They threatened to impound the junk! It was utterly preposterous!" Even Joshua, tall, calm, steady-handed Joshua began to splutter. "I've already sent an email to the legal department at the RYA."

Oh, okay, Donny'd got it now. This attack had Inspector Jake Flint's slime trails smeared all over it. Whoever had actually been on board the Maritime Authority vessel when she hove up to challenge *Strong Winds*, the fat policeman would have been lurking in the background; bribing or bullying, abusing other people's official powers for his own crooked ends.

Being grabbed by Toxic at the end of Friday afternoon must have been part of their plan. All that stuff about sending out 'mai team'. She'd known that Edward was away. So either her lot would have come and made trouble if *Strong Winds* had stayed in Gallister Bay, or Flint's lot if she moved. And Toxic would have guessed that the prospect of Flint's Boxing for the Fatherless would have made him want to do a runner if the threat of fumigation hadn't been enough.

She was meant to do welfare but her skill was the exact opposite. She made bad worse.

Lottie had told them how Toxic had visited her in hospital when she'd just given birth to Vicky. She had been sore and exhausted. Bill was in custody, the other children on the At Risk list and everything about to be taken by debt collectors. No-one had visited her with cards and flowers; no-one had helped her run a comb through her tangled hair and propped her up on the pillows for a celebratory photo. The nurses were busy. She was on her own.

Then Toxic had arrived, immaculate in one of her designer outfits and gushing with superficial sympathy. The Mal-fairy. Somehow, during that visit, she had convinced Lottie that the best thing she could do for her children was to abandon them.

Then Lottie had walked straight into the clutches of the Tiger. He ran a cleaning company that was like slave-labour.

"I discovered that I wasn't the only one. Most of the other women had been visited by Toxic before they decided to join Pura-Lilly. Not the ones from abroad – they belonged to the Tiger as soon as they arrived – people like me, outcasts in our own country."

"That's hardly surprising." June had been there. They'd all been sitting around talking, trying to understand what they ought to do. "Lots of those women would have had children taken into care or children getting in trouble. Denise Tune would have all the information – who'd been in prison, who was in debt, who had addictions. She didn't actually hand you a Pura-Lilly card, did she?"

"I found it on the bedside table after she'd left. Anyone could have put it there. Pura-Lilly send temporary cleaners in when the hospital services can't cope."

June had looked keen.

"That's good. That's the sort of detail that can be checked. We need to investigate who signs those cleaning contracts, where the payments are made, who has named responsibility for quality control."

She noticed Xanthe rolling her eyes.

"You might think it's dull but it can be deadly. Ask anyone who's been tax-inspected!"

Xanthe had recently grown taller than her mother. She patted her on the head.

"Aged Parent," she'd said kindly. "You've lost the plot. We're talking global piracy here, not annual audits."

"Innocent child," her mother had answered. "These people are exploiting and mistreating others to earn themselves big money. But they're not being paid in pieces of eight. Their profits could be traceable."

Donny thought over that conversation again as he sat in *Snow Goose's* cockpit watching the wave shapes grow steadily more distinct, as daylight strengthened and the world seemed to open up around them. Joshua was at the helm and Donny was keeping a lookout for the Armada buoy, the first indicator that they were nearing the southern tip of the dangerously shallow Cork Sand.

The fake *Hispaniola* had left her mooring this weekend of all weekends. But she hadn't chased out to sea after *Strong Winds*, she'd gone in the opposite direction up to Ipswich. Why?

And where was the Tiger now?

"The Armada's unlit. It shouldn't present any problem as long as we stick to our course. The South Cork itself should soon be visible: six very quick flashes and one long one every ten seconds. But it's as well to be sure."

They'd hoisted the yawl's full set of sails and she was slicing keenly through the tossing waters. Joshua had arranged that he would call Gold Dragon on his VHF when he was approaching the Black Deep. She would then bring *Strong Winds* back to meet *Snow Goose* and he would transfer June and the passport. Skye could be reassured that Donny was okay and they would go their separate paths.

"I thought you told me that the problem with VHF was that all your transmissions were public? Anyone who happened to be listening on the right channel would hear everything that was being said. Even if you were planning a barbecue on a beach."

Joshua glanced up the mainmast as if he wasn't quite certain that *Snow Goose*'s topsail had been properly set.

"That's true," he agreed. "And for the first transmissions, when your great-aunt was venting her anger and informing us of her intention to leave territorial waters, we communicated clearly and on maximum wattage. Then later, we used different channels … and perhaps, not the same ship's names."

Donny liked that. If he couldn't go to Holland with Skye and Gold Dragon, staying with the Ribieros would be okay.

More time passed in comfortable silence. He stole a glance at Joshua's dark, clever-looking head. The neurosurgeon was wearing a navy blue woolly hat and a cream silk scarf inside the turned-up collar of his all-weather jacket. Plenty of texture there. He might even get his art homework done.

Not that Joshua looked relaxed exactly. There was a short frown-line between his eyebrows, and once or twice his lips pressed together and the corners of his mouth twitched as if he was thinking of things that he didn't want to say.

Donny looked out to sea again. They'd passed the South Cork buoy and were approaching the North East Gunfleet. There had been the usual massive container vessels lumbering along in the distance in the deeper water and three smaller ships, not going anywhere. Joshua said they were at anchor, probably waiting for a pilot or a tide. Otherwise the sea appeared empty. No schooner coming after them. No masts.

"Wow! Look at that!"

A very large bird was flying low over the waves, about fifty metres to port, powering upwards to gain height before plummeting down in the most spectacular dives. It was white underneath and dark on top. Too big for even the largest type of gull. And he'd never seen a gull scythe into the water like that, with its neck outstretched and wings tucked tight against its sides.

Then there was a second giant bird: pure white with black wing-tips. It too dived like a Stuka and came up with a flash of silver struggling in its beak. The first bird tried again. Then they both fished together before flying off into the distance with the rising sun gleaming on their under-plumage.

"Gannets," said Joshua. "Probably parent and child. It's time we reduced sail. The wind's getting up and we're over-pressing the yacht."

They worked together as companionably as the gannets had fished, taking in one of *Snow Goose*'s two jibs and bringing down her topsail. If he had sailed with … Hermann, would it have been like this?

"Thank you," said Joshua. "I should have taken that action some time ago. I have an important meeting at the hospital later this morning and am anxious to be punctual – but that's no excuse for poor seamanship."

"Meeting?"

"I handed in my resignation on Friday and I have to explain my decision to the management committee."

"Huh?"

He knew that Joshua had been brought in to develop a centre of excellence in neurosurgery and he sort of knew that the Ribieros hadn't planned to stay in Suffolk for ever. He'd no idea that the job was going to finish so soon.

"Is that what you want to do?"

"I can no longer continue to work in a system where something as basic as cleaning is allowed to put people's lives at risk."

"Oh." He remembered there'd been some sort of crisis last Christmas when Joshua's unit was threatened with temporary closure.

"Do you have to? You know, like, resign?"

"It's my department. I cannot continue working in such chaos."

"Oh. Do Xanthe and Maggi know?"

"Not yet. Neither does June. I've talked to her, of course. She insists that I should carry on fighting. I can't do it. Too many of my patients have become ill. We have had unnecessary deaths. I intend to go abroad."

"Oh," said Donny. He was going to lose this whole family. "Is it time to make the call?"

He took the helm whilst Joshua used channel 73 for Motor Vessel *Spray* to communicate with Fishing Vessel *Larky Lass* over the relocation of a misplaced line of lobster pots. Then he woke June and Xanthe. It wasn't long before the creamy sails of *Strong Winds* were visible fine on the starboard bow and the two yachts closed for the handover.

The sky was heavily overcast, those gleams of morning sun no more than a memory. The wind continued to rise, flinging the waves angrily upwards when they met the shoal waters of the Long Sand.

The two boats hove to as close to one another as they dared; then Donny helped Xanthe launch the inflatable so she could row June across to *Strong Winds*. He waved to Skye – wide cheerful gestures to show he was okay.

But he wasn't okay. Wasn't okay at all. What was it with adults that they thought they could do as they liked the whole time? Go for a holiday or chuck up their jobs – Mr McMullen, Edward, Joshua – simply push off whenever it suited them.

He hated Joshua.

For a moment he even hated beautiful *Snow Goose*. *Strong Winds* was his ship and that was where he ought to be.

He helped Xanthe climb back on board and dragged the inflatable out of the water. It fitted neatly on the cabin roof; each varnished fastening so thoughtfully positioned.

The two yachts dipped flags in farewell.

Donny watched *Strong Winds* spread her broad sails like wings. He watched as those winds began to fly her away from him.

He made up his mind.

He jumped.

And when Joshua immediately, instinctively, threw him a line, he folded his arms and kicked away on his back, refusing to catch it.

"Tell Gold Dragon that I'm having a Sinbad moment," he yelled up to Xanthe.

CHAPTER NINE

Reality Check

Off Long Sand Head, Monday 16 April 2007

The waves seemed much larger down here than they had from the deck of the yawl. One slapped him in the mouth as he shouted and, by the time he'd spat it out again and shaken his head and tried, ridiculously, to wipe his face with sopping wet hands, *Snow Goose* was several metres further away. Then another wave came up from behind and crashed right over his head.

His lifejacket had inflated as soon as he'd hit the water. It was holding his face upturned so there would be a chance for air to continue to reach his lungs even if he was unconscious. That was what it was meant to do. By leaning his head even further back and kicking away from Joshua he was simply inviting each curling wave to break onto his face. He needed to twist away, look where he was going and take them one by one.

The water was really cold out here. This was only April. There'd been no long summer days to raise the sea temperature. Not like that evening in September when he'd been in the water once before waiting for his great aunt to come and rescue him. The flood was pouring slightly west of south, through the Deeps and up into the great throat of the Thames. The wind was doing the opposite.

Splosh. Donny misjudged another Eiger-peaked wave. It pushed him under for a moment and spun him round so he felt completely disorientated. He couldn't see *Snow Goose*; he couldn't see *Strong Winds*. He was achingly cold.

If *Snow Goose*'s lifeline had been beside him he'd have grabbed it with a gurgle of relief. He'd got to swim or his circulation would be gone. He'd got to take every single sea hill at exactly the right angle and he'd got to keep his face out of the water. *Snow Goose* must still be there, somewhere, and surely Xanthe'd have radioed *Strong Winds* by now?

But when Donny next bobbed upon a crest and glimpsed the yawl, Xanthe hadn't moved. She was still standing on the port side of the cockpit, holding the shrouds with one hand and pointing at him steadfastly with the other.

Of course she couldn't move!

If you were a person with an eye-line to the casualty (aka utterly crazy idiot) you didn't go scampering off to use the VHF. You didn't grab the tiller, help with the sails or start the engine; you didn't do anything: you simply hung on there, looking and pointing, knowing you were that idiot's single thread of hope.

He stopped his craziness of swimming away from *Snow Goose* and tried his best to keep his wet white face pointing in her direction. Trying to meet each wave right so he didn't get swamped again. Single combat with an endless queue of contenders.

Snow Goose was still sailing away from him. Not fast, because Joshua had loosed all the sheets, but steadily because the wind was pushing at her superstructure. Or was it that he, Donny, was being taken away from her by the cold, unceasing tug of the tide?

Why wasn't Joshua radioing or bringing the yawl round?

'When there's a man overboard, always gibe.'

Donny knew, as clearly as if he could see it printed on a page, that this was what Great Uncle Greg would have done. Surely Joshua, Vice Commodore of the RO&A, knew that too? The tall man seemed to have gone slightly mad. His first throw with a line had been good but Donny had ignored it.

Idiot him.

Swiftly Joshua had followed up with a life belt and another. They were heavy and didn't go so far. One had a sort of flag on it, which was good. Donny tried swimming in that direction but he couldn't make any headway. His calf muscles were starting to ache. He'd pushed his trainers off a few moments ago. His feet had hurt furiously as the cold seemed to chew its way through his socks.

That fierce pain had stopped now. Or moved up a bit. He wasn't sure he still had feet.

Donny kept kicking. Trying to. Every time he was between waves, he focussed really hard on where he would come up again. This way he could keep catching glimpses of *Snow Goose* in a sort of freeze-frame sequence.

One frame had Joshua stooping to haul in the line he'd thrown at first. Mustn't risk it fouling *Snow Goose*'s propeller. So maybe the engine's running? Gives him control.

In the next frame Joshua wasn't there at all. The heavy boom was thrashing wildly side to side. Had he been knocked overboard?

Donny slid into a trough. That would be the end.

No. Joshua was still there. He was throwing cabin cushions into the sea one after another with the speed and strength of a bowling machine, not bothering to look for Donny, just following the line of his daughter's outstretched arm. Did he really think that a sopping, semi-submerged cushion was going to be any use or was he suffering some sort of deranged hissy fit? A couple of fenders followed and a spare mooring buoy, florescent orange, very distinctive.

Donny got the next waves wrong and was smothered twice. So he didn't see the surgeon pull a handheld VHF set from the grab bag in the cockpit locker and make a fast, carefully worded call to the distant *Strong Winds* (aka *Larky Lass*).

He didn't see the junk's battened sails come cracking across one, two, three as Polly Lee wore her around 180 degrees and started back, close-hauled, on a reciprocal course with her engine leaping into life.

'When there's a man overboard, always gibe.'

Great Uncle Greg's book had said nothing about throwing cushions and fenders so when Donny saw the first of them drifting damply towards him, he ignored it.

It was different with the life-belt. That had a flag. He wanted it. He was tired. He was afraid his calf muscles were about to seize up completely. He must hang on to something.

With what felt like all his remaining strength, he struggled towards it. Never mind trying to keep *Snow Goose* in sight. His eyes were stinging with the salt, his face was frozen and his hands felt as if they were going the same way as his feet. Going … gone?

Donny hadn't seen Joshua push the MOB button on his GPS. Or use the handheld compass to take a swift directional reading. He didn't realise the importance of the other items of flotsam in helping establish the precise set and drift of currents in the area.

Bodies which have become too cold and tired to do any more than cling, eyes closed, to a horseshoe life-belt, fitted with a dan-buoy and a drogue, behave much more like sodden cabin cushions than like buoyant, manoeuvrable yachts. Joshua had got the message that Donny would refuse rescue from *Snow Goose*. He was doing all that he could to mark out the area where *Strong Winds* would operate.

Skye had been looking astern at the disappearing yawl and saw *Snow Goose*'s sheets were let fly. Something was wrong. She mimed a bird with drooping, quivering wings. Her meaning was as clear as if she'd shouted.

"*Larky Lass, Larky Lass*. This is MV *Spray*. Item of your equipment adrift. Trademark Sinbad. In sight but not retrievable by us. Drifting approximately 199 degrees from initial position 049° 60' N: 001° 32'E. Over."

"MV *Spray*. This is *Larky Lass*. Proceeding to collect item with all speed."

Skye was lookout, ready to point or to call. Polly Lee was on the helm and in charge, whilst June refastened the rope ladder that she herself had used to climb aboard. Once it was over the ship's side, she followed the captain's instructions to minimise *Strong Winds*' sail area.

When they finally reached Donny, after what seemed hours to the watchers on *Snow Goose*, but was really less than ten minutes, he was in no state to manage the rope ladder.

"Doh!" he heard, as he clung to his fluorescent life-belt, "Doh!!"

His brain must have got a bit frozen too. He had forgotten why he jumped. He had to struggle to open his eyes to check that she was there. The salt began to sting again so he blinked hard several times.

Then he saw her, though his reddened, half-shut lids. She was crouching towards him from the high deck of his home, stretching her arms down through the guard-rails. She couldn't reach him, and he definitely couldn't manage to climb the rope ladder to reach her. It was amazing that he'd got so cold so fast. He had thought people went swimming in April for pleasure.

He tried. He let go the life-belt and launched himself towards the junk's high heaving side. That could have been another very bad move if he hadn't managed to hook one of his uselessly numb arms in between the two bottom rungs of the ladder.

"T – too c- c- cold," he stuttered though teeth that began to chatter as soon as he quit clamping his jaws together.

June made a big bowline on a bight of rope and lowered it towards him as Gold Dragon slashed the cod-line which kept the rails taut. Skye signed that he should wriggle his free shoulder in the loop and try to get it right across his body.

He smashed against *Strong Winds*. Even if you were numb it hurt. But he got hooked on. One arm in the rope ladder: the bowline round his body.

Then Skye used all her frantic strength to pull up the ladder whilst June found a sheet winch to help her tighten in her rope. Between them, slowly and bumpily, they hauled Donny up onto the broad side decks where he lay sodden and bruised and dazed with relief.

Great Aunt Ellen looked as if she'd like to chuck him straight back.

"Get him below," she snarled at Skye, who didn't need hearing to understand what was meant, and to June, politely, "Perhaps you'd radio *Spray* to let them know all's well? Then, if you wouldn't mind wielding the boat hook, we'll see how many of your family's possessions we can fish out again before we get back on course."

Dried, warmed and with half a mug of hot sweet tea inside him, Donny fell asleep in Skye's arms.

It was mid-morning when they were summoned back on deck. *Strong Winds* was about to enter the Noord Hinder Traffic Separation Scheme.

"It's not that you've escaped a thorough keel-hauling, reduction to the ranks for six months, docking of pay for a year and bilge-scrubbing duty indefinitely," said Gold Dragon.

She had two deep new furrows running south-north between her eyebrows.

"It's more that you and your mother have the sharpest sets of eyes on board this vessel and I might be found to be in breach of regulations if I neglected to make use of you for the next few hours. Since you're unexpectedly available, that is," she said, pausing to scowl ferociously at him before she carried on issuing orders.

"Visibility's reducing fast and I expect heavy rain showers. Collect harnesses and full sets of oilskins and position yourselves on the port side. Traffic headed down-channel will be bearing somewhere around 40 degrees but we'll be crossing at right angles so expect to see them broadside on. We'll hardly have time to take bearings. The big fellows'll be coming down at about twenty knots. That's a mile every three minutes and, by my reckoning, visibility's less than two miles already."

"Have you not considered fitting a small radar set?" June

enquired. She had not looked at Donny or spoken to him. She was still very angry.

"Money. Plus not expecting to be harried off by a scavenging pack of scurvy bureau-rats. I wasn't even carrying enough diesel for a full trip such as this."

"Why are we using the engine now?" Donny enquired timidly. "There seems to be plenty of wind."

"And plenty more to come. We're using the engine because we're expecting some fairly unpleasant beam seas. We have to cross the TSS at 90 degrees. Best to get it over quickly, then we'll bear away, switch the little donkey off and take them on the quarter."

It didn't feel like morning anymore. Everything was sludgy brown-grey with heavy charcoal clouds billowing up to starboard, and a thick wet haze obscuring the difference between sky and sea.

"Gold Dragon, Mrs Ribiero … I need to tell you something. And Mum as well."

June looked at him coldly but didn't speak.

"Spit it out then," said Great Aunt Ellen.

So he told them about seeing the *Hispaniola* slipping up the river on Sunday morning in the deadtime before the dawn; about searching for her but not finding her and about her continued absence from her Shotley mooring. He told them about Toxic too, the questions she'd asked him on Friday afternoon, the threatened visit to *Strong Winds* and the information she already had. He even told them about her plan to send him to be bashed up by Flint after school on Mondays.

"No wonder you jumped ship," said June speaking to him

for the first time. She'd pulled the hood of her heavy weather jacket down so its peak shadowed her face. Her voice was cool; he couldn't read her expression at all. He assumed that she despised him.

"Actually," he said. "That was about the only thing I wasn't thinking of when I decided I needed to be back here with my mum. With my own family. I …"

He stopped again. He couldn't start telling her how … dismissed he'd felt when Joshua began talking so casually about his intention to walk away from his problems at the hospital and to take his family to live abroad. Maybe it was good that he had felt he could talk to Donny like that, the two of them, in the early morning, sailing a boat together – but he'd so obviously had no idea that it might matter. That Donny might … mind.

Time to change the subject.

"I know I'm needed to be keeping a lookout but could I take a quick look at the chart? I thought I sort of knew about it – from reading the book – but there wasn't such a thing as a Traffic Separation Scheme in Arthur Ransome's day."

"Nor when I last pointed my bows in this direction, either," Gold Dragon agreed. The North Sea might look featureless but it wasn't. Not when you couldn't quite remember whether you were navigating in the twentieth or the twenty-first centuries. Whether you existed now or in some odd time warp.

They were two cables away from the official start of the TSS and her own keen sight had registered nothing problematical as yet. She brought her logbook down to the chart table. She'd been using the GPS in the cockpit to check their position. It was time she transferred that data to the chart. A neat line of position-fixing crosses. Sinbad would like that.

He'd gazed at this chart so often, choosing it from the rack of charts, almanacs and pilot guides in *Strong Winds'* cabin, plotting fantasy expeditions during those long winter evenings. Now he was here, bruised and nervous, doing it for real, while the junk rolled gut-wrenchingly from side to side and the drumming of her engine pushed her determinedly ahead.

"If you were the Tiger and you were planning to attack," he asked. "Whereabouts would you do it?"

"Why the hell did you think I didn't want you on board?" Gold Dragon asked him in reply.

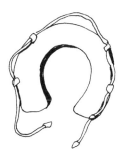

CHAPTER TEN

Mayday!

Southern North Sea, Monday 16 April 2007

"What sort of answer is that? If this trip isn't safe enough for me, it's not safe for my mum either. Or for Xanthe and Maggi's mother. What is it with you, Gold Dragon? What do you know about these people? They wanted to make you turn and run and now you have. Why isn't that enough? You say we're in danger … well, why?"

Gold Dragon looked ancient and exhausted: she also looked angry.

"Put a locking hitch on your tongue, young man, before I'm tempted to slip one round your neck. Do you think I haven't asked myself that question? You think I press-ganged your mother and June Ribiero to sign on for this voyage, knowing that there might be more than dirty weather in prospect? You're way off beam."

"So why did you want to leave me behind?"

He knew he was sounding like a kid but that was how she was treating him.

"Apart from the little matter of the passport? Because, with you dutifully turning up at school and the doctor to his hospital, we still have a stake in the System. They know we're going to come back so they've got to keep it legal. That's what I'd hoped – before you came floundering across."

He supposed she'd had to make decisions pretty fast.

"So you didn't know about Mr Ribiero's meeting? He resigned from his job last Friday and he's seeing the manager or someone today to confirm it. Then the Ribieros are all going to leave as well."

"Does June know that?"

"Not that he's definitely resigned, no."

"Then that's the second piece of rank bad news you've lugged on board."

For a moment she stood there, indecisive. She even seemed unsteady.

He'd never seen Gold Dragon look this way on board *Strong Winds*. Hesitantly he stepped towards her and held out his arm. She gripped it hard with her one good hand. Then they heard the sound of the engine being throttled back.

The junk's momentum slowed dramatically and she began to roll so hard it felt as if she was wallowing herself into a pit. Great Aunt Ellen snapped back instantly into Polly Lee and headed for the companionway.

"You still haven't answered my question," Donny called after her. "What exactly do you know?"

Gold Dragon looked back for a moment. Her bright blue eyes were sad.

"I'm eighty whatever-I-am," she said. "My memory's shot full of holes. I know there must be a connection but I simply can't remember what it is."

June had slowed the junk to give clearance to a super-tanker going south down the traffic lane. Its low black hull seemed to go on forever as it passed. Then, as it pulled away, Donny realised how swiftly it was travelling. They'd better not take time off for a single blink.

When the tanker's wash came rolling by, the waves seemed to double in size. June turned the junk to face them. *Strong Winds* began to take huge, twisting leaps as the water heaved beneath her. June reached into her pocket for a packet of Stugeron, passed two to Skye and took two herself.

"What about you?" she asked Donny. "Have you taken anything?"

"Um, I'm probably okay," he said. "Thanks."

Gold Dragon was hoisting something white and cylindrical to the top of the mainmast. Donny gazed upwards. The mast-head seemed to have taken on a life of its own, scribing parabolas against the clouds like some gigantic etch-a-sketch. Watching it made him feel weird. Maybe he should have accepted a couple of sea-sick pills. His great-aunt was wearing a safety harness but hardly seemed to need it: her balance was extraordinary.

"So you do have a radar reflector!" June commented, as if there might have been some difference of opinion earlier.

"Damn silly things. Wouldn't make a blip's worth of difference to a big chap like that."

"But you've decided to hoist it all the same. Why's that, I wonder? New-found respect for the regulations? That would be a surprise!"

The warmth was creeping back into June's voice.

"I've decided to go public. I'd hoped to slip across unnoticed and, as you know, a wooden boat makes a very poor target for radar. But young Sinbad's brought as much bad news as a Jonah in reverse so I want to plant a dot on the coastguards' screen.

From now on any VHF transmissions that we make will be full power on Channel 16 and using correct identifiers."

A survey team on a low-flying helicopter had already noticed the junk. For two of the three-man crew she was simply a curiosity: a brief unexpected diversion during a routine data-collecting exercise in the Southern North Sea. For the third man she was a shock. He stopped his meticulous annotation and stared down at her. A powerful sense came over him that something which was lost could be found and that there was truth in dreams.

Gold Dragon was telling June why she thought Donny's failure to turn up at school plus Joshua's resignation from the hospital had put them in danger.

"I'll dance a hornpipe if I'm wrong, but I've lived with pirates. One sniff of weakness and they're streaking for the kill. We've cut ourselves adrift and it might suit them if we never make it to the other side. Our only comfort is that it won't be the power-boat in these conditions, it'll be the schooner. She's got powerful engines and she's tough as they come, but we should see her masts a half mile or so before she sees us."

"What then?" asked June.

Donny was almost too scared to want to know but he kept on signing to Skye. They were all in this together. She needed to understand.

"A soon as we spot those three tall masts we'll send a nice loud Pan-Pan message claiming engine trouble. We'll sound – god dammit – feminine! We'll get the authorities out looking for us. Okay. Action stations. All eyes peeled."

But no-one spotted the fake *Hispaniola* as they rolled their way across the TSS. Donny was positioned at *Strong Winds'* bows, June amidships and Skye in the cockpit gazing fixedly over the junk's high stern.

They didn't see her when Polly Lee steered them with pin-point accuracy to a gap in the long West Hinder bank and took them through with breaking water metres away on either side.

This wasn't the route for Rotterdam. Gold Dragon had set a new course south-east towards Belgium. They should arrive off the coast at twilight about two hours after low water. Then, if they had the strength, they could take the flood up into the Westerschelde and spend the night at Vlissingen, before entering the Dutch canal system the following day.

"And if we're impounded on arrival, *tant pis*. You can all go back to England and I'll sit it out eating schnitzel and frites until Edward gets home from his holiday. We all stay safe and the Tiger can go gnaw knucklebones."

She caught them in the shallows just as night was closing in. She must have been shadowing them all day. Possibly she'd been one of that scatter of ships anchored beyond the Sunk, apparently waiting for the tide. *Snow Goose* could have passed her on the return trip into Harwich but Joshua and Xanthe wouldn't have known.

Nor would Skye, watching steadfastly out over *Strong Winds'* high stern, have recognised her, even if she'd seen her.

Which she didn't because the fake *Hispaniola* kept out of sight. She was low in the water now so she could hide behind the earth's slight curve.

The ex-schooner no longer had three tall masts. It had taken less than an hour for a waiting crane to lift them out in Ipswich dock early on Sunday morning. Then she'd been winched up onto a cradle underneath a high tarpaulin. When she'd emerged she was no longer rusting red and white; she was gunmetal grey. That tint which blends so well with the colour of the sea – or with the no man's land that merges sea and sky on a louring, stormy day.

Neither was she nameless. She was MV *Pride of Macao*. She had S band radar, two full tanks of diesel and a gun. You'd have thought she was ready to enforce national or international law in dangerous waters. Not that it was she who was setting out to make those waters dangerous.

Strong Winds' crew was tired. They'd endured a blustery crossing and had been on high alert for hours. Finally they were nearing safe havens: Zeebrugge to port, Oostende to starboard.

The wind had dropped. If they could creep a little further in, they would begin to feel the benefit of the tide flowing into the thirsty mouth of the Westerschelde. Even when it was fully dark, they would be able to pick their way from one flashing buoy to another, ticking them off on their chart, until finally they would slip into the yacht basin at Vlissingen – or Flushing, as Gold Dragon continued to call it. It would be a slow four or five hours but then, oh bliss, they could sleep sound in their bunks.

No one had given more than a glance at the motor vessel that was closing their port quarter. Might she be official?

"Hell's teeth," Gold Dragon muttered, "If she's some Belgian bureau-rat coming to tick us off for motor-sailing in the TSS without an up-turned cone, I might need you to lash me to the mast for their own protection."

"Looks more like Customs & Excise to me," said June, trying to stifle a yawn.

And Donny, remembering the warlike *Valiant* he and the kids had seen in Ipswich – how many years ago? – was about to agree with her when something about the shape of the bow triggered a memory.

No bobstay now and a hefty double fluke anchor where the bowsprit had been.

He borrowed June's binoculars to read her name.

"*Pride of Macao*," he said. "Never heard of her."

Then he saw the flag stream out, orange and green, from the stumpy signal mast and a small man pulling a stocking over his face. The mystery boat surged forwards.

"It's the Tiger! He's going to ram us from astern!"

Half a minute ago they'd been sailing on a broad reach towards a low-lying coast that was barely visible in the gathering dusk. They'd noted reduced soundings as they crossed the Groote Bank and the Akkaerte Bank and had agreed that they would continue until the 10 metre contour before starting to think about supper. Now, suddenly, they were in extreme danger.

Gold Dragon gave an odd grunt. The colour had drained completely from her face, leaving its criss-crossed lines stark as pack-ice.

"Not *Pride of Macao*. That's HMS *Beckfoot*!"

Donny gawped. Had her brain hit climate change? She was pulling a yellow plastic barrel from behind the mizzenmast and breathing quite quickly as she unscrewed its red lid. But her voice was audible and her instructions crystal clear.

"Sinbad," she rasped, "take the helm double quick and bring

her up into the wind. Then round. Don't let her lose way. I want 180 degree reciprocal course – or whatever you need to take us down his starboard side. Get your mother to do the sheets. June – VHF Channel 16. It's a Mayday! Though I'm not sure whose."

She grabbed something from the yellow barrel with her one good hand, gripped its end in her teeth and twisted. Then, as Donny and Skye swung *Strong Winds* through the first 90 degrees, she crouched down by the high aft deck and slammed the thing against the starboard gunwale.

A streak of bright white light went rocketing towards the gunboat. It hit her wheelhouse with a solid bang and a shower of sparks.

Donny didn't dare stop concentrating. The junk was turning through the eye of the wind. Mainsail and mizzen were both a-quiver but Skye was putting tension back on the foresail to bring her head round quickly. His mum was good. All those days sailing *Vexilla* while he'd been stuck in school. *Strong Winds* was already paying off on the port tack.

Donny looked at the enemy. He didn't know what other name to call her. She was much closer now. There was a big scorch mark on her newly painted upper works and her course might have wavered. The glass in the front of her wheelhouse was soot-blackened but there was a side-door open and the person at the wheel was bringing her round and at them again.

Skye kept the sheets taut. Donny could hear June from inside the cabin.

"Mayday! Mayday! Mayday! This is yacht *Strong Winds*, yacht *Strong Winds*, yacht *Strong Winds*. Mayday *Strong Winds*. Our position is …"

The two vessels were terrifyingly close. The gunboat was far faster than the junk and hadn't the impediment of sails. She was turning all the time, turning directly into the wind, coming for them. She was going to hit them square amidships. And she was heavy. Solid metal with that anchor like a ram head.

She'd sink the junk. No doubt of that.

If Donny luffed up to port at the last moment, it'd be a glancing blow: she'd catch their stern, carry away the steering gear. They'd be helpless but they'd gain time. Only minutes. Was that what he should do? It wasn't what he'd been told.

Gold Dragon let off another of her rockets. He knew what they were. They were distress flares. This one was red and went up high, exactly as it should have done. Telling a lifeboat where to find them.

"Engine, Sinbad. We'll take him to port. DON'T bear away until I give the word. Full throttle then and let the sheets fly."

She shot an orange smoke, which landed in the water between the two vessels and began to fizzle.

The gunboat didn't slow. Nothing, it seemed, would stop the Pride of Macao lining up on her helpless target. Three women and a boy. Behaving crazy. Too terrified to think, maybe?

"Okay," Gold Dragon sounded as if she might be finding it difficult to breathe. "Full throttle and bear away. Hard-a-starboard and let those sheets fly."

She'd grabbed a couple more flares from the barrel and was scuttling up the junk's port deck, crouched low. Her hook hand was clutched to the centre of her chest and her pallor was alarming.

Strong Winds spun like a war-horse. All three sails swung out, spilling their wind, as Donny engaged the engine and shoved the throttle forward as far as it would go.

As soon as she was round, Skye began trimming the sheets again. The junk was sailing, sailing beautifully. She skimmed the length of the gunboat's hull without a touch. You couldn't have fitted a fender between the vessels without it rolling up again, squeezed by *Strong Winds*' velocity.

Donny forced himself to watch his steering. This was the biggest thing he'd ever done. He had to keep her steady.

Then, as the junk's cabin top slid past the enemy's wheelhouse, he couldn't resist a glance at Great Aunt Ellen. He saw her twisting another flare between her teeth to disengage the safety mechanism. He saw the Tiger running from the far side of his wheelhouse. He was fast. With a single supple movement, he threw.

Gold Dragon banged the rocket's base and fired. Then she was falling backwards onto the deck and the Tiger was doubled up and screaming.

Donny couldn't leave the helm. Mustn't let the boats' sterns touch. Not now. But June was there, up from the cabin and scrambling towards Gold Dragon.

The ships had passed.

Donny eased back the throttle and let the sails take charge. *Strong Winds* could look after herself now. He and Skye hurried to the side deck as the Pride of Macao careered wildly away. The Tiger was down, injured. Someone else was at her wheel and they weren't coming back. They knew the distress flares would have been spotted and if they'd had a radio on they'd have heard June sending out the Mayday.

Gold Dragon was unconscious. The pack-ice of her face had

congealed to a single stark white sheet, glazed with a film of sweat. There was a knife embedded deep in the solid teak of the junk's port bulwark. Not a sailor's knife: a killer's knife, sharp both sides.

"Chrissakes!" said June. "I can't feel a pulse. Help me move her to the cockpit then get back on that VHF. Tell them we need a defibrillator and immediate transport to the nearest hospital. You say 'Pan-Pan Medico'. Very clearly. Three times."

CHAPTER ELEVEN

The Winch-Man

Off the coast of Belgium, Monday 16 April 2007

When a Mayday message has been broadcast, all vessels in the area are required to keep silence and a listening watch until they are sure that the message has been received by the rescue services. They should write down the distressed ship's name and position and, if they hear no official response, they should re-transmit the Mayday as if they were part of a relay system. The emergency may be so desperate that the distressed ship cannot continue to transmit for herself or her radio may be damaged and not functioning at full power.

If other vessels are near enough to lend a hand, they are legally obliged to do so. A ship can sink very fast and not everyone has a fully equipped life-raft or can manage to launch it in time. At the very least, vessels within a few miles of the Mayday should alter course in that direction and stand by in case they are needed to pick up survivors. The law of the sea demands co-operation when lives are at risk.

This applies to countries too. Nations may try to insist that their territories extend a certain number of miles beyond their coasts but the swirling salt-water is shared. People cannot breathe in it or stand its cold for very long, wherever they were born.

Belgium, France, the Netherlands and the UK all co-operate with search and rescue operations in the Southern North Sea

and the entrance to the Dover Straits. These are usually co-ordi-
nated by one or other national coastguard service who may
request help from a navy or an air force – as well as from volun-
tary organisations such as the British RNLI or the Dutch KNRM
– or from anyone in the area at the time of need.

So, when the Belgian duty coastguard received *Strong Winds'*
Pan-Pan medical distress call so soon after the Mayday, it seemed
an almost everyday piece of good fortune that a helicopter from
the Dutch Ministry of Public Works and Water Management
should have been flying only minutes from the area. The casualty's only chance of survival lay in immediate evacuation to hospital and there was the helicopter, already airborne and with
paramedic equipment on board as standard.

The duty coastguard sighed with relief. She didn't care what it
was doing there. She was just glad she wouldn't have to call up
one of her own machines all the way from their base at Koksijde
on the French border.

Strong Winds' Mayday had given the coastguard a headache.
Pirate attack, the caller had claimed! This wasn't the coast of
Somalia or the South China Sea. Smugglers, yes, and maybe ter-
rorists – but not pirates. She was experiencing some difficulty
persuading the Defence Ministry to take her seriously.

The Oostende lifeboat had been launched as soon as the first
red flare had been sighted and had radioed back from alongside
the distressed vessel. The lifeboat crew reported an elderly lady
undergoing cardiac resuscitation and a nasty looking knife in
the ship's side. They didn't want to touch either of them. They'd
ascertained that the person giving the cardiac massage was a
qualified First Aider and there was no other damage to the

vessel. From what they'd learned it was the alleged attacker rather than the victim who might require assistance.

The duty coastguard located MV *Pride of Macao* on her radar screen. She had left the coast and was travelling north at speed. Her course was certainly erratic but she hadn't asked for help and she wasn't responding to her radio. The duty coastguard tried to make contact but soon gave up. If neither the police nor the navy could be bothered to give chase it wasn't a job for the rescue service either. She'd concentrate on the obvious emergency.

Three women and a boy on an antique junk. Sailing for Vlissingen.

Pirates indeed! It had probably been a near miss in the fading light or some other close-quarters situation that had caused the first caller to over-react. If she had ten Euros for every time some yachtie shouted "Mayday" because of something stupid like running out of fuel … well, she'd be going somewhere a good deal more exotic than Blankenberge for her summer holiday.

The boy was her contact now. His first Pan-Pan transmission had been a bit panicky and she'd had to ask him to repeat. Then he had calmed down. She could hear an English-speaking member of the lifeboat crew joking with him, calling him "Capten" and "Mijn Heer".

He sounded quite a sensible boy. She advised him that the adults on board should report the alleged incident to the police when they reached their destination port and she instructed one of the lifeboat crew to take a photo of the alleged knife. The helicopter was almost in position.

Then she ordered the lifeboat to stand off and return to station once they were satisfied that the medical rescue was completed. They had assured her that the area was already correctly marked by an orange smoke flare.

Skye and Donny had helped June to lift Great Aunt Ellen off the narrow side deck and into the cockpit.

"Is it okay to move her?"

Nothing felt okay while Gold Dragon lay unconscious on her own ship. One moment she'd been fighting off the Tiger and now … she wasn't there.

"Technically she's damn near dead so I don't see there's much more harm to be done. I can't work on her where she is so we haven't any choice. Just get that Pan-Pan message sent."

Dead?

Delta Echo Alpha Delta?

Donny's hands were shaking and there was some huge lump in his throat and his brain was jumbled. The first time he tried giving the Pan-Pan message it came out completely wrong.

He'd sort of expected that the coastguard would be a man but she wasn't. She was a woman who sounded a bit like a teacher at the end of the day, with a really dumb class and inspectors watching at the door.

He took a deep breath, shoved his thumb on the press-to-transmit button and tried again. Then he spotted that the basic distress message had been typed out and stuck on the bulkhead in front of him. All he had to do was read it and include details of their position, which June had already noted in the log.

Then he needed to explain about Great Aunt Ellen having no pulse.

Not … dead. But … no pulse. I spell. November Oscar. Papa Uniform Lima Sierra Echo.

The teacher turned into a receptionist, putting him on hold. Then he had to tell a doctor. All the details: the unconsciousness, the pallor and the sweat.

The no … pulse.

"Do you have First Aid personnel?"

"No. Yes. She says we need a defibrillator."

He didn't even have to spell it. The doctor's English was amazing for the words that mattered.

"Ja so," said the doctor and handed him back to the receptionist again. She must have been listening all the time because she said she had a helicopter already on stand-by.

She was brilliant really.

Then he needed to work with the lifeboat crew. It got busy and, in some strange way, almost jolly.

That was as long as he only looked at Skye or the rescue team.

June was kneeling over Gold Dragon, her arms straight, pressing rhythmically down on the breastbone and then stooping to blow air in, mouth to mouth. Her mobile, sympathetic face was set in a frowning mask of concentration: five compressions – one breath – five compressions – one breath. She was giving it everything. So far she'd achieved nothing.

Donny couldn't look at the limp figure on the folded blanket. He'd seen Granny Edith dead: that was enough.

All this while *Strong Winds* had been sailing herself, sheets perfectly adjusted, rising and dipping in the light evening swell as if she were on auto-pilot.

One of the lifeboat crew had climbed on board and began

giving Skye detailed instructions. Donny intervened and found himself turning the engine on, altering course, listening to the handheld VHF and signing to his mum to get the sails down and clear everything possible off the decks.

"You must make ready quick now," the lifeboat man explained. "When the helicopter is here it will be very noisy. And the downwards wind very strong. You must do exactly as they say."

Obviously. But what if it wasn't in English? Steering *Strong Winds* and signing to Skye whilst holding the radio set was going to be hard enough: if the crackly voice from the set started speaking in Dutch he wouldn't have a hope.

"It's okay. The Hollanders can speak English. Almost as in Belgium. You must not touch the line until it is plunged into the sea. Don't worry, Capten, you do well."

So many jobs to be done. And *Strong Winds* to steer! She must stay completely steady, the man told him.

Donny didn't think he could cope. The lifeboat man was almost grotesquely jolly. But he was about to leave. He climbed nimbly back into his own vessel and saluted – or that's what it looked like.

"Goodbye, mijn heer, goodbye."

Maybe Donny'd dreamed that bit. It was in his favourite book. The one where John Walker crossed the North Sea in a storm, in the dark, in a much smaller boat, the *Goblin*, with no engine and no adults until the end. Cop on, Donny-man! If John can do that: you can do this.

The helicopter was close by. The air was starting to shudder and the radio set to crackle.

Donny almost dropped the set as he struggled to throttle back and hold his course and wave for Skye to come into the cockpit where she would be safer.

Then he realised he was being stupid. He'd noticed the mistake John-in-the-book had made. John assumed that, because he was the eldest and a boy, he had to do everything. He hadn't organised a watch system when they were crossing the North Sea. He'd gone on steering through the night until he'd fallen asleep at the helm. That was dangerous.

Gold Dragon hadn't organised a watch system either. Everyone else on *Strong Winds* had had some sleep, except her. She was too used to being on her own. They should have forced her to rest.

When she was lying on the deck, before they moved her into the cockpit, June had lifted up her eyelids and the pupils were completely dilated. That meant the heart had stopped.

The helicopter was almost directly above them now. Its downdraft was flattening the sea and its noise was unbelievable. He had to get this right.

His mum could take the tiller. She'd do it better than him. Noise didn't bother Skye at all and she would be rock steady as long as she knew what to do. Then he'd have his hands free for everything else.

The lifeboat man had set their course. Wind 30 degrees on the port bow. Thank heavens it was calmer now. He hoped Skye wouldn't be frightened when the winch-man came down.

He glanced at June. Her frown had eased. Was there maybe a little colour around the edges of Gold Dragon's face? Her eyes were still closed, her lips were blue and shrivelled and all the skin seemed to have fallen away from her cheeks so her nose jutted outwards like the peak of Darien.

Donny wanted to smack himself around the head. Peak of Darien indeed!

A weighted line was coming from the helicopter. He knew it had to touch the water well away from the junk in order to earth the static charge from those whirling rotor blades. A powerful searchlight beamed downwards. *Strong Winds* was an island of light in the darkening sea.

He checked Skye. Would she panic?

"Great wind bird," she signed, mainly using her shoulders and elbows, without taking a hand from the tiller or her eyes from the illuminated compass.

Go, Mum!

He made a sign of power and listened to the VHF. He was being instructed to gather in the slack. No sooner had he hooked the hi-line into the cockpit than the wire began pouring down and he saw the dark shape of a man sitting astride a folded stretcher.

These people weren't wasting any time. And they expected him to be pretty sharp.

Donny realised, at the last moment, that if he didn't leave go of the hi-line and shove the radio set in his pocket and grab hold of the stretcher as it swung in, it was going to get caught or bash someone.

The noise was like a madman's metal factory, clattering invisible hammers all round them, trying to bash the air flat. The helicopter downdraft was shoving the wind straight onto the decks as if it was wanted to shove *Strong Winds* under.

She wasn't going. Every single thing that wasn't firmly

secured was trying to fly off sideways but the boat herself was solid and buoyant.

A moment later the winch-man landed. Donny had expected him to be wearing some sort of helmet but he wasn't. The brilliant light showed that he had long black hair tied in a ponytail; his skin was copper-coloured and his broad strong cheekbones and a beaked nose were extraordinarily familiar.

The winch-man took two quick steps towards Skye and put both his hands on her shoulders.

"I have dreamed you all my life," he said.

Was that really what he'd said? If Donny wasn't majorly good at lip-reading, he wouldn't have believed it. It was so crazy.

Skye, of course, said nothing. She stepped back, staring at him. Then she took one of her own brown hands from the tiller and laid it against his brown cheek. Their skins matched.

But she needed to keep the boat steady. Wind 30 degrees on the port bow.

A crackle from the radio on the winch-man's jacket coincided with a furious exclamation from June.

The winch-man smiled at Donny – a totally untranslatable smile – then shifted the stretcher into position and knelt beside Gold Dragon. June had moved her into the recovery position and pulled a corner of the blanket over her.

"I have to take you to hospital," he said.

There was no recognition in the Gold Dragon's bleached face but her eyes had opened slightly and June was rubbing her outstretched hand. The winch-man grasped the blanket on both sides and began to slide it across onto the stretcher. June tucked the hand away and tried to help.

Suddenly Gold Dragon began to struggle: her eyes flashed open, she fought to roll away.

"She's the Captain," Donny cupped his hands either side of his mouth and shouted. "This is her ship. She doesn't want to leave. She'd rather die."

"Ask her," the winch-man shouted back, June heard him too, "if she owns the swallow flag or the campfire kettle? Tell her that I am the child of the *Houdalinqua*. She should trust me."

"He's from the *Houdalinqua*!" Donny leaned forward and yelled. "He knows about the swallow flag!"

Gold Dragon's eyes blinked briefly in the fierce light. Then she gave another of those awful groans and clutched her hands to her chest. Terrible pain carved up her face.

"What the hell are you trying to do?" June was incandescent. "Finish her off?"

"We have a defibrillator in the helicopter. And oxygen. I want her to come with me. We will take her to the port hospital in Rotterdam. If she comes she may live. If she stays she will die. It is her choice."

Donny didn't think that helicopter rescue men did choices.

"The rest," added the man, more quietly, "I don't understand so much more than you do."

Donny stared at Skye. Who was this man? It couldn't be … Hermann?

His mother appeared completely calm. If you'd had a protractor to check her wake you wouldn't have found a half-degree of waggle. Her woolly hat had been whirled away and wisps of hair were fighting to escape from her plaits. She was beaming at Great Aunt Ellen.

A hook pushed its way fractionally towards the edge of the stretcher.

It was enough. Quickly and gently they lifted her across and strapped her securely. Suddenly Gold Dragon seemed very small.

Then the winch-man reattached his harness and made a sign to whoever was watching from above. He put his feet on either side of the stretcher and used his weight to keep it steady as they rose rapidly away from *Strong Winds*. He was gazing down at Skye as if he wanted to pull her upwards too.

"I'll call you in Vlissingen!"

He doesn't know she doesn't hear, thought Donny.

Seconds later the stretcher was inside the helicopter, the door was closed and the searchlight extinguished. With a final burst of turbulence, the black-and-gold machine lowered its head and set off like a charging bull. A bright light began to flash from its underbelly as it curved away north-westward.

Strong Winds' stressed and jerky motion took a long while to subside. Donny, June and Skye were left confused and breathless in the sudden night.

CHAPTER TWELVE

Gateway

Xiamen, March 2007

Min forced himself to walk down the path away from the apartment block in the direction that he hoped would take him towards the bridge. As soon as he'd gone a few paces he looked back, willing himself to memorise the concrete doorway. A few paces further and it disappeared behind the next tall building. The houses looked so similar it was frightening. He counted each block as he passed.

Finally he was out of the huddle of apartments and into an empty space. He didn't remember it from last night but it had been so dark and he had been following Kai. The earth was bare and rutted. There were some heaps of what looked like construction materials but no-one was working here. He hesitated on the edge. The buildings were grouped so close; this area was so wide. So bare. He walked a little way then turned and looked back to check he wasn't lost.

Now that he had moved away from the buildings he could see beyond them. There were mountains in the distance. Green wooded mountains rugged against the sky. Beyond them, many hours beyond them, in higher mountains and with small fields and streams and narrow rushing rivers, was the village they had left. Min felt a pang of longing for Grandmother and the neighbours, the chickens and his own small room.

But this was nothing to the journey his mother had made. He turned and walked back through the houses the way he'd come, counting in reverse. Then out onto the empty space again. He could do this.

Kai had told him on the bus last night that they were crossing between islands. If he walked in the direction of the bridge and kept straight he would surely reach the water. He could look across at that towering magical city that had bedazzled him when they arrived. Then he'd work out where to go next.

Xiamen means Gate of China. People enter and leave by many different routes. Not all of them are legal. People who have money and all the correct papers can travel comfortably. They can go anywhere and return whenever they choose.

People who have money but no papers can buy them from the *she-tou*. They do not always travel comfortably but the *she-tou* is well organised and has many different routes.

People who have no papers and very little money will find that the gates are closed to them. Min couldn't see how he was going to slip through.

He hadn't eaten all day. He had discovered that the wide road crossing the bridge over the harbour was a super-highway mounted on pillars. It didn't seem to come down anywhere but he knew that it must. He had watched the tops of vehicles travelling high above him. Most of them were lorries. Container lorries. He remembered that when he and Kai had got off their bus they'd walked by the side of the highway and into the factory area. There must be an exit there.

Once he had worked that out, he had turned away from staring at the bridge in order to move closer to the water. The road here was dotted with trees and the apartments were new and thirty storeys high. They looked expensive. The view across the river delta was like nothing that he had ever seen. Busy tugs and ferries, traditional sampans and modern yachts, enormous ships stacked high with containers. If he could get on board one of them, surely he could travel anywhere?

Kai was late home and tired. He wanted to drink a beer, watch TV and sleep. They ate noodles and fish paste and the rest of Grandmother's rice balls. He said Min could walk with him to the factory in the morning but he'd need to get up early. Then he relented a bit and said he had a bike that Min could use if he wanted to explore further. The bike had taken months of saving and Min had to be careful that he didn't get picked up by the Au Gong, the city police. Children shouldn't be out on the streets during the day. They should be in school. Or possibly at work. They'd definitely ask questions if they saw Min hanging around the railway station or in the shopping streets and the tourist areas.

"Though it's very beautiful in the city on the other side. There are gardens and sports grounds. Historic buildings. I'll take you when I get a day off – if I'm not too tired."

Min couldn't come into the factory. Not unless he wanted to work there. Maybe he should think about it? He could lie about his age and try and find something on the assembly line? Kai could ask the boss. The work was hard and boring but it was a start. He could eat in the cafeteria, which was cheap, maybe move into one of the dormitories and start sending a bit of money home.

This crazy idea about getting to England – it wasn't going to happen. No-one would lend a kid like Min any money – certainly not enough for a *she-tou*'s deposit. Maybe in a few years when he'd grown a bit and got some work experience. Meanwhile Kai couldn't afford to feed them both full-time until he'd got next month's pay packet. The money in Grandmother's red envelopes wasn't going to last long. Old people didn't understand how expensive everything was in the city.

"I have my own life to think of, little cousin."

"Please don't worry about me, Chen Kai. I hope I won't trouble you for long and I have a small appetite. I'm very grateful for your kindness. And for lending me your bike."

When Kai was in the village he always laughed a lot, played jokes, made the old people laugh as well. Kai Xin, they called him – Happy Heart. He was different here. As they walked to the factory in the morning he didn't speak to Min at all. There were many other people walking in the same direction. They were queuing to check in. You could lose half a day's pay if you were a few moments late in the morning.

Kai's factory made sport equipment. Its products were packed onto pallets and sent over the bridge to Xiamen port. There they were loaded into containers and lifted onto ships. Some of those ships would deliver their cargo to the Country of the Ghosts.

"You can't get into the port," Kai told Min. "There is a fence all round and strict security at the gate. Too many people have tried to leave that way. They have equipment to scan the containers before they are loaded onto the ships. To check there is no-one hidden. Better to wait until you're older and you have some money. Then you buy fake papers and a tourist visa."

Min had found the entrance to the port. The men in uniform looked like police. They stared at him. One of them stepped forwards.

Min pedalled away in a panic. He took a wrong turning and found himself cycling past a school. Everyone was inside. They would be studying.

That's what his mother thought he was doing. His father had died because he wanted Min to have a good education. His mother had left home to earn the money for him to learn. His grandparents had paid for his textbooks and the uniform. The prices had gone up and their earnings had gone down. Some of their land had been taken. But they hadn't told him to leave school: they had borrowed from the money-lender to make it possible for him to continue and to take extra lessons.

Grandmother couldn't keep up the repayments after Grand-father had died so his mother had borrowed from the English *gong-tou* to help her. Then she was afraid and couldn't ring them any more. But still no one had said he should go to work in the factory.

Min began to wonder whether he had deserved so much. His teacher had said that if he continued to work diligently he would pass the exam to High School. High School would be more expensive and he would have to study every moment he was there because if he did not get a high score in the exam for university, all his family's sacrifice would be for nothing. There was sure to be a good university here in Xiamen, somewhere among the beautiful gardens and the sports grounds that Kai had talked about.

"If there is no dark and dogged will, there will be no shining accomplishment," his grandfather used to say. "If there is no dull and determined effort, there will be no brilliant achievement."

University wasn't free. What good would it do to win a place at university if there was still no money to pay for it? But if he ever reached his mother, would she be angry that he hadn't stayed at school?

It was foggy in Xiamen next morning. A thick wet fog. Everything was dripping. Even the container lorries on the super-highway were driving slowly. So slowly that Min could follow them on his cousin's bike. This was his chance to get closer to the security gate.

He chose one. He couldn't tell if it was grey or blue. The colour faded as soon as he dropped a few metres behind. The fog was so thick that there was no chance the driver would see him in his mirror. They were over the bridge, curving round and down to the port. The lorry stopped at the barrier and Min moved back but not too far. He wanted to see exactly who came to check.

No-one came. The driver got impatient and sounded his horn. He got out and walked across to the cabin by the gate. Or where it would be if Min could see anything. Then there were shapes thickening the gloom. Voices.

Min stepped back hastily and felt himself pressing against

twigs and wet leaves. Ornamental bushes clustered round the base of the port entry sign. He pushed Kai's bike behind the bushes so he could move more easily. Hide if he had to. There were two men walking to the back of the container. He could hear one of them coughing in the damp air. Couldn't tell what they were doing.

The dull slam of the cab door closing, then a red rear light blurred by mist. The lorry was about to move.

Min ran to the back of the lorry and jumped up. There were toeholds at the base of the container and he clung to the metal rods that locked its doors. He felt the engine starting and flattened himself against the cold surface. The lorry jolted into life and moved ponderously through the gates. Min was wearing faded jeans and an old grey anorak. He kept his face turned inwards. Nobody shouted and the lorry didn't stop.

It was a long road from the entrance. His hands felt as numb and cold as the metal rods on the back of the container. His arms ached as he held himself still and close, bracing his back against the lorry's movement.

Then the lorry stopped. The fog swirled and steadied. He could hear another engine. Rumbling. Heavy. Coming closer. It was a mobile crane. Min didn't wait to discover what it was going to do. He slid clumsily to the ground and ran away. Couldn't see properly. Cannoned into the corner of a stack of metal containers. Fell to the ground gasping. Crawled away to hide between them.

Time passed. The fog didn't lift. Min picked himself up and began moving through the lines of containers. He was bruised and cold. He was only moving because he was too miserable to stay still. Out of habit he continued to count the stacks. The metal containers were different colours, travel-stained and faded. They had different logos painted on their sides.

Min started to look for patterns, as if he were within the walls of a giant Mah-Jong game. Three containers of the same colour and logo, *pung*; a three-colour, same-logo sequence, *chow*. Unusual logos were flower and season tiles. His grandfather had loved Mah-Jong; he had loved his grandfather.

He began to think that there was something cooking nearby. Was that the hiss and sizzle of fish balls? Perhaps he was hallucinating. The warm smell of *geng* tinged the grey air golden. There were men talking. Were they actual or imagined? Were they playing Mah-Jong or bending forward to spoon soup into their mouths? Thick tangy soup. They would chase around for noodles, savour each last succulent morsel of meat or fish. They would wipe the bowls clean. Nothing would be wasted. If this was a hallucination, Min wanted to be in it.

He finished making patterns. Four sets and a pair. Mah-Jong! he declared to himself. Then he chose the nearest gap in the walls of parked containers and walked through the fog towards the smell.

It was a gamble that should never have paid off. One of the containers had been converted into a snack bar for the workers. The soup was *rou-geng*, viscous and shining, with a world of delicious fragments suspended in its translucent depths. There were a few chairs and a table in the narrow space but Min wasn't looking anywhere except at the big man in a crumpled chef's outfit ladling the soup into bowls. There was a wok beside him, steaming sweaty and fragrant; dumplings warmed on the side of a griddle, fish balls sizzling in the heat.

Min's lucky money was next to his skin. His hands felt big and awkward as he fumbled under his clothes, opened the zip, took out the red envelope and extracted one crisp new note. He didn't look at the other customers. He thanked his grandmother, silently and held out his money to the chef.

For a moment he didn't think the man would take it. No-one spoke. Min knew he shouldn't be there. All he wanted was some soup before they called the port officials and had him thrown out. Or worse. The chef's face was violently scarred. Min saw knife handles protruding from the pocket of his apron and a cleaver on the chopping board. Could you get such injuries from a kitchen accident?

"Please, sir, may I buy some soup?"

The chef stared. Min wanted to run. But he wanted the soup more. He stood there, looking down politely, still holding out his grandmother's note.

The chef laughed. "You youngsters have all the luck at this time of year. You're Feng Gui's boy aren't you? I haven't seen your father for a while. Still with the police I suppose?"

Min kept his head bowed. Should he tell the chef that he'd made a mistake? That his father was a rural farmer who tried to work in the city? That he had died when Min was three?

"My father says little in my hearing, honoured sir, but I'm sure he would wish me to pay my respects. I try to follow his example as closely as I am able."

"A little copper, eh? You must be older than you look. In fact I wouldn't be surprised if you were about his business now. Good thing I've got my licence stamped and none of my customers has anything to conceal."

Min could feel the other men slipping away. He stood where he was, head down, hooked by his hunger and the chef's strange lies.

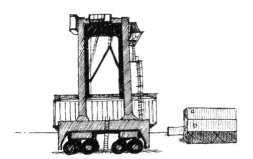

CHAPTER THIRTEEN

Oostende

Gallister High School, Suffolk, Wednesday 18 April 2007
June had refused to take *Strong Winds* any further that night. It was very late and they were exhausted. *Strong Winds* was low on diesel and they wouldn't be doing Gold Dragon any favours if they put her boat at further risk.

She had automatically assumed that she was *Strong Winds'* skipper. Donny wondered whether he should mutiny. He tried claiming that he'd been to Vlissengen / Flushing before – but he hadn't, only John-in-the-book had. Whereas June and Joshua had actually taken *Snow Goose* into Oostende as recently as last summer. It was the nearest port and that was where they were going. June wanted to make sure that whoever had been on board the *Pride of Macao* was arrested and charged as soon as possible. Donny couldn't see that happening. He thought they should follow the helicopter.

"There's also a regular ferry service from Oostende back to England," June added, in the same firm tone he'd heard her use to Xanthe.

"But Gold Dragon's been lifted off to hospital in Rotterdam, and that guy said he'd call us in Vlissingen. He'll have news. Anyway, he'll want to see Mum."

It had been churny seeing that unknown guy gazing at his mother like she was totally amazing. Which she was, of course, only he'd never seen anyone else see it before.

"Mum," he'd asked, trying to keep the crazy hope out of his signing "Was that Hermann? Was that … my dad?"

But it wasn't. The man who came down from the helicopter had said he was the child of the *Houdalinqua*. That was the name of Skye's parents' boat. Was he a friend of theirs? Some sort of relative? Yet he obviously didn't know Skye all that well because he hadn't known she was deaf.

"Who was he, Mum? He said he'd dreamed you."

"Ojibwa. Of my father's people. They know much in dreams."

"Had you dreamed him?"

"Maybe."

"My mum needs to see that guy again," Donny said to June. "And he thinks we're going to Vlissingen. He said he'd call us there. Gold Dragon would have carried on."

"Your great-aunt just nearly died, in case you hadn't noticed," said June. "Partly, I suspect, because she was already at the end of her tether before that … pirate tried to ram us. Oostende is part of the continent of Europe. It has a telecommunications service. And trains – which we will use if you're allowed to travel any further without ID. If you're not, we will have to decide whether you're sufficiently mature to be allowed to return to England on your own, or whether your mother or I have to escort you back. To make sure you don't do anything else unbelievably stupid."

"Oh." Donny had forgotten all that stuff about how he came to be on board *Strong Winds* in the first place. "Um, Mrs Ribiero … er … June … you saved Great Aunt Ellen's life. If you hadn't been here, she really would be dead."

They had spent the rest of that first exhausted night alongside a pontoon belonging to the North Sea Yacht Club in Oostende. June was so efficient that she even had a few euros with her to buy fresh bread and milk the following morning. She said they always kept a supply of currency on board *Snow Goose* in case of emergency landfalls. She would have sent Donny to the shops but the immigration authorities were already on his case for arriving with no passport. Apparently Gold Dragon should have been carrying some official crew list and he wasn't on that either. They accepted June's explanation that the reason for *Strong Winds*' arrival in Belgium was that she was on passage for Rotterdam where her owner had intended to clarify her paperwork but that still didn't excuse Donny's presence on board. June didn't even try explaining that he'd jumped over the side of her husband's yacht and had refused to be rescued.

"Couldn't you like tell them that I'm my mum's interpreter or something?"

Nothing she had said made any difference. He was to be sent back to England on the first available ferry and meanwhile he was not permitted to leave the port area. If June didn't guarantee his compliance they would consider taking him into custody.

She switched to asking what steps had been taken to arrest the captain and crew of the *Pride of Macao*? The immigration authorities said that was a matter for the police but when the police came they were unenthusiastic. Attempted Ramming didn't seem to be on their list of criminal offences. When June pointed to the Tiger's knife they re-photographed it and took everyone's fingerprints. Then they wrapped it in some sort of plastic and took it away. June insisted on making an official witness statement but Skye couldn't tell them what she'd seen and Donny was quite relieved that they didn't ask him. He wasn't sure what he would have said about Gold Dragon shooting the Tiger in the stomach with that flare.

Strong Winds' voyage was over. As soon as Donny had been deported June and Skye would hurry to Rotterdam hospital by train. The harbour authorities advised them to move the junk to a more secure berth. This was two basins further in, through lock gates and three sets of lifting bridges. It wasn't going to be cheap – they didn't dare think about who would pay – but she'd be safe there while the lawyers argued about her status and her skipper battled for survival. Donny wondered whether *Strong Winds* would feel abandoned amongst the cluster of GRP yachts and small motor vessels. There was an impressive museum ship there, the *Mercator*, but she'd stuck her bowsprit to the skies and fallen asleep, knowing that she'd never go sailing again.

June vented her frustrations in a furious telephone call to Joshua. Then they had tidied *Strong Winds* as best they could. They hauled down her flags, closed the stopcocks, turned off the electrics, then locked the cabin doors and checked the mooring warps one last time before leaving to meet the Ramsgate ferry. Skye and Donny packed their clothes and Donny had all his schoolbooks weighing down his rucksack.

Was there anything he could leave behind? He'd finished re-reading *We Didn't Mean to Go to Sea*. This time it had depressed him. John-in-the-book had managed everything, virtually unaided, whereas Donny couldn't see that he'd been much help to anyone. June was so experienced it had been natural for her to take command and Skye had steered as if she'd been lashed into the chains since birth. No surprise father had leapt from his ship to save them (that was his favourite bit in the story) and now he was being sent back to Erewhon Parva vicarage while the others went on to Rotterdam.

He heaved the book out of his rucksack. Then, on an impulse, he decided to lay it in the berth where Gold Dragon should have slept. A pledge for her return.

"Something for Ellen to read in hospital … what a good idea," June smiled, taking the book from him and packing it. Donny couldn't quite get his face to smile back.

He was haunted by his last glimpse of his great-aunt. She'd looked so fragile, strapped to her stretcher, then hauled away into that whirling, clattering, machine. And who was that strange bloke who had asked her whether she owned the camp-fire kettle or the swallow flag? The swallow flag had come from her sister, Eirene, Skye's mother. He wasn't sure about the camp-fire kettle. Was that Granny's?

When June was about to lock up the junk Donny dived back in to the cabin. He grabbed *Secret Water* from the ship's book-shelf. He knew it was his great-aunt's special favourite (apart from *Missee Lee*) and he hadn't had any time to ask her what it had been like, that last weekend, revisiting the actual location. He'd read the book as quickly as he could, then send her a proper letter sounding really interested. Maybe he'd copy her some maps.

"I can't believe you didn't discover what happened to the *Pride of Macao*." Xanthe sounded accusing as she swung her book bag off her shoulder and let it fall on the dining-hall floor with a thud. She was officially on study leave but she'd chosen to come and work in the school library instead of staying at home. She and Maggi hadn't said much but the others knew that the Ribieros had had a terrible argument when June had telephoned from Belgium. She'd accused Joshua of cowardice in resigning from his job, especially for doing it without telling her. The girls agreed with their mother and were extra-outraged that neither of their parents had given them any hint what was going on when it was them who'd have to change schools and leave all their friends if their father took a job abroad.

Mr Ribiero was staying at home that day to think about application letters. Xanthe said she didn't trust herself to be in the house with him.

"What chance did I have to do anything?" Donny protested. "I wasn't allowed to leave the port and then I was marched onto that ferry as if I'd committed some sort of crime." The ferry didn't normally take foot passengers but the police had ordered them to make an exception in his case. He wasn't allowed to move from the saloon and everyone treated him as if he was some sort of delinquent. Rev. Wendy had met him at Ramsgate and driven him back to Suffolk in her little car. She hadn't said much. "I thought the coastguard might have tracked her on the radar but I think she was too busy trying to sort us out. Getting the helicopter and all that. The police did say that it was an offence *Pride of Macao* not waiting to offer help when *Strong Winds* was in distress."

"They didn't understand the problem at all?"

"When your mum said we were under attack by pirates?

No. I don't think Belgium's that sort of place. Or they don't think it is."

"To be fair I wouldn't have expected to find pirates in Suffolk either," said Maggi. "Not till I met you and your family. Fancy a pasta salad, Anna?"

"Not all that hungry, thanks. I wonder where she is now."

"Who?"

"*Pride of Macao. Hispaniola* as was. She's obviously got some good hiding place wherever it was that we couldn't find her. But you'd have thought that she'd have been spotted coming back into the harbour. I mean there's obviously radar and there's all those Port of Felixstowe webcams and you'd think the coast-guards and harbour authorities and immigration people here would be pretty hot shot, wouldn't you?"

"Except for any of them who are being bribed or intimidated or just plain fooled by Flint." Donny was having two big-break-fast panini with salad, beans and pasta topping. He only wished the school's healthy eating policy would allow him to add chips as well. Except then he'd probably end up as gross as the fat policeman. "There must be some who do what he says or they wouldn't have managed to set up that ambush for *Strong Winds*. It would have been really early morning again when she did come back. If she did. Could have slipped past if there was someone looking the other way."

"We'd have kept watch on the river ourselves if you'd told us."

"Sorry. Other things on my mind. Don't get at me, okay?"

"That helicopter winch-man sounds cool." Maggi was changing the subject.

"Deus," agreed Anna.

"Don't you mean dude? Or 'well fit' as you and Mags might say when you're prowling the streets of Ipswich getting your shopping fix."

Xanthe was so grumpy today. Maybe it was pre-exam stress. Now she was getting at her sister for saying, at least twice during the past three months, that she'd rather go into town with Anna on a Saturday afternoon than be out on the river in the freezing cold doing extra capsize drills.

"At least we're half way sociable," said Maggi. "You never look long enough to see whether someone's male or female. You're too busy trying to work out where you can tack across them or take their wind."

"Anyway," said Anna, "I meant to say *deus*. I mean, this guy could well be cool but from what Donny's been saying, he's at least over thirty. So, maybe not. I meant *deus* as in *deus ex machina*, a god out of a machine. They used to have them in Greek and Roman plays. They'd come down from a pulley or something suspended over the stage and, like, rescue the heroine or change the course of a battle or something. He's a helicopter winch-man. I mean, neat or what?"

"You've been swotting again," Donny accused her. He really hated it when he thought of her taking that scholarship to her new posh school. "You should get out more, Anna. Get a life."

She pressed her lips together and went to buy a smoothie from the vending machines.

"Your mum was amazing, by the way," he said for the millionth time to Maggi and Xanthe when everyone had finally got their food and the atmosphere had lightened up a bit.

"Obviously," said Anna. "But if you hadn't been there they

wouldn't have had any warning at all about the *Pride of Macao*."

"Or what Dad was about to do," added Xanthe. "Lily-livered surrender monkey."

"But there've been more infection-related deaths from his department than anywhere else in the hospital," said Maggi. "And neurosurgery shouldn't carry that type of risk. I mean it's not like it's a medical ward where people might come in being infected already. Well they might, I suppose, but Dad's been doing extra-thorough pre-op tests and they're not."

"It's got to be the cleaning."

"Pura-Lilly!" Xanthe spat. "Even the name stinks."

"But if Gold Dragon's really taken out the Tiger …?"

"No Tiger, no Pura-Lilly …?"

"You wish," said Anna. "It won't just be him you know. Remember how my mum said she got suckered into working for him. It was Toxic. As it is, the whole situation, poisonous."

Maggi was still thinking about her parents. "Maybe, when Mum comes home, they'll have one of their long after-supper forget-to-turn-the-lights-on conversations and we can make out we've got work to do and leave them to it?"

"Maybe," said Xanthe, gloomily, "if they're talking at all after those things she said to him yesterday."

Donny didn't like to think of the Ribieros having that bad an argument. "Is Rev. Wendy okay?" he asked Anna. "She hardly said a word all the way back in the car last night. Not as if she was cross. She just seemed slightly out of it."

"She was probably bothered because she wasn't chairing the Mothers' Union AGM or something. There's some Diocesan Mission thing for the flood victims in Indonesia."

Anna chucked her bottle into the recycling bin. "You're going to want to go back to Oostende. Or Rotterdam. Do you fancy a quick trip to the library and we'll go on-line to see what you need to do to get yourself a passport?"

"Thanks. And tonight I'll search the camper van to find my birth certificate. I'm sure to need that."

"Biometric prints, more likely. And money."

CHAPTER FOURTEEN

Hoi Fung

Xiamen International Port, March-April 2007
"It's okay," said the chef. "I know your father's not with the police. I don't know anything about your family. I wanted my customers to leave."

He spoke with such a heavy accent that it was difficult to understand. Min hadn't said anything. He was too busy eating. When the bowl of soup was empty, the chef gave him a plate of noodles together with some of the fish balls Min had heard sizzling. Sweet spicy noodles. Min felt them curled contentedly inside his stomach.

"Thank you," he said. The chef hadn't even asked him to pay extra.

"The last time I cooked noodles for a boy with an appetite like you I was far away from China."

"Where is your home, sir?"

"Guangdong Province. I was born into a nest of sea scorpions in Bias Bay. I am a ship's cook."

"But you have not chosen to go home?"

Min had been about to quote one of his grandfather's favourite sayings, "falling leaves return to their roots," but he realised that this might seem discourteous. Those scars made it impossible to tell how old the chef was really.

"No. But we are not discussing me. It's you. What are you

doing here? This city may be your home, I don't know, but the port is no place for a boy. You should be in school. Or possibly at work?"

"I have only just arrived in Xiamen. I'm staying with my cousin. I need to find my mother and I can't think how to do it."

"She won't be here in the port."

"She's in England. She can't come back to us because she owes money to the *gong-tou*. I want to go to her."

Min covered his mouth with his hand but it was too late, the words were out.

The chef frowned. "The Country of the Ghosts can be a dangerous place for those who owe money. My name is Hoi Fung. You should listen to my advice."

"I am Chen Min. I am eager to find help."

The chef looked hard at Min and then he laughed, a sudden, wide, rumbling laugh. "So, if my advice is don't go, stay here in your own country, finish your education or see what you can do to get a job, you'll thank me politely and go away. But if I tell you how to hide yourself in one of these metal boxes: if I help you spend three or four weeks in the stinking dark, sick and frightened and hungry, to reach a country where you're unwanted and illegal; a country where your own countrymen will exploit and enslave you as they've exploited and enslaved your mother, then you'll give me a big grin and do anything I say!"

Min wished that he could speak Cantonese. Hoi Fung's deep voice expressed such an extraordinary mix of passion and kindness but his words were so difficult to understand. Min's native language was a form of Hokkien but his Mandarin was clear and formal, a good student's speech. At this moment it seemed safest to say nothing. Just look straight up into the chef's brown eyes and smile. There were laughter lines travelling from the corners of those eyes as well as the terrifying scars and a complicated criss-crossing of wrinkles.

"The boy who helped me escape was a boy your age. It would be better if we can help your mother to come home."

"I'm not sure exactly where she is and I don't know how much money she owes."

"But I have a good friend in the Country of the Ghosts. Ai Qin knows many people and can pass messages secretly. I'll take you on as my kitchen boy – some of that money from your red envelope will buy you an entry permit from the gate staff – and you can fill your stomach with soup and noodles every day while we wait for news."

Min began to thank him but Hoi Fung was frowning again.

"Let them think that your father's a policeman. I can send you round the port to do deliveries but you don't want people asking too many questions. You're not a good liar so you must learn not to speak. I don't have friends here and I don't want them."

"I can use my cousin's bicycle. I make a delivery and then I pedal away quickly. We'll do more business too."

Min enjoyed working for Hoi Fung. The food was very good. It was cheap and it was always hot. They fixed a plastic box to the handlebars of Chen Kai's bike. It had a tight-fitting lid and polystyrene packing for insulation. Min got to ride all round the port and whenever he started a new area the chef offered a special deal to the foremen and other officials so they didn't have to pay. If anyone asked Min any questions he looked awkward and didn't answer. People suspected he might be some sort of spy so they took the good hot food and were glad when the delivery bike was gone.

Hoi Fung sent a message to England. He didn't tell Min how this was done. He still had *guanxi*, connections, he said.

Spring came to Xiamen as they waited for Ai Qin's reply.

It was the wrong answer. Or, more exactly, it was an answer from the wrong person.

Hoi Fung was lying on the ground. There were men surrounding him. Kicking, punching and shouting. All in Cantonese. Min couldn't understand what they were saying. He'd just got back from a delivery. The container café had been trashed: food tipped out, tables and chairs overturned. Any customers had disappeared.

One of the men had a knife. He was slitting through Hoi Fung's white chef's trouser to the leg beneath. He cut the straps of the leg and pulled it away. Then he threw it into the path of a loaded straddle carrier.

Sixty tonnes of heavy machinery ground the limb to splinters.

"Stop it!" Min shouted and rode towards them. One of the men turned and sprinted at him. Pushed him off the bike so violently that he hurtled through the air and landed hard on the packed earth. They slashed the bike tyres and kicked the chef some more. Then they ran off, shouting threats.

Hoi Fung stole from the Tiger in the Land of the Ghosts and this is the Tiger's revenge. Or it is the beginning of revenge. Hoi Fung owes money and the Tiger wants it back. If he doesn't get it the attackers will take the other leg, the living one.

The Tiger is a *gong-tou*, a gang-master. His name is Zhang. Hoi Fung offered to buy the debt of one of his workers. An Englishwoman. Her daughters gave him the money but he didn't hand it over. The woman escaped and so did he.

The Tiger was very angry. He used his own *guanxi*. He sent messages to triads and snake-heads all along the coast and they had found the chef.

"You'd better give the money to them," Min advised anxiously. "The snake-heads and the money-lenders know everyone. They know the criminals and the police as well. You can't fight them on your own. They'll ruin your business and … they might do worse. You can earn more. I'll still help you."

He felt a bit shaky as he said that. He hadn't even realised that the sea-cook had only one leg until he saw it torn away from him.

Hoi Fung had dragged himself up into the container café. Min had pulled the rear doors shut as if they were closed for the day. He'd picked up a couple of the chairs and lit a lamp. Hoi Fung was drinking home-brewed rice wine.

"I didn't keep the money. I left it with Ai Qin to help others return home to China."

"People like my mother?"

"It's possible, but you don't know where she's working and we've no more time to wait. Those men will be back and they've seen you. You'll have to travel now. My network will help – if it's not been broken. You get to Suffolk and you find Ai Qin at the Floating Lotus. Then you ask her to take you to the Dragon …"

"Who's he?"

Tigers and Dragons! This was beginning to sound like one of

Grandmother's fireside tales. Except that Hoi Fung's breath was rasping where the attackers had kicked his ribs. His face was swollen, one eye shut and his artificial leg was crushed into the dirt.

Min was bruised and aching too.

"Jin Lóng, Gold Dragon as she is called in English – or Hai Lóng, dragon of the sea – was trained by the greatest of the Chinese pirates, Madame Li Choi San. But Jin Lóng never fought for gain. She was a legend of my boyhood – the Englishwoman who helped fugitives. Even against her own country's ships. Then she took a new name and sailed round the world. There is no-one else for whom I would have done this. You must go to Jin Lóng. And you must go now. I'm sorry for your cousin but it's best you don't go back to him. We'll leave tonight from the new port."

"Are you coming with me? To the Country of the Ghosts?"

Min wouldn't be afraid at all if he and Hoi Fung could travel together.

"No, my friend. You saw those men. I put us both in danger. I will see you into the care of an old sea-scorpion. He sails tonight for Rotterdam. It's far from here but near to Suffolk. That is Ai Qin's province and also the new home of Jin Lóng. She is a powerful lady. I'm sure she will protect you."

"But what about you?"

"I am a falling leaf. It's time I returned to the root."

CHAPTER FIFTEEN

Defoe

Erewhon Parva Vicarage, Wednesday 18 April 2007

A single dream-catcher, cobwebbily suspended over the sliding door, reminded Donny of the summer when this camper van had been his and Skye's home. Maybe he should move in again? But Wendy and Gerald had assumed that he'd be using his old bedroom in the vicarage and someone had even managed to organise him a temporary bus pass so he could travel to and from school with Anna. That must have been Lottie because they'd have had to pay for it. He hadn't spent any time in the camper since he'd helped Sandra, the social worker, collect their clothes, bedding and books when the van had been released from the police pound last autumn.

Luke and Liam used it as a den. There were crumbs and three-quarters-empty plastic bottles and completely empty crisp packets. They collected junky toys and plastic weapons left unsold at the end of jumble sales or donated to them by the tidy parents of more sophisticated children. They hoarded guns and cowboy outfits, indestructible monsters from forgotten TV programmes and elderly copies of the Beano. They'd dumped all their camping stuff inside the van and someone, probably Lottie, had taken everything out of the bags and had spread them out to air. Donny was surprised how much mud and grass they seemed to have brought home from Mrs

Everson's field; bits of string and sweet wrappers too.

Donny sighed, and began searching through a box of papers that hadn't been taken on board *Strong Winds*. Lottie must have been through it already when she was looking for his passport. Had she looked in this folder, marked 'John' in Granny's small neat handwriting and with a papoose pictogram?

A papoose! His hands shook a bit. If he found his birth certificate, surely he would discover his father's full name? Did they do addresses on birth certificates?

The certificate was there. All the spaces relating to his father were blank.

Donny felt that same sick sense of loss and anger. How could Granny and Skye have let his dad get 'lost'? All that stuff about dancing in the Northlands and the breaking of the chain. He didn't understand his mother's story and he didn't care. His dad should have known that he had a child. And he should have known his dad.

The cushions in the camper van were faded by the sunlight and flecked with mould. Donny chucked them across the crowded space, pushed a couple of sleeping bags aside and plonked himself onto the bench. He noticed Granny's blackened old kettle: the one that had stood by the door of their bungalow in Leeds, the place where they kept their house-key. They used to take that kettle on holidays with them. It was special to Granny in some way. He didn't know why. You wouldn't exactly want to use it.

There were other things in the folder: some baby teeth, a fair curl – his, presumably – plus a shrivelled, black thing in a plastic peg. With a shock Donny realised that this must be some vestige of his umbilical cord. Ugh! How could Skye keep these grisly souvenirs and lose his father?

There were papers too: all the letters to solicitors, letters from Leeds SS, medical records, Assessments and Re-Assessments – all weapons from the bitter fight old Nokomis had fought to save him from being taken away from his mum and adopted. All the reasons why he should be grateful to her and not angry.

A worn brown file contained newspaper articles about the Baltic Revolution in the 1990s. That seemed a bit random. Donny read a few headlines. Then he got more interested. Some of the protests had involved lines of dancers.

There had also been police charges, violence, arrests and deaths.

When Donny opened the last file – the one that contained copies of all the letters that Granny Edith had continued sending to authorities in Riga and Tallinn, almost until the day she died – he finally began to make some sense of Skye's story.

It took a while. The camper van battery was flat but he had a torch in his rucksack. Granny had written to ask about ships in Baltic ports, crew lists, police detainees and casualties. She'd gone on asking for years and years but no-one had sent her anything except silence and dismissals. She'd subscribed to a slim newspaper called the *Baltic Eagle*, presumably so she could check it for Hermanns. Occasionally a face in a photograph was circled but then crossed out.

Donny began to feel certain that something bad had happened the night that his dad and mum were separated. This was definitely not the sort of holiday romance he'd imagined.

He was sitting there, staring at pages in the dark, when Anna came rattling at the door.

"You've missed supper," she said. "But there's some left in the kitchen. You missed a call from Toxic to Rev. Wendy – wanting to make it quaite clear that there would be no public funding for your stay at the Vicarage this taime – it's so funny seeing how Wendy doesn't give a toss about Toxic any more. When you think what she used to be like! You missed June Ribiero as well. She rang to say that Gold Dragon's still too ill to be visited. She's in intensive care but they think she'll pull through. It'll take a long time and she won't ever be the same etc etc. I expect they always say that. Anyway she and Skye are staying in Rotterdam and they've met up with that bloke again, the rescue-man. He's a hydrographer mapping tidal streams – which is why he and his team happened to be buzzing about in a helicopter when the coastguard needed someone. There was some reason to explain why he'd also had medical training but I can't remember what it was. The thing is that he's been drawing pictures for your mum. June wants you to ring her back as soon as possible. She urgently needs to ask you what the pictures mean. She wants to know if Skye could ever have had a brother?"

Rotterdam, Holland, Wednesday 18 April 2007
"My mother was a story-teller." June and Skye and the winch-man were sitting in the lounge of a hotel on the Haringvliet, as near to the port hospital as they could afford. He had soft cartographer's pencils and a large pad of paper headed The Delta Project. He was using it greedily to communicate with this woman who he had dreamed for so long. He hadn't known she couldn't hear. It didn't matter.

He sketched a man, a woman and a child. He gestured that the child was himself. "My mother called me Ned," he explained to June. "But I prefer Defoe." He drew his family living in a fertile clearing amidst luxuriant vegetation. "The Cocos Islands. Before they were made a national park and all the human inhabitants had to leave."

The older man was standing apart looking away into the distance. He was brown-skinned with long black plaited hair like Skye herself, or like the winch-man, except that Defoe's long hair was pulled high and sleek into a pony-tail. The woman had plaits but she was small and pale and her plaits were fair, or possibly even grey.

Defoe drew a curving line right out of his picture. He began to sketch the outline of *Strong Winds* and Gold Dragon lying on the deck. The line twisted into a question mark. It was obvious he was trying to connect Ellen to the small fair woman. "My mother," he said to June. "Eirene. Her name meant peace. They had crossed the ocean to find peace. She would never tell me why and neither did my father. He was a seer and he had built a sailing canoe, the *Houdalinqua*. Since they died I have spent my lifetime studying the ocean currents, wondering why they settled on an unknown shore, like castaways. Wondering if they had left anyone behind them. My mother told many stories of children. Especially stories of two boys and three girls who loved sailing and camping and making more stories. The Swallows and their adventures with the Amazons, two girls and with the Ds, a girl and a boy."

He was drawing as he spoke; an island and a lake, tents and dinghies, children in old-fashioned shorts and aertex shirts; a fat man, tumbling from a plank, squashed into a cage. Skye was watching his every line. "When I saw the junk earlier that day – you were crossing the TSS – I was certain that she had sailed straight out of one of those stories that my mother told me. I was never sure which of them were made up by someone else and which ones were her own."

He drew another curving line, pulling *Strong Winds* towards the story-pictures. Again it twisted into a query.

He looked at Skye, wanting her to understand. "There were other stories. Stories of two brothers who had died in the icy sea and two sisters left to guard a treasure. One sister was given a blue flag with a swallow: the other had a campfire kettle. The third sister sailed away. She took nothing with her.

They weren't such good stories. As if my mother wasn't certain what had happened in the end. She never told them when my father was there. I think they'd made a promise to each other that she sometimes found hard to keep. I told her about my dreams. My dreams of you," he said to Skye, drawing the contours of her face with complete certainty, then curving a connecting line back to the figure of the father as if to say you look like him.

"My father understood much in dreams," he said to June. "My mother needed words."

Skye had taken the pencil from him and was sketching dark, cruel scenes of disease and death. Two people fleeing from grief into emptiness. A canoe launched into the waves. A baby left behind. An old woman bent over the child; a kettle on the campfire. They weren't detailed pictures but they were powerful.

June had seen the swallow flag, flying at half-mast in *Strong Winds*' rigging but she didn't know anything about Skye's parents, Henry and Eirene. She'd never met Granny Edith or seen the blackened kettle. She couldn't draw the final line that took the *Houdalinqua* from leaving baby Skye in England with her aunts, far across the Pacific Ocean to the Cocos Islands and the birth of a second child. Not until Donny had rung her from Rev. Wendy's study that night and told her the story that Great Aunt Ellen had told him in the quiet of *Strong Winds*' cabin.

Then all of them understood.

His mother had a brother. No wonder their skins had matched when Skye had laid her brown hand against Defoe's brown cheek.

Donny had never seen anyone who looked like Skye as Defoe had looked like her.

And no-one who'd ever looked at Skye in the way Defoe had looked at her.

"And, if my mum's got a brother," he said excitedly to Anna, "Then I've … got an uncle!"

Gallister High School and Rotterdam Port Hospital, April 2007
To begin with, Donny's grand new acquisition didn't make a heap of difference to his everyday life. Skye and June stayed in Rotterdam until they had seen Gold Dragon and given her the wonderful news that her sister Eirene had found a new life and had had another child. Then they returned to England: June to campaign for access to the hospital's cleaning records and nag Xanthe about her revision: Skye to share Donny's small bedroom and spend as much time as possible with Anna's little sister, Vicky, and Hawkins, the rescued canary.

Defoe spent every moment that he wasn't at work sitting by Ellen's bed in Rotterdam's *Havenziekenhuis* trying to get used to the fact that he had found a family. He was in such a daze of happiness, so eager to hear her retell some of those childhood adventures, that he didn't notice the other uninvited visitors. The silent, hostile watchers who never introduced themselves and who might, had it not been for Defoe's oblivious presence, and the vigilance of the nursing staff, have been tempted to pull some vital tube from Gold Dragon's arm, or slip a pillow over her face and hold it there.

When Mr McMullen had seen Donny at registration, that first Wednesday morning back, he'd been decent about the absence authorisation, but as implacable as ever about the need to catch up with the work Donny had missed during his two days off.

Only two days off schoool? For all that!

"You still have to take SATs next month and I don't want to hear from a single one of my colleagues that you've blagged your way out of homework with the excuse that you weren't there when it was set. Use Miss Livesey's planner."

He'd smiled at Donny from within his bushy beard. But Donny didn't smile back. If his tutor was truly friendly, he'd have bothered telling him that he wasn't going to be at the school much longer. Like Edward bunking off on his fishing holiday or Joshua chucking in his job and preparing to take his family away as if it didn't matter to anybody else. The word 'homework' had made him remember the art lesson. 'Draw your Dad!' There wasn't an adult male in his life who he could be bothered to look at for the length of time it would take to sketch the single outline of their untrustworthy heads.

Or so he had thought then. Once he knew he had an uncle he'd changed this mind as swiftly as if he'd been roll-tacking Maggi's Laser round a racing mark.

Someone, probably Lottie, had bought Gerald a teach-yourself Sudoku book – presumably to wean him from his hopeless attempts at cryptic crosswords. Every evening he and Rev. Wendy were to be seen sitting next to one another at the wiped kitchen table, their mugs of Horlicks growing steadily colder as they struggled to put numbers into squares. Donny guessed that Wendy must be skipping meetings but he didn't like to say anything as the two of them appeared so strangely happy.

Not that they were doing well at Sudoku. He heard their embarrassing Wizard Whimstaff / Miss Snufflebeam joke once or twice, but generally both brows were furrowed, and Donny could glimpse lots of rubbings-out and lines of numbers in margins with question marks. Occasionally Anna was driven to offer help but Wendy turned her down quite snappily.

"It's our senility that needs sending into remission, not yours. Er, thank you, dear."

That's when he could do his homework and sketch Gerald. Gerald, who would always Be There for them, fussing away about meals and hygiene, struggling to keep up with the washing and recycling systems and regularly prevented from listening to his beloved Radio 4 by Luke and Liam's temper tantrums. There wouldn't be a lot of texture in his bleached, clean-shaven face and fading hair but it would do. Maybe he could con the two of them into attempting a Killer Kakuro, accentuate those furrows a bit …

How old were Gerald and Wendy anyway? Did they have a family? He'd never seen any photos.

"Who did you draw for Art?" he asked Anna. It wouldn't matter if she'd done Gerald already. Art was one of the very few subjects that he maybe had the edge. Not that he was talented or anything but he was a bit more patient than she was, didn't get so irritated if it wouldn't come right first time.

"I was going to ask Mum for a photo of Dad but then I thought I'd surf the net for a picture of my great-uncle, Oboe." She pulled her new Macbook out of her bag, sat down on the living room sofa and opened it as if she'd remembered something urgent. "Both of them are dead, so I'd only be observing the texture of a more or less poor-quality image, whichever I chose." She was already logging on. "As far as I'm concerned, my dad's death was a pretty well unmitigated disaster whereas Oboe's has actually helped quite a lot. So (a) I owe him enough to be interested in what he looked like and (b) I'm less likely to splosh tearmarks over the page. Okay?"

Donny wouldn't have dared to disagree.

"Maggi sketched some random sailing instructor. She called it study in purple and blue. It was so cold she didn't even take her gloves off when she was doing it. She and Xanthe are so fed up with their father that they're refusing to be in the same room as him. Except he's been away from home so much, they're not sure he's noticed their protest. I do wonder whether anyone will tell that stupid teacher how much grief she's managed to cause. It was obviously some spur-of-the-moment idea because she'd forgotten to think up a proper assignment. Usually when they want us to look at texture they get us to collect rocks or driftwood or something."

"Mmmm."

Maybe he'd go find the other kids or read *Secret Water* or something. There was this crazy little person sort of leaping about inside him, flourishing something that looked remarkably like Skye's ravelled standard on its bamboo pole and chanting, "I've got an un-cle! I've got an un-cle!" Over and over.

Gallister High School, May 2007

The crazy little person was possibly a bit of a figment but he'd got some assertiveness about him. When Ms Spinks called Donny into her office, a couple of weeks later, to yell at him for his failure to attend Inspector Flint's Bonding Initiative, Donny's inner uncle sent him straight along to his tutor to complain.

"I know I'm still on the SS list but I told my social worker that I didn't need to go and she completely agreed with me. My mum's come home from Holland now; I'm living in a house full of different-aged people. I've got friends AND, as soon as I've got my passport, I'm going to meet my uncle. That'll be when my great-aunt's ready to travel. Probably in about another month or six weeks."

All this was true and Sandra had been pleased for him.

"By the way," he'd dared to ask, "What happened to that other social worker? I can't remember his name ... Clang or Wang or something? He hasn't been round in ages."

"It wasn't Clang, it was Zhang. He was from an agency. I think he's gone off sick."

Donny tried to look sorry.

"It's okay," said Sandra. "I know you don't like us. You're not the first. I sometimes think that one of our main uses is giving our clients something definite to be angry about. Instead of simply angry with Life."

That was a bit too deep for Donny. He could have tried it out on Mr McMullen but he needed to stick to the main point.

"But Ms Stinks, sorry, sir, Ms Spinks, says I'm invalidating my Care Plan and there will be Consequences at the next meeting if I've failed to attend. I'm not going to the Boxing Club and that's that. I've only come to ask you whether they've really got a meeting?"

Care Review and Planning. C.R.A.P. Mr McMullen had to be invited to the SS meetings for as long as he was still Donny's tutor. So he'd know if there was one coming up and what was the worst they could do if Donny refused to play punch-bags with Flint. If they tried to take him away from Skye and send him to some hideous Home, he had an uncle who'd stick up for him. A glorious vision of being plucked away by helicopter made him think it might almost be worth it.

"Hmmm," said Mr McMullen. "You may perhaps have overlooked the economic aspects. Helicopter rescue doesn't come cheap, you know. It's possible that the Dutch navy or hydrographic office or whoever pays your uncle's fuel bill may not see springing a disgruntled fourteen-year-old from English SS accommodation as one of their prime objectives. They'd also have to consider the little matter of invading another nation's air space … even within the European Union."

"Oh," said Donny. He hadn't intended his tutor to take him quite that seriously.

"On the other hand there's also an economic aspect to taking young people into residential care. Accountability.

Expenditure of public money. Difficult to justify in this case I'd have thought. Especially now that your relatives can mount a legal challenge. That'll push the costs up and even Ms Tune has a budget to observe."

"O-kay?"

"The authorities think you should join something, something that brings you into contact with a new group of people, something, slightly … macho? What if we were to find you some regular commitment on Monday evenings? Something that, unavoidably, happens at very much the same time as Inspector Flint's initiative but which doesn't involve any demand on the public purse. No travel costs to Ipswich, for instance."

Donny said nothing. It felt safest.

"As it happens," continued Mr McMullen, "I have a long-standing involvement with the local sub-aqua society on a Monday evening. In fact I'm their principal instructor. It's one of the hobbies I'm planning to extend in my retirement. If you decide to join the society I feel quite certain that our regular meetings will prevent you from travelling into Ipswich on the same evening. Not when you have homework to fit in as well. As your tutor it will be my duty to advise you against over-filling your extra-curricular time in this pre-exam period."

Of course Donny should have said thank you. Instead he stood up and backed towards the door of the DT office.

"So it is true …what Toxic said. You are planning to leave! Thanks for mentioning it. Not. You'd have been the only person who I like who was still here next term. Once my best friends have all gone. Or didn't you think it mattered to anyone except yourself?"

Mr McMullen took a moment to catch on.

"Surely everyone knows that I reach retirement in July? When my new group was assigned to me in Year Seven I told them, and their parents, that I'd only be seeing them through Key Stage Three. I reminded them again at last summer's prize-giving and again by letter at the start of this academic year. There's nothing sudden about my departure. I've known when I was going to be sixty-five for, well, the best part of sixty-five years."

"But …"

"But you weren't here in Year Seven and you weren't here last summer and you weren't here for the first week of this year either. So you didn't know. I'm sorry. I suppose I feel that my expiry date is so obviously stamped all over me that there's been no further need to mention it."

"But …"

"But someone told you of Denise Tune's pathetic little plot to force me to leave early? If I thought you took any notice of her I'd begin to suspect you'd been drinking seawater, not just living on it. Even basic snorkelling can be useful if you need to check your boat's hull or remove a rope from round her prop. Or so my daughter tells me. It's entirely your decision."

" …I mean, yes! Of course I'd like to do sub-aqua. Is there, um, an economic aspect?"

"None whatsoever. I'll see you next Monday. School pool, seven o'clock. We'll leave Ms Spinks to convey your regrets to Inspector Flint, shall we?"

Donny thanked his inner uncle from the bottom of his heart.

CHAPTER SIXTEEN

Buddha Jumps over the Wall

Off Xiamen, May 2007

The moon was full and low. The sea glittered silver and the shape of every passing sampan stood out black and clear.

"You couldn't have chosen a worse night, one-leg," grumbled the shrivelled fisherman who had ferried them discreetly away from the floodlights of the port and the illuminated city buildings out into the wider waters of the Taiwan Strait.

"Tiger Zhang picked the night, not me."

"Zhang," the old man spat. "I remember when he was smuggling ladies' underwear. Makes his money out of people now, does he? I wouldn't have thought he had the brains."

"He's hooked himself onto some powerful ghosts."

"And you've cut across them once too often. Why did you do it? I'd heard you were nicely set up in some cushy restaurant with a flock of pretty waitresses to protect."

"Cage-birds flying free, most of them. Yes, it was a good set-up but I'd always planned to come home in the end. Then Jin Lóng arrived."

"Jin Lóng! I thought she was dead way back."

"So did we all but she turned up in that junk of hers, cool as you like, with a crew of children and some long-lost niece."

"That should put a mouse-dropping in Zhang's porridge."

"Dollops of dragon's dung, I hope. So, when she asked me to

do a job for her, I was honoured to oblige."

"He who sets out to poke a hornet's nest must carry a long stick."

"I've no regrets."

The two men fell silent then. Min had been watching a long black patch that he thought might be an island, perhaps with street lamps. Except that it was moving steadily towards them, blocking out the shimmering waves and the bobbing lights of smaller boats.

"Transport's on its way. We'll put you on the tug first, youngster, then you'll be up and into that tanker and non-stop for Rotterdam. Yu Wan, the cook, is a friend of mine so make yourself useful. Be sure to give him this." He pulled a folded paper from inside his shirt. "He's been after it for years."

"What's that?" asked the fisherman.

"My special recipe for *fo tiao qiang*. It's payment for the lad's final hop."

The old man burst out laughing, a wheezy cackle that was soon drowned by the engine of the approaching tug.

"Why's that funny?" Min needed to know. The swelling on Hoi Fung's face made smiling even harder than speech but he did his best.

"It's a local speciality soup. They call it 'Buddha jumps over the wall'. Yu Wan'll tell you the story on board. Now remember young one, lock up your tongue when you can't speak truthfully and seek the protection of Jin Lóng as soon as you arrive in Suffolk."

Suffolk, May 2007
Donny spent more time with the younger boys at Erewhon Parva

than he did with Anna. She was obsessed with revision for her scholarship exams and then, once they were finished, she usually chose to shut herself away with her mother in the evenings.

There was a new TV in the sitting room – much approved by Liam who could now record the late-night football matches and watch them when he came home from school – but Lottie preferred Rev. Wendy's study where she'd installed a state of the art keyboard, headphones and recording equipment. Donny didn't really know what she did during the day. Made plans for the family move to Bawdsey Manor, he assumed. She was always charming and efficient and affectionate but it seemed as if her heart was somewhere else.

The two mothers got on remarkably well. Once Vicky had been put to bed Skye often sat beside the cot holding one of Vicky's feet as the child fell peacefully asleep. Lottie stayed downstairs into the early hours practising complicated small patterns on her guitar or working out song ideas at the keyboard. Skye hung dream-catchers over Vicky's door and window and drew picture-stories which she stuck around the bedroom walls. Lottie had begun learning sign language so that she and Skye could talk and sometimes, when she was playing her guitar, she asked Skye to sit beside her and put her fingers on the resonating wood as if she understood about hearing by touch.

Anna took up coffee-drinking. Once she'd finished her revision she followed her mother every evening into what she now styled Rev. Wendy's sanctum. When Donny accused her of becoming a poser as well as a swot she shrugged irritatingly.

"Maybe yes, maybe no. I expect you'll get the point one day."

Because Anna had once been on the other side – the child side

– she knew how much private adult conversation you could hear from the dark landing above the hall. The study door was solid wood. It fitted snugly into its heavy frame. With Anna on the inside, nothing leaked out.

Which was why Donny was as shocked as Luke and Liam when he dropped into the boys' bedroom to say good night one evening and discovered what these conversations had been about.

"It's our Dad," Luke said. "He's due to be released early. Anna's lawyer's been making a fuss."

"Wow!" said Donny. "That's … really great!"

But why did Luke sound as if somebody'd punched him and how come Liam was right down his bed with his face to the wall and his Man U duvet pulled right up so only the top of his head and one ear of his Flopsy Babbitt was visible?

"Um, when's it going to be? Will you all be going up to, like, collect him? Bring him back here?"

Now Luke collapsed, his face buried in his pillow, his skinny body heaving with the sobs that he was fighting to contain. The sound of his crying got Liam out of bed. Blubbered and crumpled, he sort of dived across like a half-blind torpedo. The brothers were hugging each other, desperate in their need for comfort.

Were they frightened of their father? He remembered Anna saying that Bill had got drunk. There'd been rows. Maybe violence.

"Hey, you two, this isn't good at all. Hang on a minute and I'll fetch Lottie. Sounds like you need to talk to her."

The boys shook their heads and sobbed harder.

So Donny sat there and sort of patted them and comforted and said there-there, don't worry, it'll be okay, honestly it will. Come on Lukey, come on Li, cheer up, we'll sort it out. Whatever it is.

Until finally they were so exhausted they began to make some sense.

Their dad was coming out of prison but he wasn't coming home. Not here to the vicarage and not to Bawdsey Manor either. Lottie had told them the news when she'd tucked them into bed and they'd nodded without comment and asked for a story as usual.

Between her going downstairs and Donny coming up they'd understood what this meant – which was more than she or anyone else had done.

From the moment Bill Whiting had been arrested, a few months before Vicky was born, through his time on remand and his time on trial, through the black day of his conviction and the first year of his sentence, Luke and Liam had been surviving on hope. It was much more than hope: it was an expectation. Something someone had said had given them the idea that when all this was over, when their Dad had served his time (they were both too young to be sure how long this might take) then they'd be together again as a family.

This expectation had kept them going through their stepmother's absence, their life in care and the miserable monthly journeys with Gerald or Wendy to the prison visits centre. It had helped them in past the sniffer dogs and their handlers, through the body searches and the suspicious stares, and then it had helped them out again. They'd mostly managed to say goodbye to their dad without tears and had allowed themselves to be driven away without looking back or even saying much until it was time for the next month's visit. At school they'd told lies without feeling guilty and they'd got really, really good at looking blank and focussing on something else when it was Father's Day or 'All About Me' class projects.

They'd been hanging on to the idea that when people were sent to prison they did their punishment and after that it was a Fresh Start.

"You know, Donny, all of us living together. Us an' Dad an' Lottie an' Anna and Vicky. Like we did before in Low'stoft."

"We didn't care if it were only a caravan and there was all them rows."

"We know our Mum's never coming back because she's dead."

"But we thought it would be different with our Dad."

Donny got Skye to come and sit with the boys when he reckoned they were calm enough. Then he went storming down to the study to ask what the hell had been going on.

They were all waiting – Lottie and Anna, Gerald and Wendy – sitting in silence with the study door open, as if they'd been listening upwards.

Lottie stood up as soon as he came in. "Thank you, Donny," she said, "Thank you so, so, much."

She looked exactly like Anna. Anna at her sweetest and most manipulative when she knew she was in a totally tight spot.

"For doing your dirty work? For picking up the pieces after you told the kids that you're dumping their dad? Didn't get given much choice, did I?"

All the questions he'd planned to ask and the hard things he was going to say suddenly got jumbled up and stuck like logs in a dam, somewhere between his mind and his mouth. He looked at them all, looking at him: worried, concerned, affectionate, ready to explain. Ready to help him understand and forgive. He turned round and went out, slamming the door behind him.

He'd get right out of this house. To the river? No. To the camper van. Yes. He could lock it from the inside. He wished he could drive.

It wasn't until he'd pulled the metal door shut that he realised how stupid he was. This wasn't about him. It was about Luke and Liam and he hadn't picked them up a single bit of explanation. He'd have to go back to the study and ask.

"So do you want to understand what's going on or don't you?" came Anna's voice from outside. "Because I'm not going to hang around if you don't. You're just proving my theory that male emotions … suck!"

"What the hell do you mean?"

He opened the door with a furious heave, hoping that she'd topple in and look silly. Instead she was standing there with a bit of a smirk on her face.

"I thought that might get to you," she said, pushing past and closing the door with exaggerated care before settling herself on one of the benches. "In my experience blokes are so useless at expressing themselves that, once they've past the crying stage, their only resource is to slam out of the room or thump someone. Obviously I'm hoping that your testosterone hasn't reached that level yet."

Her smirk stretched into a grin. He almost smiled back. She was his best friend, he remembered.

"Get on and explain then. It had better be good. I've never seen Luke and Liam so upset. It was horrible."

"It is horrible. Bill's being let out because our lawyers have proved that his sentence was too long. They haven't managed to get him declared innocent."

"Is he innocent? I don't even know what he did."

"Mum thinks he is. She thinks he's innocent and scared. More scared about being released than staying in. It's him who doesn't want to come home as well as us who don't want to have him. He thinks he's a danger to us: we think he's right."

"Because whoever put him inside is still around and could be waiting for him. Has Lottie told Bill that Gold Dragon got rid of the Tiger? The Tiger's called Zhang by the way. He's gone off sick."

"Mum's stopped visiting. They faked a row last time. Now she can only send messages through Wendy. She's not going to let the children go in again either."

"That's so cruel. He's their dad. They, like, love him."

"I think," said Anna, "that you must have forgotten how truly frightening these people are. With your sub-aqua sessions and your Dutch uncle and your jolly jaunts up and down the river. They'll think Bill's been let out because he's grassed – which, unfortunately, he hasn't. I wish he would. Until then he needs to disappear."

"We got your mum away from Pura-Lilly. She hasn't had to go into hiding."

"Hoi Fung has. The chef from the Floating Lotus. Handed Ai Qin the money and then bunked. And don't think that Mum isn't keeping a lookout. That's partly why she's being such a pillar of the parish; helping Wendy collect for the Diocesan Mission, locking the car from the inside when she does the school run, staying in at night, not singing in pubs or anything. Wonders all the time whether she'll be snatched."

"Oh."

"And if Bill comes out of prison and then disappears they'll be watching her more closely than ever. That's why she faked the row. I've never understood what she saw in him anyway but normally speaking they'd have given it a go. For Vicky's sake."

"You and Vicky are paying for Bill's lawyers."

"Not directly. It's being done through some Justice Fund. Edward organised it: the Trust just donates. Keeps us at a distance. Mum and I are taking the line that we don't mind Bill being let out but we're much too grand to want to have anything to do with him. Ladies of the Manor, etc."

The two of them. Anna and her mother. Answers for everything. He was fed up with them both.

"So doing what your mother just did to Luke and Liam was all part of the big sassy act? Do you think you might possibly have missed something? Like recognising that the kids do have feelings – even though they're unlucky enough to have been born male?"

"We got that wrong." She wasn't smiling at all. "We had no idea they would take it so badly. That was why Mum was trying to thank you. You were totally the right person. They'd never have said all that to her. She's gone up to them now. She's trying to make them feel better – without actually telling them anything different. They can't keep secrets, you know."

"I think," said Donny, "that you're one hundred per cent wrong on that as well. I think they've been keeping a really serious secret for years. And you and your mum only just found out."

"Okay, so you're one hundred and one per cent right but it doesn't alter anything. Flint and Toxic and Tiger What's-his-face are running some racket. It's criminal and Bill knows about it.

That's why they got rid of him. They're vicious. Don't you remember them killing the blue bird? And that fight in the Oriental Xpress?"

So it wasn't only Bill and Lottie who were scared: Anna was scared too. But he wasn't. Which was almost certainly wrong, as usual.

Donny shrugged and sat down.

"What do you and your mum think we should do?"

"More of the same. Behave as if we're too cushy to care. Take the kids' minds off things. She wondered whether it might be a good idea to go on holiday? There's half-term coming up."

"Sort of like where? Skye and I don't have any spare cash. She's giving all her weekly money to Gerald and Wendy for keeping us. I suppose we could clean out this van and go somewhere but it would be a squash. And not exactly in line with your new image."

"No-oh …" She sounded thoughtful. Devious. "But I suppose there's *Vexilla*. And Luke's tent … And I could always buy another one for me and Vicky. And some really top thermal sleeping bags. And a cooker."

"You mean you and your mum and Vicky might come camping?"

"The boys would like it. And Gerald and Wendy could have their house to themselves for a few days. Be all touchy-feely in the evenings and keep checking the answers without worrying that I'll notice. If we went to a proper campsite there'd be facilities for washing and …everything."

"Whenever Mum and Granny and I stayed on what you'd call a proper campsite it wasn't much fun. People were always staring at Mum. They didn't seem to have anything else to do. Couldn't we just go somewhere like Mrs Everson's field? Then you could swim when you felt dirty and – well, you take a spade and dig a big hole and then you put a bit of earth back each time. You can have a sort of seat to put over it if you want."

"Yuck. It'd have to be somewhere amazingly special before I could stand doing that."

Donny thought about what she'd said. Somewhere amazingly special.

"The Desolate Shores! We'll go to Great Aunt Ellen's Desolate Shores. Where she went with her brothers and sisters when they were children. Where she and Mum were prospecting before they got ambushed. I've got a chart and a book and I was going to read it then write her a letter. Come on, Anna, let's have an adventure!"

CHAPTER SEVENTEEN

The Desolate Shores

Rotterdam, Saturday 26 May 2007
"You're saying that Tiger Zhang is dead?"

Yu Wan, ship's cook on the bulk oil carrier that had brought Min to Rotterdam, couldn't believe what he was hearing. He bought his informant another beer and one for himself and Min as well. Min didn't like beer. He left it untouched beside him. Yu Wan would drink it quick enough. He needed to listen and understand what they were saying.

It was crowded and noisy in this bar. People were drinking and gambling. It was the sort of place where deals would be done. The sort of place where he'd rather not be. So lonely. So far from home.

"That'll be good news for Hoi Fung, if it hasn't come too late. The Tiger had a contract on him. How did it happen? Fight?"

"Accident at sea is the official line. Then he went into hospital in England and died from an infection. Shockingly low standards over there."

"And what do the wise men say? Unofficially." Yu Wan took Min's beer and pushed it towards the other man.

"They say," the man lowered his voice and looked from side to side, "that the attacker was Jin Lóng and that she has moved into his territory on the other side."

"That can't be good for the *she-tou*."

"Tiger Zhang was only a manager," said the informant, hurriedly. "His boss lady's been over here since. She's a *gweilao*. It's business as usual their end and no concessions. She wants the throughput stepping up. They'll be using agency carriers to clear the backlog."

It was people they were talking about, Min realised. Human cargo. Like him.

Walton Backwaters, Essex, Saturday 26 May 2007
The five children and Skye had been walking and playing and paddling on this strip of wet sand for almost two hours. It wasn't sunny and there was a brisk on-shore breeze, which took their breath and slapped their faces as they leaned into it. It must have been some time between six and seven o'clock in the evening. Tea was hours ago but no-one had suggested that it was time to begin thinking about supper. This sand felt like a sort of miracle, which you needed to enjoy while you could, because you knew it wouldn't last.

It hadn't been here when they arrived. Or, Donny amended mentally, it hadn't been on show. The sandbank had been underwater, waiting for the ebb. Probably it had existed for centuries guarding the entrance to these creeks.

In some places the sand was rippled by the prevailing tide and in others it might give a little as you trod on it. Mainly it was smooth and hard. If a ship grounded on this sand with a high wind blowing and a falling tide she would be pounded to pieces as surely as if she'd struck any of the other shoals that had built up along the coastlines of the Southern North Sea.

Donny thought of the Long Sand where *Strong Winds* had waited for *Snow Goose*, or those ragged underwater banks off the coast of Belgium where the *Pride of Macao* had caught them. At least a crew stranded here would be able to escape. This sandbank ran all the way to the shore in a thin peninsula. Even with grey skies piling overhead it didn't feel dangerous at all: it felt exciting, shivery, magical.

It helped him forget what he'd seen.

Snow Goose had sailed from Pin Mill late that morning to deliver the campers and their equipment. This was the place Great Aunt Ellen and her brothers and sisters had explored as children and had nicknamed the Desolate Shores. It was Flint Island in her book but it wasn't an island, it was another peninsula, almost, but not quite, cut off from the mainland by marshes and a muddy dyke. On the map it was called Stone Point.

There were no roads here. A boat was the only way to arrive – though June did tell them that it was possible to walk right along the beach until you reached the Naze. She gestured towards low cliffs and a distant tower. The children didn't take much notice: they were busy taking possession of their new world.

And trying to forget that the Tiger was back.

His ship was, anyway. They'd seen the *Hispaniola* on her Shotley mooring as they'd come surging joyously down the Orwell.

Snow Goose was revelling in the fresh breeze and making light of *Vexilla*'s weight as she towed the day-boat astern, ready-loaded with camping equipment. They'd reached the first of the Felixstowe quays: those steps down to the river where the sharkboat liked to lurk. No worries there. They'd known that the black-and-white monstrosity was secured to the RO&A pontoon and there was no sign of its outsized owner. Not even in the bar.

Maggi and Xanthe had stayed behind, cheerfully packing up their dinghies for their trip to Weymouth.

The younger boys were gazing at the row of cranes, comparing them to dinosaurs, watching the containers sliding outwards and down onto the waiting ships. Or being lifted up and away if they'd reached the end of their long sea voyages.

Donny had glanced casually to starboard. Saw those three telegraph-pole masts; that flat hull re-painted garish white and crimson; the aggressive bow, re-camouflaged by a jutting sprit and bobstay. Exactly as he'd climbed it.

June and Skye were staring too. All three of them had seen her, slate-grey and mast-free, driving at them out of the twilight. Intent on ramming, sinking, drowning everyone on board *Strong Winds*.

All three had watched Gold Dragon fight off the Tiger. Had been appalled by the price she paid. They remembered their attacker sheering away into the darkness and had allowed themselves to hope that they'd never set eyes on her again.

"We won't go any closer," said June, although no-one had suggested it. "But I begin to understand how they manage the disguise. I think," she said to Joshua, "that there are more questions we can ask …"

"Not now," Joshua had answered without looking at her. "Not while we're here with the children. We'll do whatever's to be done after the weekend. For now, is it possible we might simply be allowed to take a holiday?"

There was something hard and wrong in the way he spoke. June had disappeared into the cabin as if she couldn't trust herself to answer.

The Desolate Shores were part of a nature reserve. There wasn't anything remotely resembling what Anna considered a proper campsite. No facilities and not even any obvious clear space to pitch the tents. Instead there was an amazing mixture of sand dune and sloping beach, mud and marsh, saltings and seawalls.

They'd all explored for a while before settling into a smallish sandy hollow surrounded by low dunes. There was an alternative site where other people had built barbecues but their place felt more private. From inside the hollow it was easy to forget that there was anyone else in the world. Or that there was a world at all. When you were sitting or lying down, all you could see above the sand dunes was the sky. If you peeped over the rim you might see the top of a boat mast entering or leaving the channel but the people on board definitely wouldn't see you.

The only problem was that the sand was so dry and fine it was impossible to get the tent pegs to stay in. It probably didn't matter because both the tents had integral frames and ground sheets. They could put them up then weigh them down from inside with their bags and all the tins and water bottles they'd brought with them. But it was quite windy and it seemed amateur not to try to lash the tents down with ropes and pegs as well. In the end Donny suggested they tie each rope to a heavy stone – or bricks or rocks, if they could find them, which wasn't easy. Then they should dig holes and bury the stones as deeply as possible, heaping loads of other stones on top. It seemed to work okay.

Snow Goose had left in the middle of the afternoon. The campers had food and water for three days. If, after that, they wanted to stay longer they would have to take *Vexilla* up to the town of Walton and re-stock.

Anna and the adults had agreed easily to Donny's idea.

Far too easily, he thought later.

First Lottie had made a big thing about clearing the camper van and taking it off to be serviced and MOT-ed. She re-did its insurance as well. He couldn't really see why. She already had a new Toyota hybrid and Donny kept telling her that he couldn't see anywhere in the area that they could take the van, unless they went to one of the big caravan sites in Walton. Skye wouldn't be happy and he didn't think it was the right choice for Luke and Liam either.

"I thought we were trying to maybe give them something different to think about. What good's a caravan site? That's not an adventure."

Lottie had agreed as soon as he made her look at the map but she didn't seem a bit bothered that she'd spent all that money on the van for nothing.

"Oh well," she'd said. "It needed doing. Maybe you and Skye might want to be hitting the road again one day."

We might, might we? When you and your family have moved off to your grand new home, maybe? He still wasn't sure about Lottie.

A few days before they were due to leave she said she'd changed her mind. She wouldn't be coming with them after all. She didn't exactly say why. He'd asked Anna straight out what she was up to but he'd had to believe her when she'd said that she didn't know.

"My mum is telling me most things now and I think she trusts me. But she might not be telling me everything."

"You don't think it's strange that she's still letting Vicky come? When Great Aunt Ellen was that small, her mother always kept her behind. She only went with the big ones about once."

"Maybe Mum's not like that. She knows Vicky'll be okay with me. And there's your mum. And even if Maggi and Xanthe join in they won't be bringing that crazy dog. They've finally decided to re-home it with Mrs Everson's daughter. She lives on a farm."

"S'pose that leaves them freer to emigrate," said Donny sourly.

There were six of them, that evening, walking on the sand that seemed to come lifting out of the water. It made Donny think of all those old stories about islands that turned out to be large-backed whales.

He glanced back warily the way they'd come. He couldn't see their camp and he couldn't see *Vexilla*. She was loaded with their spare equipment and had a waterproof cover rigged over her boom so she too looked like a tent. She'd been anchored close inshore in the lee of a little bay and he knew she'd be safe there. All the same, the tide would soon turn and it was his responsibility to look out for risks: his job to keep everyone safe and happy.

Liam was practising one of his endless ball routines and Skye was drawing pictures for Vicky on the blank wet surface. Luke had brought a spade and was digging for cockles.

"We could live on these," he said. "If we'd been marooned for endless long years."

"You couldn't," said Anna. "You'd go mad – or madder – and all your nails would go black. You'd have to look for special grasses on the dunes with vitamins to stop you getting scurvy."

She'd been standing some way away from them, staring out to sea with her hair tangled in the breeze. He'd wondered what she'd been thinking. Not about Defoe and Gold Dragon in Rotterdam, eighty miles due east, she was more northerly than that. She wasn't looking back to Harwich and the *Hispaniola* either. She was more – Donny took a surreptitious fix with the waterproof combined barometer, watch and compass, which she'd given him as a very late birthday-and-Christmas present – more north-easterly.

It must be Bawdsey. Anna was probably imagining the curve of the coastline towards her new grand home with its pines and minarets. He was glad it was getting dark. She wouldn't be able to see it any longer.

"Come on, Luke. I'll race you back. Liam too. Anna can have the spade. She can dig our lonely graves when we've all died from unhealthy eating."

"Ben Gunn didn't die," said Luke seriously. "Nor did Crusoe."

"But they smelled so bad that even the wild goats ran away," said Anna. "And what did they do with disposable nappies that aren't disposable at all?"

She couldn't have been standing there thinking about – hygiene?

"That's the reason they made out they were always digging for treasure because they were too embarrassed to say what they were really burying. Leave it out, Anna. Mum took Vicky's nappies off ages ago. She's potty training without the potty. Tide's definitely coming in. Race all of you. First one back cooks supper!"

"And the last one washes up," she yelled, not waiting to be loaded down with spade or football.

What a cheat! Gerald had made a huge bean and sausage stew, and Lottie had gone out early to buy freshly baked baguettes, which they could dunk in their bowls and use to scoop the hot food straight into their hungry mouths. Supper only needed heating, not cooking. But there would still be washing-up. There was always washing-up.

Walton Backwaters, Sunday 27 May 2007

It took ages to get everyone moving next day. Donny was determined that they should unload all the rest of the supplies from *Vexilla* so that they could go for a really good sail. He had Gold Dragon's book and the map, which was part of the story, and he told them as much of the old *Secret Water* adventure as he could remember. Tried to show them where the island was and the crossing of the Red Sea.

As soon as they returned to their camp Luke and Liam found the stickiest stretch of mud and rolled in it.

"We're Eels," they shouted, "we eat ship's babies for tea!"

Maybe he was getting middle-aged before his time. Donny and Anna drew mud stripes on each other's faces and coated Vicky's legs with a sophisticated sand/mud mix. Then they plaited headdresses while Skye tidied the camp. After supper they invaded the barbecue site and built a brief fire from driftwood and dry plant stalks and danced around it with fierce energy.

"Sensitive, seldom and sad are we," they shouted, as they leapt up and down in their mud and rushes. "By the desolate shores of the silent sea."

"Oh so seldom and sad / So sensitive, seldom and sad!"

The yachts that had anchored during the day had left and no other boats had arrived. If there had been any ramblers or birdwatchers they too had gone home. Stone Point was completely deserted. They could be as wild as they liked.

But not stupid or irresponsible. Donny was sure that they'd trodden the fire out before they went to bed. And tipped water on the ashes.

So why was he smelling smoke?

He'd no idea what time it was. Not morning yet. Not even dawn. The tent he shared with Luke and Liam was a mess and he wasn't sure that he could find his posh watch without waking them.

He needed to investigate. He knew he didn't want to.

The wind had eased off but the cloud cover was low. When Donny crawled reluctantly outside he found that the night was very black. It took a while before he sorted out his sense of direction and stumbled away from the tents until he stubbed his toe on the stones beside the barbecue. The ashes were completely cold. Not a flicker of heat, let alone smoke or flame.

"Er ... hello?"

There wasn't any answer. He didn't know why he'd expected one. He crept carefully back to the tents feeling puzzled and uneasy.

The smell of smoke refused to leave.

Donny snuggled back into his sleeping bag, trying to recapture lost warmth. He imagined himself in his bunk on board *Strong Winds* and Gold Dragon in her cockpit, puffing her pipe beneath the hidden stars. A thin blue-ish ribbon of Fisherman's Friend trickling downwards into the cabin. How good would that have been!

But this smoke was cigarette smoke and he'd crawled through it in the space between the doorways of the tents. As if someone had left it hanging there.

CHAPTER EIGHTEEN

Signals or Trophies?

Walton Backwaters, Monday 28 May 2007

It must have been his mum who'd been smoking outside the tents. Donny knew that Skye had sometimes shared an evening pipe with Great Aunt Ellen, especially when she was recovering from her alcohol addiction, but he was shocked to discover that she was smoking cigarettes.

Maybe it wasn't Skye. Maybe it was Anna. After all the health warnings they'd had at school! He had heard that teenage girls were more at risk than boys. She drank coffee now and he supposed she might have been under a bit of stress with all that extra studying. All the same it wasn't right and he'd have to speak to her about it. Though since when had Anna ever taken any notice of anything he said?

Because if it wasn't Skye or Anna, who was it?

Donny fell asleep feeling gloomy and woke late with a headache. He scrambled out of the hollow not seeing much and walked up the beach. Anna, Luke and Liam were heading back. Liam was whirling a spade. They'd eaten their breakfasts ages ago and caught the early morning appearance of the magical sand.

"That was well fun! Anna was chief engineer and me 'n' Luke digged. We digged a whole system and when the water came back it fairly rushed into our reservoir. It filled right up. But then it carried on and flooded. So we watched for a bit more and then we came back."

"It was chasing us!" said Luke. "Snapping at our heels and Liam saw two crabs."

"They was massive! And Anna says we can do it again tomorrow and if you get out of bed we can do it much bigger."

"We did try but you was sort of muttering and then you punched the pillow."

"An' then you started snoring."

"Louder 'n the fog signals off Low'stoft pier!"

The brothers looked at one another. But it was okay. They could say Lowestoft without bad feelings.

"Have you been smoking?" Donny asked Anna who was standing with them, looking windswept, flushed and happy.

They'd all been on the sand without him. Having fun and making jokes while he'd been kept awake with worry.

"I so have not," she flashed back. "Don't you know what's in those things? There's benzene, nitrosamines, formaldehyde …"

"… and hydrogen cyanide. I went to the workshop too, you know. So it must have been Mum. She can't read the warnings. I'll have to search her tent."

"Some one's crawled out of the wrong end of his sleeping bag ! We know where everything is in our tent because we keep it tidy and I'm certain Skye doesn't have cigarettes. So why don't you shut up and get yourself a cup of tea? Skye and Vicky were heading back to camp to put the kettle on and I need us to make plans. Xanthe and Maggi might arrive this evening and then we have to decide whether we're going home. I mean, the weather's not too great and we'd have to get more stores but the kids have got so many things they want to do that maybe we ought to think about extending?"

"We're going to dig a huge pit and cover it with wood and trap people. Or mammoths."

"No, we ain't. We're going to dig a huge pit and make it into our special den. And invite our Treasure to tea."

"If we haven't caught any mammoths we won't have no tea to give her."

"But if we ain't got a den we can't ask anyone round anyhow."

Luke and Liam were glaring at one another. Anna's cup of tea suddenly seemed like a good idea. Especially if there was any breakfast left. Or even a packet of biscuits. He could tackle Skye about her smoking later. Maybe she'd picked up the habit when she was in Holland. Maybe his uncle smoked? He hadn't looked the type but how could you tell?

Because if it wasn't Anna or Skye, who else could it have been?

"We could dig two big holes," he suggested. "One for living and the other for trapping. And if we gathered a load more wood we could maybe have a really good bonfire when Xanthe and Maggi come. Cook our supper on it, if no-one else turns up."

"We'll fight 'em off," said Luke.

"'Cos we've been here first," his brother agreed.

Donny and Anna had read the local sailing club notices near the barbecue site and knew about the permission process but they didn't bother saying anything. It had been great having this place completely to themselves: they couldn't really expect it would continue. It was half-term after all. Surely other families would soon be arriving?

Donny didn't have time to waste on tea. He sent Luke and

Liam to the camp to fetch apples, biscuits and a water bottle, then settled down to dig.

"Know something, Anna?" he said later. He stretched his back. This digging was tough work. "The barometer on that mega-watch you gave me shows that the pressure's fallen by almost ten millibars."

"Since when?"

"Er, since I last checked it."

"Which was …?"

"Last night? No, yesterday evening. I mean afternoon. When we got back in *Vexilla*."

"So what does falling ten millibars mean? How normal is it?"

"Dunno exactly. I should have been checking every few hours. Then if you notice a sharp fall or rise in a short space of time you know that there's bad weather coming."

"Also I noticed that it's been flooding for ages and the only boats that have come past have gone straight on up the river. No-one's stopping here. Maybe they know something we don't?"

"Maybe."

Donny looked out to sea. The on-shore wind, which had dropped in that black time of the night, had been rising steadily all morning and seemed to be changing direction. Low flat clouds were building to the north-east.

"Have you got your mobile?"

"It's in the tent."

"Let's ring Weathercall. Luke, Liam, we're going to take a quick break in the camp. Have a drink. See whether Skye wants help with lunch?"

The younger boys didn't take much persuading. They'd been

digging their great pits with intense concentration and the word lunch made them realise how hungry they were.

"What were they doing anyway?"

"Who?"

"Mum and Vicky. I haven't seen them all morning. I know I woke up late but I thought you said they were heading back to the camp but I never spotted them."

"Not sure. Skye was making patterns when we were out on the sand. She was collecting shells and pieces of wrack then finding places where there were worm casts or sand ripples and laying them down in sort of intersecting curves, like knobbly weaving. Vicky was fetching things for her. Round the other side, towards the Naze. They're probably still doing it. Or they're back at the camp."

But they weren't.

Luke and Liam demanded two large slabs of chocolate then agreed to find Skye and ask about lunch while the others rang Weathercall.

Anna's mobile had been left switched on all night and the battery was completely gone. Then the boys raced back to say that Skye and Vicky weren't Anywhere.

"They must be. One big lady, shawls and braids, tendency to wave arms around: one small lady, red hair, no nappies, tendency to shout and throw things. You probably missed them in the crowd."

"Go look for yourself."

There wasn't anywhere much to look but he couldn't find them. The tide was high so there wasn't much beach between the water and the dunes. Skye's artworks would have been washed away. He couldn't believe that she and Vicky had been washed away as well. Anna ran to check the boat but *Vexilla* was lying sweetly to her anchor about five metres out into the channel. The rope they used to haul her in was as they had left it. They could see there was no-one on board.

That meant they needed to look again. Everywhere.

First, the beach on the seaward side. Anna fetched her new binoculars but they weren't necessary. Everyone could look along its narrow, empty length. Grey waves were breaking against the tide-line, almost bursting through the low dunes, but there was not so much as a dog-walker in sight, the entire distance to the Naze cliffs. Even the seabirds had flown elsewhere. The high streaks of hurrying cloud were getting lower and thicker but visibility was still good. They could see that there was nobody walking the raised seawalls that crossed the marshes. They knew there was no-one on the steep foreshore by the channel because that was where they had been.

Which left the entire complex of deep dykes, small creeks and swampy islands plus a small lagoon. All full of water now.

Suddenly they were certain there had been a terrible accident – it only took a few inches to drown a toddler, they all knew that.

Skye, absorbed in her pattern-making. Deaf. Vicky wandering away, tumbling into the steep dyke, struggling, terrified, drowning. Then Skye … missing Vicky, searching for her … unable to call out clearly or hear a cry for help.

Anna began to shake. Her teeth chattered. "I sh-should n-never …"

"Our Treasure!"

Donny forced himself to breathe carefully, speak calmly.

"We'll start from the exact spot where you last saw them, Anna. Can you take us there? As near as you can."

She swallowed hard and nodded. They walked back without speaking to the seaward side where the sands had vanished beneath the water. No-one hurried or called out.

In part of Donny's mind he was wondering how to get the news to Lottie. He scanned the desolate scene wildly hoping for help. Adults! Anywhere?

He stubbed his toe, painfully, on a large pile of rocks. Huh? How could they have missed this lot when they'd been struggling to find sufficient heavy weights to secure all their guy ropes?

Such an unworthy thought to think at such a time.

Except … His toe really hurt. It felt broken. He'd skinned his ankle too. They couldn't not have seen such a jagged heap.

Especially as this pile of stones had a stick protruding from the top and the stick was flying two coloured ribbons: one a deep crimson and the other, buttercup yellow.

Signals or … trophies? Suddenly he remembered that smell of smoke. Who could have tracked them to these Desolate Shores? He'd felt so safe.

"Over here – quick!"

They were slow, at first. Then they came running.

"Footprints," said Luke. His eyes were huge, his breathing rapid. "On a desert island you get footprints!"

"You won't get any here, this sand's way too dry."

"We ought to be lookin' for 'em," said Liam, instantly siding with his brother.

That's those Crusoe stories I've been making up, thought Donny.

"And grab them ribbons. Skye and Vicky might be captives!"

"Like whose?" Anna's face was pink with delight. You'd think she might be about to dance. "They're having a game with us. How idiotic do I feel! Hel-lo, you can come out now!"

There wasn't any answer. Donny didn't bother mentioning that Skye wouldn't hear her shouting and Vicky's language skills were still pretty basic. He hadn't told Anna about the smoke. She couldn't know that there had been someone in their campsite as well as them. He glanced round desperately. If Flint or the Tiger were here, there would surely be a boat? They would have had to overpower Skye to make her go on board. She was strong. She would have fought.

Unless they'd threatened Vicky …

Anna untied the ribbons, carefully, and stood beside the stones waving them.

Luke and Liam were casting around – Luke had slipped into tracker-dog mode, and Liam had armed himself with a musket-shaped piece of driftwood and kept dropping to one knee to take careful aim at suspicious clumps of marram grass.

Donny stayed where he was, trying to be rational. The word 'cairn' had come into his head but it wasn't a word he thought he knew. Had Granny Edith used it once when she'd taken him and Skye to the Pennines? He remembered when they'd walked and walked in the clear light until they could see right across the other side of the hills to the distant blue haze of Morecambe Bay.

Donny knelt down on the beach. Slowly, stone by stone, he began to dismantle the cairn.

Rotterdam, Monday 28 May 2007

There was an argument going on among the people who were being hustled out of the back on an anonymous truck and into a shipping container. It was a hopeless argument from people who didn't like what they were being ordered to do: who felt cheated and frightened; against people who knew that what they were doing was wrong but were going to do it anyway and knew that the other people had no choice but to submit.

"But I have paid 60,000 yuan," one man said. "I had expected I would be going by air."

"Why are there so many of us all going together? I've been waiting for weeks. Surely it's safer to go in small numbers?"

"Why must we be put into crates? Surely we can move around on the journey?"

"It's for your safety. The crossing is not long but it's sometimes rough. There's heavy furniture packed in here. It could shift."

"If you want to come to England, get a good job, this is what you have to do."

"If you don't like it you stay here. Beg in the streets. We won't help you anymore."

"You have no passport. You have no work permit. You'll soon be picked up and sent home and who's going to help your family then?"

The snakeheads punched and kicked the loudest grumblers: grabbed others by their clothing and manhandled them into the crates. Most of the travellers were resigned. They knew they had no choice. And it wasn't so much further now.

Min said nothing at all. For the rest of his life he would remember the sound of the electric screwdriver fastening the migrants into the packing cases. Then the clang as the container doors were shut and sealed and they waited in silence until they felt themselves lifted up and loaded.

An hour later the ship began to move.

CHAPTER NINETEEN

The Eyes of Pauguk

Walton Backwaters, Monday 28 May 2007

A flattened cigarette packet with a crowded message written in blue biro on the cardboard side. FOLLOW THE SIGNS IF YOU WANTS TO SAY HELLO. THERE IS NO NEED IF YOU DO NOT FEEL CORDIAL. DON'T GET SEEN. YOUR LOVING DAD (OR STEP-DAD) BILL

"Cordial's for you, Anna. It means you don't have to come if you don't want to."

"He's got my sister, hasn't he?"

Luke and Liam had dropped their pretend games at once. The note had been written for them. This was their loving Dad, their personal, returned ex-convict.

"What about you, Donny? You coming? You don't even know our dad."

"I suppose I could say the same as Anna: he's got my mum. Hey, of course I want to meet your dad. Question is whether he'll feel okay about meeting me?"

"We told him about you already." Liam was taking big breaths as if he needed extra oxygen. "When you was living at the vicarage first time. About Hawkins and *Treasure Island* an' all."

"Then we're all in this together. Come on, everyone. Let's get looking for the signs."

"At least this weather means that we won't get seen – because there's absolutely no- one anywhere to see us," commented Anna, using her binoculars methodically.

"Sticks," shouted Luke. "Two of 'em and weed. Could be an arrow!"

"Gotta be," said Liam.

After that, the trail was easy. They found themselves hurrying further along the beach towards the Naze, following arrows formed from driftwood, pebbles, weed and shells. Then a heap of dried reed stalks directed them to turn inwards and take the first of the curved paths that led across the saltings. It was slightly higher than the surrounding marsh and gave good clearance above the flooded dyke.

Liam, running ahead, stopped suddenly beside the remains of a flat grey punt. It would never float again, but whoever had abandoned it had cared enough to make it fast to a stake, and turn it upside down on a couple of crates so that it would resist the worst of the weather for as long as possible. Bundles of reeds stacked against two of its sides suggested that some enterprising birdwatcher had used it as a hide.

Vicky was enjoying it, as she scrambled in and out of the low entrance, and played peek-boo with the two adults who were sheltering from the wind on the dry grass of the bank. She wanted Liam to come inside at once. Skye was equally at ease. Lottie's finger-spelling must have been far more advanced than she'd ever let on.

The children's father was a short, broad man wearing a black woolly hat and a new-looking donkey jacket. His jeans looked new as well. They were about a size too large. Maybe someone else had bought them.

What happened about clothes when you went to prison? Did they take your stuff away and give back to you when you were let out? Or did you wear your own clothes or overalls or something?

Whatever you'd worn in prison, you'd surely never want to wear again. Lottie would have been the one who'd done Bill's shopping and chosen these new clothes for him. Maybe he wasn't as big as she remembered.

Why wasn't Lottie here?

When Luke and Liam sprinted forward to hug their dad, Bill struggled to his feet awkwardly. Looked over his shoulder and from side to side as if he was about to make a getaway. He stood where he was but didn't reach out, didn't speak or smile.

Liam flung his arms around his father's waist and hung there, ecstatic, face completely buried in the thick cloth of the donkey jacket. Luke stopped before they touched.

"Hello, Dad."

"Hello, Son."

Even in the fresh breeze Bill's face was colourless. He and Luke stood staring at each other unable to find words. Bill let out a long exhausted sigh and slipped an arm round Liam. Held him close; brought his other hand to touch his son's fair hair, so carefully.

"Your sister's grown," he said to Luke.

"Yeah. And she talks a lot more too."

"Not too much, I hope?"

His voice was suddenly harsh. It took the boys a moment to understand what he meant.

"No, Dad, honest. It's only us as understands her most of the time."

"She says 'doh' mostly …"

"Like Homer Simpson."

"Your step-mum says you two can keep a proper secret now." He stopped again. Donny noticed that he was avoiding looking at Anna.

"I'm sorry I didn't come, Bill. When you were in …"

"Her Majesty's Parlour? You didn't exactly miss much. Did she, boys?"

Luke and Liam didn't answer.

"I shouldn't be here," Bill burst out. "If yer knew … how I wanted … all of yer!"

He had to let himself touch both his sons together, just his hands resting on their shoulders. He looked at Anna then gazed at Vicky.

"Wasn't even there when she were born. Thought it wouldn't matter. Being a fisherman and that. Used to be off on the trawlers three months at a time – when there was trawlers. Couldn't cope with this, though. You could be proud to have your dad a deep-sea fisherman, even when he weren't around. Not a …"

He couldn't finish. His eyes were wet and it wasn't the wind.

"You're still our dad," said Luke.

"Why ain't you coming home, Dad?"

"Because it ain't safe. Thought your step-mum told you. Never mind that I wouldn't exactly fit in with your new big house an' all … it just ain't safe. There's a bloke out there strangles budgies for his party trick. He could hurt you, any of you."

Anna stood exceptionally still. Tense with wanting to know more. Tense with trying not to ask.

"He's why I shouldn't have come. Him and the others. But

Lottie's leading 'em a dance in her flash car and I'm parked up at the top in this lady's van."

Skye had scooped Vicky into her arms. She was quick to sense distress.

"He says you lent him the camper," Donny signed. "Did you know all about this?"

"He has seen the eyes of Pauguk," she answered. "He is frightened." Her hands conveyed her pity and sadness.

"Dad's scared because of us," Luke told his brother. "Thinks we might let on to them bullies. Then they'd try an' rough us up to get at him. If we left you inside, Dad – pretended to – we wouldn't have no problem looking a bit sick an' not saying much if anyone was to ask. Today, it's like we're on our desert island. It ain't regular. So you don't have to be our dad today; you can be like our Man Friday."

"It's Monday," Anna corrected automatically.

"An' he is our dad. Every day. Wherever he's been. You said."

"I know I did, Li. An' he is … but you know when people start asking stuff. Like that lady who catches us at school – that old yeller-headed witch – the one who gives you bad feelings."

Toxic didn't only call at Gallister High; she could visit any of the schools, pluck out the unhappiest children, probe their scars with her painted nails.

"So, if we leaves our dad back in that visiting room, then this bloke's our Man Monday. An' we don't get in no muddles, see? Even if the yeller-headed witch or that fat copper come asking us who we might have been meeting."

Liam saw at once. Bill more slowly.

Donny and Anna were impressed.

"How do, stranger!"

They greeted him one after another, slapping high fives and jumbling their stories. They assured him that they were the solitary inhabitants of these Desolate Shores and they enticed him back to their camp. Skye made him tea – just as Granny Edith would have done – and then she cooked a pot of pasta, mixed with sweetcorn, tinned tuna, egg and tomato and some shreds of bright green samphire that she'd gathered while she and Bill and Vicky had been waiting to be found.

Afterwards the boys wanted to show their father the pits they'd dug and then walk out with him on the slowly uncovering sands.

"'Course if you'd have brought a good flat net you could go after them shrimps. Or you could anchor that little boat of yours some way out and hope to hook a few dabs or a plaice."

"Luke did try cockling but he didn't get many."

"Cockling … that's hard. There ain't so many as there was. An' you need a sieve. Still, mix 'em up with whelks an' mussels an' you'll get yourself a panful."

"Yuck," said Anna.

"You ain't changed then," said Bill, forgetting that he had never met her in any other life.

"I think I have, you know."

Donny felt sorry for Bill. His fear was like those flat bits a little way up the beach, which looked as if they were covered with smooth sand. Then, as soon as you stepped on them, you found slippery black mud straight underneath.

Bill couldn't keep up the Man Monday game. They walked down to *Vexilla* and he turned straight back into an ex-fisherman, making suggestions how Donny should keep her safe if it should come on to blow in the night.

"Reckon you'll want to be well out of here tomorrer. Forecast ain't getting any better."

"I wanted Anna to ring Weathercall but her mobile's out of battery. Don't suppose you've got one?"

"Nah. Well, that ain't exactly true. Lottie did give me one but I told her I weren't going to switch it on. Not when I'm near here. They can track you by a mobile, you know. I met blokes inside that had been done that way."

"But …" Anna sounded unconvinced.

"Don't start, Anna," Donny interrupted. "There are some things we don't want to know, remember? If Maggi and Xanthe turn up, we'll use theirs and, if they don't, we'll batten down the hatches anyway. Except we haven't got any – hatches, I mean. Look at the sky. Someone's getting well wet out there."

The clouds on the horizon were massed gun-metal grey. Dark rain veils linked sky to sea. Night was coming early.

"Time I was off," said Bill. But he didn't go.

They went back to the camp and drank more tea and Bill checked the guy ropes and reminded them about not touching the sides of the tents if it did come on to rain.

"It was you, last night, wasn't it?" Donny asked him. It was difficult to be sure which questions could be asked and which would have Bill skidding on the mud of fear again. "Round our tents. Smoking."

"Might have been."

"I only wanted to be sure that it wasn't … anyone else."

"Bad habit I picked up. I've told Lottie I'll stop. I'd seen you from the tower, when you was out sailing. Then I spotted a couple of coppers. They was only buying ice-cream but I made meself scarce. Moved the van a couple of times and came back when you was all asleep. Felt a bit emotional … Packet's gone now."

"The cairn, whose idea was that?"

"Your mum's. I'd been holed up since early. Watching. Then young Vicky came along and found where I was. She wouldn't leave go, bless her. So I wrote the note and your mum laid the trail. She thought you'd enjoy a bit of a game. You took long enough. I reckoned Lottie'd made a mistake and the kids didn't want to see me after all. Wouldn't have blamed them."

"You should have done," said Luke, firmly.

"You're our dad. We keep saying."

"Bill," said Anna. "I'm sorry about … how I used to be. But I think you should explain. Why did you and my mum have those terrible rows? You kept getting drunk and once …"

"I hit her. I'm sorry for it. I'm sorry every day. Luke, Liam. Don't ever get like me, do you hear? What Anna says is right. That was when I realised how low I'd sunk … Because I was wrong. Not wrong like they said, but wrong all the same. It was when I was working at the docks. Container handling. I didn't have no skill – not like a crane driver or anything. But the baby was coming and Lottie couldn't work and we needed the money."

Donny watched Anna now, leaning forward, intent on hearing the truth.

"So when I'd been there a bit and they told me about the bonuses I was well pleased."

"What bonuses? What did they give you bonuses for?"

"Observation. If you spotted a container with a special mark you told this Chinese feller and it was hundred quid in your hand and the next day off. Unofficial, so you still got paid like as if you'd been in. But Lottie, she wouldn't have it. Wouldn't touch the money – the hundred quid or money for the day un-worked. She was that stubborn."

"She knew it was crooked."

"So did I. Thought it must be goods going to get lost out of the system. You know stuff ends up in markets or gets sold out of the backs of vans. Didn't want to think it was anything worse. I'd borrowed money where I shouldn't and the repayments … well, they was getting bigger all the time. But she wouldn't entertain it. So then I tried to stop and the Chinese feller turned nasty. Really nasty. That's when I reckoned it must be drugs."

"But it wasn't drugs."

"It were people. Mind you, it could have been drugs as well. They was that bent. First I tried taking the money – so they didn't think I was going to grass on 'em – and drinking it on me day off, but I couldn't get the people out of me mind. Couldn't live with meself. Let alone with her."

"That wasn't the first row."

"No, it weren't. But it were the last. Next day I went to work and found a copper and I told him everything I knew." Bill fumbled in his pockets as if he was searching for these absent cigarettes. "Picked the wrong copper, didn't I?"

"You told … Flint?"

Bill nodded. His hands were shaking. Like Skye's when she'd been coming off the vodka.

"Big man. He was always about down there. Always going on

how he hated illegals. I reckoned if anyone would want to stop the trade it'd be him."

"You were wrong."

"Couldn't have been wronger. He sat me down. Wrote down everything I'd said. All very correct. Got me to sign it, with witnesses. No intimidation, nothing."

"That's right. The lawyer checked it …"

"Then when the other coppers'd gone, he took it all out of his bag again. Kept the signatures. Wiped most everything else – except the bits that fingered me – and said, if I added as much as another word, my kids'd suffer. Then he bought his nasty little mate in and they did one of their demonstrations."

"With … a bird?"

"With a bird."

Anna didn't move or speak but Donny found there was one more thing he needed to know.

"The mark, Bill. What did the mark on the containers look like? The one you were meant to spot."

"Load a scribbles really."

"Can you show me?"

"Promise you won't none of you tell. I just need you to keep safe."

"We promise."

"Cross our hearts."

Bill leant forward.

Donny had been certain he was going to see the Pura-Lilly symbol – the one on that pile of containers where the hidden workers had had to live, the flesh-pink sign on the Tiger's van, on the Chinese cleaner's overalls. Skye had seen it. Lottie had worn it.

The sign Bill drew in the clear damp sand was the Chinese character for Welcome – the sign that Donny had remembered from the poster on his primary classroom door, the sign he'd carved on the fake *Hispaniola* that distant day when he'd rescued the dragon flag. He'd put it on top of the Chinese national flag. Left it for the Tiger.

The Tiger had tried to threaten Great Aunt Ellen: GO HOME LÓNG, he daubed and slashed her flag to shreds. He would have assumed that Donny's Welcome sign was Gold Dragon's reply. No wonder there'd been trouble.

Harwich Approaches, Monday 28 May 2007
Min couldn't know where they were when the storm struck.

Even the container ship felt it. She rocked slightly and heeled for all her massiveness. It was the noise that was terrifying. The wind screaming round the exposed metal, the small, unexpected crashes as the crated furniture began to shift. The cries of fear from people in the dark. Then came the moment when they felt their prison begin to slide. The traumatic lurch when the single container that hadn't been properly fastened slipped from its position on the exposed aft corner of the lee side and plunged forty metres into the gale-swept sea below.

It sank slowly and almost completely as the spring tide pushed it towards the sands.

CHAPTER TWENTY

Hazards to Navigation

Walton Backwaters, Tuesday 29 May 2007

Bill had stayed until it was almost bedtime. Xanthe and Maggi had arrived in their Laser dinghies so he met them as well. They'd been late leaving Weymouth and the traffic had been bad but they'd persuaded their parents to launch *Spray* and *Kingfisher* at Titchmarsh Marina. They'd come down the Walton Channel on the ebb, carrying just enough gear for one night.

"We don't need a tent," said Xanthe. "We want to sleep in *Vexilla*. I've been hankering to bivvi there ever since you did. The parentals are bringing *Snow Goose* tomorrow. They don't want you to stay any longer. Forecast's terrible. If the tide had been right or if we'd left earlier, they'd have come tonight."

"Good thing they didn't."

"Do you have to go now, Bill?" Anna said. "Couldn't you stay a bit? The boys'd squash up for you."

"Don't never want to go but I reckon I ought. That there van's conspicuous and they don't like overnighters in the car park. I can't risk having me number taken." He sighed. "Tell you what, though, I might drive back up the Naze in the morning. Have a last look from the tower. You won't see me but I'll likely see you."

"We could fly a flag," Maggi suggested.

"Not with this wind. It'd rip away. You're going to have to sit tight enough in them tents. And get your dinghies pulled well up."

"Here you are." Anna brought out her binoculars. "Use these. They're almost new. I thought I'd take up bird-watching but I haven't the patience. Go on," she insisted, "think of them as a present from the kids. The shops are full of stuff for Father's Day and I haven't anyone to buy for."

He thanked her awkwardly. Then he hugged his children and set off along the beach to the Naze, taking care to walk all the way below the tide-line.

"That's so his footsteps'll be licked away when the water comes back up," said Luke, glumly.

They did their chores, ate and got ready for bed. No-one felt like dancing about.

"Sorry," said Donny to Xanthe and Maggi, when they went to check the dinghies one last time. "This isn't quite what you came for."

"Yes, it is. Just because we haven't done some blood ceremony doesn't mean we don't stick together through thick and thin, hell and high water, sand, mud and slime."

Xanthe'd read *Secret Water* but the others hadn't. Donny told them about the blood ceremony – pricking fingers and mingling the drops. Anna said "Yuck" immediately but Luke and Liam began to look alarmingly keen.

"I bet Xanth hasn't told you why we were so late leaving Weymouth," said Maggi.

"Don't."

"Why shouldn't I? You were brilliant and the selectors were there and we were asked to stay afterwards … and they've put her on the long list to train for the Olympics! They'll confirm the place after this summer's championships but, as she and *Spray* are so amazingly consistent, she's pretty well home and dry. Or wet."

"That is so fantastic!"

"It's better than that. Because if they do confirm that she's in the squad, Dad'll have to give up looking for jobs abroad. The training schedule's seriously intense – even though it's such a long time away. And there's residency rules and stuff."

"That's the best news since … well, since we last had any best news. Put it there, Xanth."

"Atmosphere a bit muted in the car though. Him and Mum. He still insists he's chucking in the Ipswich job. We might find we're living in Dorset or Anglesey or anywhere."

"At least it's the same country. We can have holidays together and stuff."

"And I get to chill out at weekends occasionally. When she's off in some RYA boot camp."

"Don't you mind, Maggi – not being in the squad?"

"Not one bit. It's not only that *Spray*'s a better dinghy that *Kingfisher* – which I have to admit that she is – it's the way Xanth sails her. Full out all the time, even in a flat calm."

"Which we don't have tonight," interrupted Xanthe. Donny'd noticed her give *Spray* an affectionate pat – like he might give *Lively Lady* if he didn't think anyone was watching. It was a bit of a mystery why one of the Lasers should be so much better than the other; they looked identical to him.

The middle of the night was wild. No-one slept much – but no-one blew away. The wind was still directly on the shore, so their small dunes gave them some shelter and the dry sand tended to pile up on the seaward side, burying their guy ropes deeper than ever. Then, when it rained, it felt as if they were being hammered in.

Sometime between five and six it all went quiet. Everyone slept and then it was nearly eight before Donny crawled out of his tent to inspect the damage.

There wasn't much: *Vexilla* had lain securely to her anchor and extra warp. Her tarpaulin had tried to break free but Maggi and Xanthe had grabbed on to it from inside and re-lashed it as often as necessary. They'd had the roughest night of anyone but seemed remarkably unbothered once they'd made sure that their dinghies were okay.

Spray and *Kingfisher* had been hauled right up to the top of the beach with anchors buried deep. They had both blown a bit sideways and were splattered with wet sand but they hadn't lost any gear. Xanthe, Maggi, Donny and Anna pulled them back down to the water and began cleaning them off. They could hear Luke and Liam shouting long before they could make out the words.

"We went out on the magic sand, far as we could …"

"There's a big thing run aground …"

"But we couldn't get there."

"And now Skye brought us back."

"Because the tide's turned. She says we can go in the boats."

"Skye says? Says how?"

"By drawing, eejit – in the sand."

"Us and you in the boats. Her and Vicky in the camp. Big circle with two dots in the middle and the rest outside. Wavy lines for water, canoes for boats. Easy."

They grimaced at the stupidity of the older ones.

"It could be a wrecked ship and, if we board her, we could discover all the stores we need to never go home, like in *Robinson Crusoe*."

"Not *Robinson Crusoe*. You mean that family, the ones who built houses and planted crops and always just happened to find whatever they needed. Rev. Wendy told me … They were like Robinson 2."

"You mean Lemony Snicket. It's in the school library. It's called *The End*. They have a Coastal Shelf and things get stuck on it."

"No, they don't. They get salvaged and dragged away."

There was about to be a quarrel. Everyone knew the signs.

"Look," said Donny. "This is us and we're not in the vicarage or the library now so let's go check it out. As long as Skye said it was okay."

"She did, she did."

They saw it as soon as they'd rounded the promontory. It had grounded where the strip of sand continued under the waters, stretching towards the distant Pye End buoy. It must have blown on in the early hours of the morning and been stranded ever since. But it wasn't a wrecked ship: it was a container.

"I didn't think those things ever fell off," said Anna.

"Must do, sometimes," said Donny. "You have to report them on the VHF as a navigational hazard. If *Snow Goose* or *Strong Winds* hit one of those out to sea, they'd probably sink."

"We haven't got a VHF so we can't report it. And it doesn't look much of a hazard stuck out there. Nobody's not going to see that, are they?"

"Not in good visibility but what about in the dark? Or in fog?

It must have struck at high water. It was probably submerged. And now the tide's coming up again."

"It might have broken open and be full of new computers."

"Or bottles of whisky," said Luke, rather surprisingly.

"We can't take them, you know. That's what wreckers do."

"Then we'd best go hold back Xanthe and Maggi."

The Ribieros were racing each other as usual, apparently not at all held back by the wind and tide against them.

"It's not deep," they shouted, as the others reached them.

"I felt the sand with my spinnaker pole. You could stand if you wanted."

"Up to your neck."

"But we don't want, thanks all the same."

"That's probably why no-one's come out to move it yet. Or even buoy it. Because it's still too shallow."

"They'll be waiting until there's more water."

"Meanwhile it's all ours: a stranded galleon. Do you dare me to climb on it?"

"No, we do not," said Anna. "Calm down, Xanthe, you're setting my brothers a bad example."

"Anna," said Donny, "look."

He'd manoeuvred *Vexilla* until she was lying in the lee of the container.

"It's that Welcome Mark. The one Dad was on about. We have it on our door at school." Luke's voice was strangely low and slow.

"There could be people in there."

"NO! There just couldn't!"

If Bill's story had been true, spotting this container could have earned him £100 and a paid day off – thus ensuring that he wasn't on site to know what happened to it next. If there had been people … Bill would have had no idea how they had got in there or how they got out. Or where they went next.

They'd told Xanthe and Maggi Bill's story last night. Now Donny showed them the Welcome Mark.

"Quick!" said Xanthe. "Phone someone. Harwich Harbour Authority or the coastguards. Damn! I left mine in the car. Mags? Anna?"

Maggi never took her mobile on *Kingfisher* and Anna's had no battery.

"Come on! We can't just sit here like stranded starfish waiting for the tide to come back. Those people in there …"

"Are probably dead," said Anna.

Donny felt sick. Tears instantly filled Maggi's eyes and Liam began to bawl. Luke turned sheet white as if he were going to faint.

"Or they may not be." Xanthe had come to a decision. "I'm going to sail for help. Harwich is closer but the wind and tide are wrong and I don't know exactly who I'd ask. I'll get the Walton coastguard. They're just behind the beach. Mags, if you see any yachts or fishing boats, you could try to persuade them to send a VHF message. Donny, Anna, you stay here. Start tapping on the sides of this thing. You need to give the survivors hope."

She sheeted in *Spray*'s mainsail and was reaching for the Naze like a low-flying bird.

"She didn't wait to check," said Anna.

"She believed our dad. Straight away."

Liam stopped crying and looked at Luke.

"But will it be okay?" Luke asked Anna. "If she tells them it was our dad who told us. He said it was dangerous to be a grass, really dangerous. What if they find him?"

Donny didn't give Anna time to answer.

"If you think about it, Lukey, there isn't a choice. If there's any possibility that there's people in there – then we've gotta take the chance of helping. They can't get out themselves and we don't know how much air there is inside. Let's do what Xanthe said and start tapping. We could work our way round this side and Maggi could start on the other."

"There's a thing called witness protection," said Anna. "I read about it somewhere and I remembered it in the night. As soon as we get home I'm going to ask Edward if we can get it for Bill. This container – with this mark – could be exactly the proof he needs."

"I don't want there to be people," said Liam. "Even if it does help Dad."

"None of us want that," said Donny. "So if we've made a mistake, or Bill did, we'll probably get told off – Xanthe the worst – but we'll be quite pleased all the same. What sort of tapping do you think we should do?"

He knew that he needed to help the younger boys stay calm and, if possible, not think too much. The container rose above them like a crag jutting from the seabed.

"Dunno."

"I get bad feelings … "

"Does it matter?" Maggi sounded tense. "If there's anyone in there – which I truly hope there isn't – they need to know help's on the way. We could tap God Save the Queen."

"Gold Dragon made me learn the flag codes. F – Foxtrot – means 'I am disabled. Communicate with me.' Why don't we do that? In Morse. Short, short, long, short."

"Anything," said Anna, "As long as we remember to listen as well."

Maggi had set her stopwatch when Xanthe left. It was almost an automatic reaction of the sisters to keep checking and comparing times and distances. How soon could someone come?

It took just over half an hour.

It was the longest half an hour they'd ever spent. What had sounded like a simple job – tapping and listening – turned out to be much harder than they'd thought. Although there wasn't much of a sea running – nothing like last night – yet there were waves constantly breaking against the side of the container, and almost nothing to hold on to.

Donny remembered the first time he and Xanthe had run *Lively Lady* alongside the fake *Hispaniola*. There'd been a fresh breeze blowing on that day as well, but they'd been able to stay under the schooner's lee and had been lucky enough to find a loose rope dangling down.

There was nothing like that here. Maggi, on her own in *Kingfisher*, found it impossible to cope. She'd taken her sail down but the dinghy was rolling so much that her mast kept hitting the metal. She didn't have enough hands to hold steady, fend off, tap and listen.

Eventually she gave up, attached her painter to the metal bars on the container's end, and perched in *Kingfisher*'s bows fending off, tapping with a paddle, looking at the complicated arrangement of seals and padlock and getting completely soaked.

If only her parents would arrive early. She and Xanthe had

begged them yesterday not to hurry: to allow them their maximum time in camp. What wouldn't she give today to see the sleek outline of *Snow Goose* slipping out over the Harwich shelf three or four hours ahead of schedule? She wouldn't care how much of a bad mood they were in.

Donny kept *Vexilla*'s outboard motor running and set Anna to fend off while Liam tapped and Luke listened. They moved as slowly as they could, tapping and listening every few inches. But they heard nothing.

After a while they thought that they might not be tapping loud enough so Liam began banging against the container with the metal boat hook: Short, short, long, short. Short, short, long, short. Still there was nothing.

They knew that they didn't want there to be anyone trapped inside the container but it was hard not be disappointed when there was no reply. And anxious. Because that might mean that there had been people but they were dead.

"On the other hand it could mean that they're alive but physically can't answer," said Anna. "After all we don't know what else is in there. There might be crates and things. It'd give better protection."

"Only protection from some things," said Donny, looking at the angle of the container. Perhaps there was a steep edge to the sandbank. He found he didn't really want to think of heavy crates, sliding about inside. Would it have rolled over?

"Maybe Bill got it wrong."

"In which case we're mega-pleased but we're also in deep doo-doo. And Bill won't be all that impressed with us either."

The inshore rescue boat, an orange RIB, arrived at speed with Xanthe on board as well. The four crewmen didn't particularly want to talk to the children.

Which was sort of okay. They'd been worried that they'd have to answer difficult questions about the identification mark. Like who told them? And how did he know? But all the men asked was whether they'd heard any sounds from inside. They didn't seem that surprised when the answer was no.

Donny had the impression that they'd found Xanthe's story hard to believe and were struggling not to resent being called out by a teenager. They said that the grounded container had already been reported as a hazard to navigation. A salvage tug was booked to tow it off when there was more water to help float it.

Now they wanted the children to take their friend and go. She'd given them full contact details. They'd be in touch if they found that there was anything … that there shouldn't be.

Xanthe was trembling as she climbed carefully across to *Vexilla*. She looked as if she was in shock or something. Her pull-ups and sailing shoes were wet.

"Are you okay?"

She shook her head.

Donny peered at her.

She turned away and hid her face in her arms. Her shoulders heaved.

Maggi had been talking to one of the rescue crew. Talking and pointing. She looked persuasive and very like her mother. So he wasn't totally surprised that the crewman was listening to whatever she said.

The inshore lifeboat was powerful and manoeuvrable. The man spoke to the steersman and they brought it right alongside. Then he stepped out of the RIB and onto the sloping metal. He laid his ear against it. Spoke to Maggi again. Urgently.

She pointed to the locking bar where she'd attached her dinghy's painter. She seemed to be showing him how far the water level had risen.

He nodded. A bit agitated now. Clipped on his safety harness so he could brace himself and use both hands.

She freed her painter and pushed *Kingfisher* away.

"Xanthe," Donny banged her on the shoulder. He didn't mean to do it hard but *Vexilla* shifted to a wave and he lost his balance. "Maggi's telling them something. They're listening to her."

She didn't answer.

"Xanth, what the hell's the matter?"

Liam took over *Vexilla*'s helm. He loved using the outboard and had done it lots of times before but never without being asked. Anna and Luke were sitting beside one another on the forward thwart. Almost in passing, Donny noticed that they were gripping each other's hands.

One of the men in the RIB was talking on his radio: another cupped his hands round his mouth and shouted across to them.

"Kids! You've got to move away. We're going to open the container. Move right away. Now! Back to your mum. We're very grateful and we WILL contact you. Now GO!"

Liam opened the throttle at once and turned *Vexilla* away. Maggi had her sail up and was drifting alongside them.

"Xanthe!" He shook her again. "What is it?"

She lifted her head and turned to face him. Tears were pouring down her cheeks.

"It's *Spray*," she said. "I hit an unmarked breakwater and wrecked *Spray*. It was deep and she went straight down. I knew I had to get to the coastguard to save the people. So I swam and then I ran. I only looked back once. The top of her mast was showing. But, when we went past in the RIB, it had gone."

CHAPTER TWENTY-ONE

Point Horror

Walton Backwaters, Tuesday 29 May 2007

Donny thought of *Spray* when he'd last seen her, streaking across the morning waves. She had begun moving as soon as Xanthe had pulled in her sheet, she'd responded to every small shift of Xanthe's weight as if the two of them were a single being.

He knew how he felt about *Lively Lady* – yet he also enjoyed sailing *Vexilla* or *Strong Winds*. He'd sailed Maggi's *Kingfisher* once. They all had different qualities. But for Xanthe, *Spray* was everything. She was so focussed and intense. She and *Spray* were a winning team. Was it only last night Maggi'd told them about their possible selection for the Olympic squad? Would they … would the selectors still want her?

That definitely wasn't a question that he could ask right now.

"Did you … um … did you happen to throw out the anchor?" was all that he could think of.

"No. We hit so hard that it was me that got thrown out. And when I surfaced, she was already going down. I don't normally even carry an anchor. There was one, though, from last night. I supposed it's possible it could have been tipped out by the impact …" Her body sort of sagged again. "It's no good, Donny-man. *Spray*'s a GRP racing dinghy. You can't mend her with a couple of new planks or bodge her together with layers of fibre-glass. Once her hull's been smashed like that, she's finished."

Everyone had been listening. No one could find anything to say. Maggi had brought *Kingfisher* right up to *Vexilla's* lee side and had let her sheet go. She'd given Luke her painter and was hanging on the larger boat's gunwale, so she could join the conversation as the outboard moved them both along.

"You can have 'Fisher, Xanth. You know you can. Any time you like."

"Thanks."

Would that keep her in the squad? Or could the Ribieros afford to buy a new top-quality Laser? That probably depended on Joshua having a job.

"Anyway. You haven't told us what were you saying to those men back there. Why did they suddenly decide to try and open the container? Did you hear something?"

"Not exactly. Thing was, while I was hanging on there, I was looking at the way the container doors might open. I knew we couldn't do it – there were metal seals on them – but I saw how it ought to work. They'd open outwards and, with the way the thing was lying, there would be time to open at least one of them if the rescuers got started straight away. Some water might go in but it wouldn't be too bad. But as soon as the tide comes up any further, the water will be pressing against the outside. Or pouring in. There'll be no chance. I really wanted the man to have a go. So I said I might have heard … someone screaming."

"But you didn't … hear anyone?"

"Mmmmm … probably not."

Donny was confused, "What do you mean, probably? Either you did hear someone or you didn't, surely?"

"Okay. In that case, I didn't. Not with my actual ears. But inside my head. I got to thinking and that made the screaming start. I was thinking what it must have been like for people inside one of those things. Feel the darkness pressing round you and the tiny space shutting you in and the ship moving, but you don't know where. And then imagine what it must have been like when the container went over the side. Falling. Hitting the water. They could have been injured. Then tossing around and the thing slowly sinking and being certain that you were going to drown …"

"Maggi, stop! You'll give Luke and Liam nightmares."

"I hope we'll all have nightmares. Everyone in the world should have nightmares. It's every bit as foul as the old slave ships …"

Her dark skin had lost its glow: her big eyes were full of pain. She went on describing the scene that she'd experienced so vividly.

"So we don't know how long they were tossed about. Or how badly anyone was hurt. But then the motion stopped. Maybe there were crashes when the container hit that sand. A pounding as the waves kept pushing it further on. And maybe some of the water drained away as the tide fell outside. So maybe a tiny bit of hope came trickling back. Maybe they tried calling out. Being discovered would be better than being dead. But there wasn't any answer because there wasn't anyone to hear them. Then they started to feel that the water was creeping back in again …"

"Maggi, that's ENOUGH!"

She was sitting safely in the familiar white space of *Kingfisher*;

she was clinging to *Vexilla*'s sturdy gunwale; she was with her sister and her closest friends, yet Maggi's mind couldn't leave its black and terrifying prison.

Donny remembered the airless cupboard where Zhang had imprisoned him. His head began throbbing. It was hard to breathe. He lurched to the opposite gunwale and chucked up. A moment later Luke joined him.

"So when they heard you," Maggi hadn't stopped, "if they heard you – dot dot dash dot, dot dot dash dot – they wouldn't exactly have tapped back, would they? Anyone who was still alive in there would have screamed for help. They'd have screamed to you with every last gasp of their breath."

They were round the promontory, almost to the beach.

"But no-one did," said Anna.

"No," said Maggi. "I don't think they did … It was probably just in my head."

They beached the boats and scrambled out. The sisters hugged each other.

"Sorry, Mags, I don't know how I could mind for a second about *Spray*. I wasn't thinking."

"There's always a chance," said Anna.

"What chance?"

"A chance that you didn't hear anything because there wasn't anyone there to hear. Bill could have made a mistake. Or we could. About that particular container."

They took turns helping to pack up the camp and looking out seawards. Other boats came and joined the RIB: a police launch, a harbour authority launch, a tug, bringing a sort of floating pontoon which the harbour launch helped to fix alongside.

"I wish I had those binoculars," muttered Anna. "No, I don't! That's the shark-boat. That's Flint. Bad. Bad. Bad."

"And there's *Snow Goose*!"

"At last."

"But they don't know."

"They don't know anything."

"Hasn't anyone got a mobile that works? I can't bear them not knowing."

As *Snow Goose* came into distant view from behind the harbour breakwater, the watching children saw her heavy gaff mainsail swinging up and then out to catch the fair breeze and favouring tide as she set a leisurely course towards the Pye End buoy.

"They'll be ages coming at that speed. There's no wind this morning. I wish they'd put the engine on and hurry up."

Everything was packed and ready for them to leave. Donny had told Skye about their discovery of the Mark on the container; about their fears for anyone who might have been hidden inside; about Xanthe's heroic dash for help and about the loss of *Spray*. She had put her arms round Xanthe but Xanthe was controlled now. She couldn't allow herself to respond. Skye stepped away.

She went back to amusing Vicky as usual: tried to get Liam and Luke involved but they were pale and distracted, obviously on the edge or tears. She offered to unpack and make tea but no one wanted anything.

"Maybe I should sail out to meet Mum and Dad," suggested

Maggi. She didn't want to. None of them wanted to go near the container. They didn't want to imagine what the rescue team had found which had made them summon so much additional help. There were more pontoons being towed into position now. With screens.

What would Gold Dragon do, Donny wondered? If she'd been here now with her brothers and sisters? If she been one of the oldest, not the youngest, and wanted to get a message to the parents. Send up a flare maybe? But they hadn't got a flare and it might distract the real rescuers.

"Anyone got anything orange?" asked Xanthe. "Waving something orange is a sign of distress."

Liam had been fidgeting about, as if he was practising a football routine with no ball. Now he dug in his sports bag for a replica Dutch football shirt, which he fixed to the end of a stick and waved. It was tiny.

Then Skye signed that she was going to light the unused fire they'd started building yesterday … the day before … half a lifetime ago?

"Won't that make June and Joshua think we're enjoying ourselves?"

"Depends …"

She signed that Donny should fetch the tarpaulin from *Vexilla,* and that the rest of them should begin collecting the semi-sodden wrack and reed stalks which marked the highest limits of the tide.

"She wants us to send a smoke signal!"

It was unnecessary, possibly silly. It was playing. It wasn't going to make any difference to whatever grim reality was happening out there, but it stopped them having to keep thinking about it. The smoke swelled and billowed under the tarpaulin; stung their eyes and made them cough, then surged up in clumps of dirty cotton wool when they pulled the cover momentarily aside. They tried long bursts and shorter puffs – three at a time – S.O.S.

Snow Goose stopped idling. Her sails came down; her engine went on. The Ribieros probably checked their VHF. They were dropping anchor off Stone Point in less than half an hour.

Once the police and the tug and the rest of the salvage team were in position – and the screens were up – the crew of the inshore rescue boat did exactly as they'd promised, and came to find the children.

It wasn't good news. It was worse than their worst expectations. The rescuers were visibly delighted to discover that the children all had parents with them.

Lottie had arrived, even before June and Joshua. She'd run the whole distance from the Naze tower where she had parked her Toyota. She was gasping for breath, her eyes were streaming. It was a while before she could do more than hug people.

Bill had told her there was an emergency. He'd been watching from first light, using Anna's binoculars. He hadn't minded getting soaked, frozen and buffeted. He'd been worried about the children in the storm.

Bill had been the first person to report the stranded container – simply as a hazard to navigation. Later he'd watched Xanthe and *Spray* and that was when he'd realised there was something wrong. He'd used his mobile to call Lottie and to tell her she was needed. Then he'd wiped the phone and left it at the foot of the tower. He'd headed away in the camper van. She'd no idea where he was planning to go. He was desperate to avoid bringing more trouble on them.

"He's put a marker out where he saw your boat go down," Lottie told Xanthe. "He used a weighted can. There wasn't much else he could do. Although Bill was born a fisherman he's never learned to swim. He got right out along the breakwater, he said. He thought there was a goodish chance you'd find she's been jammed against it. You'll probably get her back."

"What's left of her," said Xanthe, sadly. "It was kind of him to try. Anyway, what's a dinghy?"

There had been a dozen travellers in the container … but only one survivor.

"A young boy, miss," said the crewman who'd listened to Maggi. "Not much older that yourself, I wouldn't think. He was unconscious when they pulled him out. That scream you heard must be the last thing he did. I wouldn't have thought it possible. A miracle, really."

"Only one from all those people."

"If it hadn't been for you, there wouldn't even have been one. We couldn't help wondering what made you think of listening in the first place?"

They'd had no chance to talk properly to June and Joshua, or to ask Lottie what they should say. And they had promised Bill.

"I suppose we were mainly curious," said Xanthe.

"I'd seen something on TV once," offered Maggi.

"About the places people try and hide when they're

desperate," Anna finished. "Like underneath trains and in the wheels of aeroplanes."

The crewman shook his head. "It's terrible," he said. "Absolutely terrible. Those poor souls. I don't mind telling you I'll be glad when I get home to my family."

Lottie took Vicky, Skye, Luke and Liam back to the vicarage in the car. She would have taken Anna and Donny as well but they asked to stay with Xanthe and Maggi for the moment when they had to pass the disaster site.

"We could go to the marina. Leave *Snow Goose* and the dinghies for another day. Get a taxi home. Wait until the container's been removed."

"It's in our heads, Mum. Nothing's ever going to remove it."

"Then I'd prefer you all to stay in the cabin with me. Your father will manage the yacht."

" I wonder if we'll ever meet him."

"Who?"

"The boy. The one they salvaged."

"If he doesn't get sent straight back."

"To wherever he came from."

"Why?" said Xanthe, "Why do people come? At least in your old slave ships they'd have been captured, Maggi. Those people probably paid. Paid more than if they'd been on a luxury cruise."

"Paid Zhang!"

"Then he paid Flint and Toxic."

"Then the people start paying all over again when they go to work for something like Pura-Lilly, which keeps back most of their money and makes them sleep in dumps. And their debts get so big they can't ever escape."

They shut up for a bit, and blew the froth off the mugs of hot chocolate that June had made for them, and felt how lucky they were to be together in *Snow Goose*'s cabin as she carried them smoothly homewards to her berth at the Royal Orwell & Ancient Yacht Club.

"All the same, I wonder where he did came from?" said Donny.

"And where his parents are," added June. She'd made coffee for herself and Joshua and was sitting with the Allies again. "I have heard that even young children sometimes make these journeys alone. I can't bear to imagine it. And how is this going to affect all of you? I can request counselling, you know."

Xanthe, who'd relapsed into a moody silence and was letting her drink grow cold, sat up and glared at her loving parent. "Counselling! We don't need counselling – we want REVENGE! I'll finish my GCSEs. Give them my best shot. But I'm not doing anything else. Certainly not going dinghy-racing until we've scuppered Flint and Toxic. That's not because I've lost *Spray*. Eleven people dead! And I don't suppose that anyone'll offer their families counselling. Or whoever took their money will be sending tasteful wreaths and offering compensation."

"There will certainly be an Enquiry," said her mother.

"Reporting in a few years time and recommending Safety Measures," said Xanthe contemptuously. She began using her strong and mobile fingers to tick off the steps they needed to take. "One: we get Lottie to find Bill and persuade him that he's got to tell everything he knows. Not all policemen are crooked, just because Flint is. Two: Anna's lawyer will get him that witness protection thing. Then three: when we know Bill and the kids are safe we show someone the Mark. They'll surely keep the container now. They might even have to designate it a grave or something. They'll have to believe us."

Then Donny managed to say the thing that had been worrying him for weeks.

"Do you think," he said, addressing himself mainly to June, "that if we have a go at them, they'll try and get Great Aunt Ellen into more trouble when she comes home to England? For shooting the Tiger in the stomach with that flare?"

"I was there too," she answered. "I saw him throw the knife. Who's to say that didn't make her miss her intended direction? It was a collision avoidance flare and he was on a collision course. All I am certain about is that obtaining justice in this case will not be as straightforward as my daughter believes. The survivor's testimony may be all that's needed to identify culprits and obtain convictions but I'm afraid, Xanthe, that you may be away from your dinghy racing for a long time yet."

Harwich, Tuesday 29 May 2007
Min was lifted from the container and the paramedics gave him sedatives. Some people asked him questions but he couldn't, at that moment, find the English words to answer.

He was so young, his silent distress so heart-rending, that it seemed kinder to help him to sleep. Then, when a uniformed Inspector and a charming and very senior lady from the Welfare

Services arrived to take him to a secure and purpose-equipped location, the rescuers were reassured that he would be in safe, professional hands. The Inspector and the Welfare Officer would transport him themselves. No time would be lost.

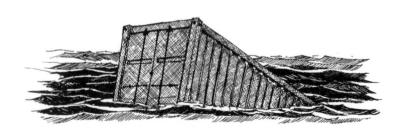

CHAPTER TWENTY-TWO

Donny draws a Map

Snow Goose, RO&A, Monday 18 June 2007

"This witness protection thing isn't as simple as I thought," said Anna. "Either Bill can go back into prison and be held in a special unit where nobody knows his name. He'd get called Bloggs and be given a number. Or him and all of us have to go to a police safe house and be surrounded by panic buttons and alarm systems and never go out until everyone he accuses – that's Flint and the Tiger, because we haven't got anything real on Toxic (yet) – has been tried and sentenced. Could take ages. Then, after that, he's still not safe because they probably have associates, so he has to be given a whole new identity. And so do all of us if we want to go on living with him."

"Wow!" said Maggi. "I wonder how often they do all that?"

"Not very often. It's really expensive because they have to wipe everything, birth certificate, driving licence, bank account. It's not simply thinking up a new name and dishing out a passport. But at the moment it's not even a possibility. Edward says that the police have got to be convinced that what Bill has to tell them is totally worthwhile – and that he's in actual danger – before they offer anything at all."

"And as he's still too frightened to talk – even if we knew where to find him, which we don't – it's all hopeless."

"Let's forget about Bill," said Xanthe.

She'd taken her last GCSE that morning but she wouldn't even go sailing for pleasure. The remains of *Spray* had been collected and were awaiting an insurance assessment; *Kingfisher* sat on her trailer in the dinghy park: *Vexilla* grew weed on her mooring. *Lively Lady* was, presumably, dangling from davits in Oostende.

It wasn't that Xanthe had banned the rest of them from sailing: they just didn't like to go when she was so obstinately denying herself. Donny knew she was missing it at least as much as he was: he'd seen her checking the breeze.

They were sitting in *Snow Goose*'s cabin, not on deck. It was too hard not to look out across the wide river, and long to see the evening sunlight slanting low into your sails, and feel the tug of the wind on the sheets, and the lift and lightness as your dinghy came to life.

"The kids wouldn't like to hear you say that about Bill," Anna told Xanthe. "They're longing for him to be the shining knight who gallops up and sorts everything. They're missing him far more than they ever seemed to do when he was inside."

"We wouldn't mind our dad shining a bit more gallantly either. He keeps going off to look at other hospitals, checking out their neuro-surgery departments."

"And how they manage their cleaning contracts. He goes on and on about accountability."

"Then, when he is at home, he and Mum are still having rows."

"That must be awful," said Anna.

"It is," said Maggi. "They've never been like this before. We have to keep being diplomatic."

"Sloshing oil on troubled waters. No time at all for sisterly bickering. When we finally get Zhang, Flint and Toxic in

Execution Dock, I'm suing for restitution of my teenage rights. I haven't thrown a proper strop for weeks."

"Feels more like 'if' than 'when'."

For all Xanthe's energy and Maggi's intuition and Anna's brains and money, they hadn't made any progress. All Donny could offer was an uneasy feeling that they were missing something. He was sure that there was something – or someone – really obvious and important that they'd forgotten.

"That's why I wanted us to come here," Xanthe explained. "Remind ourselves how we felt that day when we were lurking down below, too sick to get up on deck as we passed the container. Or even to go spit at Flint."

"You think we need reminding?" Anna had at least been talking to her lawyer.

"It's probably just me. I caught myself checking last weekend's results on the RYA website. You know those two girls from Norfolk?" she said to Maggi, "The twins no-one can tell apart? They've overtaken us in the rankings now."

"So?"

"So … nothing. And the Harbour Authority has decided to move the container. Some people suggested that it should be left there – as a sort of memorial. That idea's been turned down, so they're towing it back into Felixstowe and, when the police have finished with it, it'll be scrapped."

"Convenient for anyone who mightn't want anyone else to look too closely at it later on. If Bill ever decides to talk."

"There must be other workers who know what's going on. And the officials who helped Flint harass *Strong Winds* and looked the other way when the Tiger came back."

"Bribed or frightened?"

"Remember that man we saw through the binoculars that day?" Anna asked Donny, as if he could have forgotten. "That wasn't Bill because Bill was already in prison."

"I think," said Donny, who usually tried not to think about that sight more often than he could help, "that the Tiger kept his cage-birds on board the *Pride of Macao*."

"The *Hispaniola*, you mean."

"Yes, but she's the wrong story. The right one must have started when Gold Dragon was living in the South China Sea. You know, the story of the Three Islands. It was you that told me, Maggi and Xanthe. I know it's only fiction but everything's based on something."

"So?"

"So, not a lot. There's a character called the Tiger in that story who keeps birds, that's all. Maybe this bloke's posing as him."

"Why?"

"Make himself look scarier? I dunno."

"And Gold Dragon can't remember."

"She nearly did. There was a moment off the Belgium coast when she saw him coming at us … The shock was probably what gave her the heart attack."

"But the Tiger doesn't know that she's forgotten. So it's not surprising he got in such a panic when we hoisted her dragon flag on his boat."

"Especially as we made that mistake and put up the Chinese flag when it should have been the Australian. He must have thought the message was for him – 'You are standing into danger.'"

"That it was a threat to him instead of a warning to her!"

"Quite funny really."

"Except not." Donny thought of all the trouble there'd been. "Because I didn't tell you what I did on board the *Hispaniola* the next day. I had your knife, Xanth, the old one with the marlin-spike, and I found a piece of plank and I scratched all the welcome words I could remember and put it on top of the Chinese flag and left it for him to find, like a doormat."

"Including the Mark?"

The others didn't know whether to giggle or gasp.

"He must have gone … ballistic!"

Donny nodded, unhappily. "I think he did. But I think he took it out on his birds. Smashed the place up a bit, threw the cages about. Tipped a couple overboard. That's why we found Hawkins so soon afterwards. And there were other birds, cage birds. They were still fluttering around the Hisp … *Pride of Macao*. We saw some being blown right across the harbour. They'd never have survived."

"That's horrible," said Maggi. "Are you sure?"

"If *Strong Winds* was here I could check the dates in her log-book. But yes, I am sure. That boat gave me a really weird feeling …"

"You and your feelings," said Anna. "You're as bad as Liam."

"I dunno. I thought Gold Dragon had finished the Tiger and I didn't ever expect to see the *Hispaniola* again. I can't get her out of my head. I get fed up with it. I only want to go sailing. And draw maps," he added hastily. That bit about sailing had slipped out by accident. It was such a lovely evening. He could hear all the boats in the marina chattering to each other through their hulls and their halyards and their rigging.

"We did mind-mapping once," said Maggi. "When they were trying to teach us study skills."

"I actually meant charts. I got a letter from Gold Dragon this morning. Not really a letter – she doesn't do them – it was one of her crazy texts. I don't think she's quite grasped that the world isn't run via telegrams any more."

"Or writing with a hook isn't all that straightforward," said Anna.

Oh. She was probably right. Donny'd got so used to his great-aunt being able to do everything he'd actually forgotten that she only had one hand. It wasn't something he noticed any more.

"Get on then," ordered Xanthe, "Read it out."

"A TALE TO TELL OF THE HOUDALINQUA. INTEND TRADING CHART FOR CHART WITH YOUR ARCHIPELAGO REPORT. WAS IT WAR OR EXPLORATION?"

"That's a bit cryptic?"

"Not by her standards. She expected us to have spent more time sailing round the islands and exploring all those little creeks. She thinks I'll have drawn a map but I haven't done anything. What with school and SATs … as well as what actually happened. It's almost too late now. There was a letter from my …uncle as well. He wants me to come out to Oostende again and help him sail *Strong Winds* home."

That wasn't precisely what Defoe had written …

"I need you to agree to skipper the junk as that's the only way Polly Lee is prepared to relinquish her command. I'll sign on as your crew. Bring a friend if you'd like. And Skye, my dream-sister. Come as soon as you can. I begin to feel uneasy here. With love from Uncle Ned (though I prefer Defoe if you can manage it)."

"The thing is that I've got my passport and I've looked on our school calendar and the teachers have a day off next Friday – for marking tests and writing reports and all that stuff – and Rev. Wendy says she'll take us across on the ferry. But I'll have nothing to give Great Aunt Ellen except bad news. I ought to send her a message back but I can't think of a single word."

"Forensics," said Anna.

"Huh?"

"You wanted a single word, send that. She doesn't have a monopoly of cryptic communication. It might amuse her. The more she thinks about it, the better prepared she'll be to hear the real story."

Donny so knew how Gerald and Wendy felt. "That's a really great idea, Anna, but …"

"You have a problem with it?"

"Um … my problem is that I'm never exactly sure what 'forensics' means. I've heard it on TV of course. When they cordon off an area with that sort of orange ribbon. Or put special tents up so people don't get rained on when they're checking for DNA."

"Then you hear some interviewer saying that someone's got a 'forensic' intelligence, and you wonder if they just mean that she's a mega-brainiac? I'm not sure either," said Maggi.

"Forensics is what the Romans did in the forum. So it's any sort of legal argument or the special sorts of science and medicine that you can use as evidence. We should have taken a photo of the Mark when Bill drew it on the sand and another when we saw it on the container. And we should have noted the number of the container so that it could be tracked back to port of origin. But we did do some deductive stuff – mainly you, Donny –

and we're doing our best to be forensic now."

"Because we want to present a case with real evidence, you mean?" said Xanthe.

"Yes. And if Donny wants to start assembling our evidence on a map for Gold Dragon – I think we should all help."

"A forensic map?"

"Oh come on, Donny, don't be slow. A hunter's map's going to be different from a farmer's map."

"And a detective's chart will be different from a hydrographer's." Xanthe'd got it. "War and exploration all on the single sheet, I'd say. Stop yearning out of that porthole, skipper. It's time to sharpen the ship's pencils."

"By the way," she added, sometime later, when she'd been struggling to sketch an accurate outline of Felixstowe Dock, "Mags and I won't be arm-wrestling you for that spare berth on board *Strong Winds*. I'm going sailing next weekend and she's my PR manager."

Okay.

Donny looked at the harbour map: at the position of the red and white schooner – so strategic and yet so isolated. There was a link he was missing. He was sure of it.

Harwich Harbour, June 2007
There was a person missing too. But his disappearance had been well disguised and no- one had yet noticed.

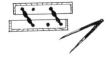

CHAPTER TWENTY-THREE

HMS *Beckfoot*

Southern North Sea, Friday 22 June 2007

As soon as they boarded the Ramsgate-Oostende ferry, Rev. Wendy hurried to find a cabin. It was only a four-hour crossing and the weather was completely okay – sunny, wind southerly force 3-4, visibility good, sea-state slight. If this lasted through the weekend, as the forecast promised that it would, they were going to have such a brilliant return voyage in *Strong Winds*.

Donny was so excited he could scarcely bear to sit down. Let alone go shut himself in some drab little cubicle and lie flat on a bunk. He wondered whether Rev. Wendy had had a bad experience that had made her afraid of the sea? There was that day that she and Gerald had been on *Snow Goose* and they'd raced from Woodbridge Haven to the Orwell. *Snow Goose* had heeled over quite far. Maybe that had put her off.

He tried, unsuccessfully, to explain that the ferry would feel completely different to a classic yacht carrying full sail on a crisp spring morning. It wasn't crowded; there were loads of comfortable seats in the lounges or she could sit with Skye on the after deck, watching the wake and wave patterns and the following seabirds.

Not that relaxing in the fresh air would have been normal Wendy activity. Normally she'd have marched to a spare table and set up her laptop to write a sermon or a progress report on the Diocesan Aid for Indonesia. Then she'd have worked solidly throughout the trip, pausing only to accept the cups of tea that she would command him or Anna to bring her. Though, come to think of it, she didn't drink tea nowadays, or coffee.

Rev. Wendy and her little car were going straight back to England once she had delivered the three of them to the *Mercator* Yacht Basin. Lottie was taking Luke, Liam and Vicky camping at a folk festival for the weekend so Wendy and Gerald would be getting two days' practice at living on their own again – which was what it would be like for them in just a few weeks' time. Anna's family were planning to move to their new home as soon as school had broken up for the summer and he'd be back on *Strong Winds* with his great-aunt, his mum and … Defoe.

His uncle had said that he'd managed to complete all that was needed on his current project so, as long as they could find him space to live, he'd like to stay a while. At least until it was over, he said. Donny assumed he meant the official enquiry into the container accident. That would probably take years.

He spread out his Southern North Sea passage chart and asked Anna if she'd like him to begin entering waypoints into the portable GPS she'd bought on her most recent shopping expedition. She'd said that it was her reward to herself for getting such high marks in the scholarship exams. Donny refused to ask how brilliantly she'd done. Never mind that the portable GPS was the best toy he'd ever played with. Even if she gave it to him it wouldn't compensate for her leaving Gallister High.

By the time they reached Oostende he'd not only followed the ferry's track and compared it with the course he remembered from his first crossing, he'd also roughed out a passage plan for their return journey, assuming conditions similar to today. He'd even made a few calculations of tidal advantage. In reality, his great-aunt or his uncle would take charge of all that, but it was an absorbing occupation and it would be interesting to see how his ideas compared with theirs. Last time he'd been on this ferry he'd felt like a deportee. Today he felt convinced that the world was his at the tip of a pencil.

Gold Dragon's long plait had gone. Her hair was thin, short and completely white. She hadn't been released from hospital because she was well again. She'd been released because there was nothing more they could do.

As a voyage it was idyllic: as a family reunion it was … complicated. His uncle hadn't entirely been joking when he'd said that Donny would be acting as skipper. He'd been expected to arrive with ideas about times to leave, courses to steer and watch systems. Donny thanked his stars for the portable GPS and resolved never to criticise Anna's shopping habit again. Defoe had dealt with provisions, fresh water and diesel. He'd also checked that *Strong Winds*' engine and all her electrical systems were running properly and had fitted a simple radar transmitter.

"Yes, even as a little boy he loved engines," said his aunt affectionately. "Eirene and the others used to tease him about the amount of time he spent below, when they had those summer holidays together. And that spaniel of his, carrying the tool-bag."

"That wasn't me, Aunt Ellen, that was Uncle Ned – your brother. I'm Defoe, remember, Eirene and Henry's son. I grew up on Cocos Island in the Eastern Pacific – hundreds of miles from the whiff of an oily rag."

"I know, my dear, you did tell me. It was Eirene's dream to reach the Pacific. I'm so happy for you all. Happier than I ever thought possible. Your dear, dear father … what a navigator he must have been! But you must remember that the reason my sister called you Ned when you were born, was because she wanted something of our brother to live on. Just as Edith called this one John," she added, gesturing at Donny. "After Ransome. Him with his charts and his leadership qualities."

This wasn't the moment to burst into tears. But where was Gold Dragon in this sweet old lady? His 'leadership qualities', indeed! Had there maybe been a mix-up in the hospital?

"It's as if Ellen's mind is circumnavigating her life," said his uncle. "When the light is shining on her childhood years, then we companions of her old age fall into shadow. But then her mind returns again and here we are in our modern shapes."

"So are you an engineer?"

"No, I'm a hydrographer; I work with charts. Ocean currents and depths are my speciality. I got a basic, all-round training with the US Navy while I was going through college. I had to work my way because I hadn't any money. Although I'd grown up on *Treasure Island* (as my mother called it) it wasn't the sort of treasure that converted into dollars. Ellen says that you're a map-maker. I hope it'll give us something in common – as well as our worshipful forebears, of course."

"Well … " Donny stopped feeling misunderstood and realised that there could be a funny side to all of this, "I'm useless with engines but I suppose I could learn and then I could give you a break when you're fed up with being Ned. You could take on the leadership qualities. That was Great Uncle Greg. We've got his book if you need to do research. I don't think I can provide a spaniel with a tool-bag though."

"Would a canary do? Because my little brother Liam truly does love engines and he and Luke – that's my other brother, the wordy one – have been training their canary to pick things up with his claws and carry them when he's flying. A tool-bag would possibly be a bit heavy but somebody mentioned rags? I'm Anna by the way. We're not related but I have a vacancy for an uncle if you find you like the role?"

Defoe smiled his amazing smile.

"To have a nephew without a niece would be like ebb without flood. I have been alone for so long, dreaming of my sister. Now I have found her and a family beyond my imagination."

Gold Dragon had said something like that. Donny couldn't cope with any more of this emotional stuff.

"Your mum and dad are dead, I suppose."

"And buried in Costa Rica. Ellen is the last of her generation. So if sometimes she wants to go travelling back and I have to be Ned and you, Greg (or John), I think we should go with her."

"Fine," said Anna. "I totally agree: so let's all join in. Skye is Eirene's real daughter and she's got a crazy name and loads of creativity so she's typecast for the middle sister. Therefore, for the purposes of this trip – and this trip only – I'll be Edith. Or Mate Susan. Whichever you prefer. Lead me to the galley! My trademark is the kettle and I demand to count your stores. One thing I'm not going to do though. I'm not going to check whether you're wearing double underclothes."

She'd meant it as a *Swallows and Amazons* joke, of course but unfortunately for her she was looking at Defoe as she said it. She suddenly saw how fit and muscular he was in his t-shirt and jeans. Those wide, dark eyes, that amazing glossy ponytail … *deus* or what? Anna went completely scarlet and fled for *Strong Winds'* cabin.

"She's not like that normally," Donny reassured his uncle. "She's really clever. She'd be a better radar operator than a cook."

"It's okay. Ellen's told me about Anna. And Oboe. We've had a lot of time to talk while she's been in hospital. I began to wonder whether she was quite safe there. There were some … characters hanging about that I wasn't sure I liked. I would have spent every spare moment with her anyway. There was so much I didn't know. My mother had promised my father that she wouldn't look back when she left her family so she only told me stories. Nothing about the real people. Ellen has explained why that was. She told me what happened to them in the war. She's not always been drifting back to childhood."

"No, she certainly has not." The sweet old lady was shaking her hook at them. "And she doesn't take kindly to being the subject of scuttlebutt. If you two don't skip along to your mess deck, I'll be resuming command, with Nimblefingers as my first mate."

Defoe beamed at Skye. Donny had wondered what language they were going to use to talk to each other but it seemed that at this moment they didn't need one.

"When are we sailing?" He asked his uncle.

"We'll have to take a look at your calculations, skipper. I'd like to arrive on the other side in daylight but that shouldn't be difficult at this time of year. Depends how hard you want to push us.

I was rather hoping you might let us take our time. I've heard so much about this ship."

They left Oostende on the evening tide, past the statue of the unknown sailor, and out into the dove-grey sea. The surface of the water was in constant sluggish motion: molten pewter, with dints of pink and lilac among the silver and grey. The sun was almost gone and the series of approach buoys flashed ruby and emerald as they guided them away from the coast.

Polly Lee took the helm for the first couple of miles but then she handed over and allowed Skye to wrap a blanket round her and tuck her into the leeward corner of the cockpit. No-one wanted to go below.

Later, Donny used the GPS to show Anna exactly where they had been when the *Pride of Macao* had caught up with them.

"That was when I recognised her," said Gold Dragon, speaking out unexpectedly from her sheltered corner. "I last saw her forty years ago, in the mid-1960s. She was HMS *Beckfoot* then, a seaward defence boat, and she was being used for covert action in Indonesia. Intercepting kumpits and sampans that might – or might not – have communists on board. It was one of those little local wars that don't get much of a mention back home. The *Beckfoot* was based in Singapore and came out on night patrol. Sometimes she was out days at a time, threading her way south through the islands towards the top end of the Java Sea. She had a couple of Vickers machine-guns mounted forward and Brens on the bridge and stern. Her brief was capture and destruction. No questions asked or explanations accepted. Her crew wouldn't have understood the explanations anyway.

They weren't exactly linguists."

Strong Winds was sailing serenely through the long mid-summer evening.

"She had a mortar loaded with illuminating flares. They'd darken ship just before dusk then steam around their patrol area, keeping radar watch. As soon as anything was spotted, anything at all, it was action stations. Searchlights and shouting and shots across the bows. The people on the kumpits were taken aboard and handcuffed to the guard-rail until they could be handed to the naval police. Then the crew of the *Beckfoot* sank their boats."

Great Aunt Ellen paused for a moment. She looked old and tired and depressed. Then she sighed and carried on.

"The trouble was that not all of those people in their little boats were armed insurgents. Some were run-of-the-mill smugglers – loaded with cigarettes, clothing and electrical goods – and others … were refugees."

"You were on a Foreign Office list," Donny remembered something he'd heard through the study door at Erewhon Parva. "You were an Undesirable Alien."

"I rather thought I might have been," she said with the ghost of a smile. "I'd changed my nationality by then. Though I still felt British. Always have done. It made it so much worse. I felt I knew those men on the *Beckfoot*. They'd been trained at Shotley, probably. Good brave lads most of them. Simply following orders."

"Attitude problem?" He wanted to lighten up the conversation. Didn't think she should get agitated.

"Bang right I had an attitude problem. Some of those families, out at night, crossing between the islands, had seen their villages destroyed. They were escaping, not attacking."

They could hear her struggling to breathe. Her lips looked pinched and blue again.

"Ellen," said Defoe, "may we have the rest of the story tomorrow? The skipper's drawn up a watch system and some of us have to go below."

"Not me." They could hardly hear her speak.

"Of course not. You're Top Brass here. You do exactly as you like."

Her breathing eased. That ghost of a smile again.

"As they do. There's not much more of the story to tell. We took that ship, Madame and I …"

"Madame?"

"Li Choi San. Queen of the Pirates. These were her Three Islands. She liked to manage her own protection business and she didn't like the *Beckfoot* interfering. I didn't like it either, for different reasons."

"You took on … the Royal Navy! You fought against machine-guns!"

"Madame had cannon."

Several moments passed while they considered this. *Strong Winds* lifted and dipped, lifted and dipped, her cream sails curving to the breeze. The moon had risen. Her sails looked ethereal.

"But … would cannon have been much use? 'Cos the Hispan … I mean the *Beckfoot* is probably steel. She's a warship after all, even if she's not a very big one. She's got those engines and, presumably, you were sailing a wooden junk? Something like this?"

"Black sails. Very fast and quick to put about. A top spec pirate ship. Built in Bias Bay."

"The *Beckfoot* had radar."

"Radar can't see through islands. We were cunning and unscrupulous and operating in our own patch of sea. She never stood a chance. We set the entire crew adrift in their ship's boats and took the *Beckfoot* as our prize. Mine, to be exact."

"Yours?"

"I gave Madame my hand for her. And for her crew."

CHAPTER TWENTY-FOUR

Crossing the Bar

Somewhere at the top end of the Java Sea, mid-1960s

It was velvety dark: warm with a breath of wind and the water rippling with phosphorescence at the slightest disturbance. A single flash of silver could have betrayed the junk as she sailed neatly and noiselessly towards the stern of the gunboat. Her black hull and black sails were otherwise invisible in the moonless night.

The *Beckfoot* had intercepted a suspiciously overcrowded kumpit. They'd floodlit her and Lieutenant Drinkwater, the *Beckfoot*'s commanding officer, had ordered the suspects to abandon their vessel before she was destroyed. They'd obeyed instantly and had been taken on board, confused and panicky. They seemed quite stupid with fear and the process of handcuffing them to the guard-rail was more awkward than usual. Most available members of the ship's company were dealing with the captives, others were lining up the abandoned kumpit. They'd be using her for target practice shortly.

Then, at some unseen signal, the frightened voyagers turned on their captors. A dozen or so reinforcements came swarming over the gunboat's stern from the black-hulled racing junk that had materialised out of darkness. The eighteen men on the *Beckfoot* were taken by surprise and swiftly overpowered. Now it was they who were cuffed to the guard-rail as their captors discussed their fate.

The pirate chief was small and dark and deeply weathered. She was dressed in black silk tunic and trousers with an old-fashioned but effective-looking gun shoved casually into the broad black sash around her waist. Drinkwater and his crew knew who this must be and they didn't much fancy their chances of survival. Madame Li Choi San's reputation had spread far beyond her islands.

There was a second woman there, similarly dressed and also small, not Chinese. English? Drinkwater tried to catch her eye. Wished he could understand what they were saying. A sinister-looking man was disagreeing angrily. Madame was listening to both. The man said something that made the Englishwoman gasp.

Li Choi San turned towards her. There was a moment of stand-off, of challenge. A tense, dangerous moment – Drinkwater felt certain their lives were in the balance. The woman looked at him and his men.

"Did you any of you know Captain Palmer – of the *Sparrow*?" she asked suddenly.

"He was my first commander, ma'am," Drinkwater was able to reply. "A tragic loss."

"I might … do it," she said, and turned back to continue negotiating with Li Choi San.

Harwich Approaches, Saturday 30 June 2007
Xanthe, Maggi and Anna were never going to be caught without fully charged mobiles again. As soon as Anna's came within range of the English coast, in the early afternoon of the following day, texts began arriving from Maggi. The first was a warning:

Shark-boat circling Harwich Harbour☹ Smelling blood? xxM

"Huh? Must be there for someone else. He can't know about Gold Dragon. Not even that she's coming home. Certainly not about how she is – or what she's remembered. Don't want him stressing her out though. Ask Maggi for updates."

"There'd be real sharks in the South China Sea," said Anna as she pressed Send.

"Why?"

"I was thinking about the blood. When they cut off her hand. She must have bled like crazy. No wonder she forgot so much about it afterwards."

"It's amazing she survived. She said the ship's cook did it really quickly with a cleaver. And stitched up the stump straightaway. The other pirate, the older Zhang, hoped she'd die. He was her bitter rival."

"If she hadn't done it all those crew men would be dead."

"And there'd have been a proper war. The Navy might have covered up the loss of a single ship …"

"Especially if they didn't want to publicise exactly what she'd been up to …"

"But they'd have sent the fleet in if that Queen of the Pirates had killed eighteen British sailors!"

"Should we tell anyone what Gold Dragon did? Like a newspaper or something?"

"Probably not."

They both went quiet for a bit. Tried to enjoy the sailing. Failed.

"As soon as she was okay she took the *Beckfoot* right out of the area to Bias Bay in Guangdong province on mainland China. Used her to pay for *Strong Winds* to be built – lived on *Strong Winds* happily ever after. Forty years!"

"This shark-boat," asked Defoe a little later. "It's the Mr Big who tried to run you down when Ellen first came home?"

"Fat Flint. Bully of the Seas. Yup, that's him."

"She'd come across from Rotterdam, hadn't she?" He was frowning slightly. "Crated *Strong Winds* in Shanghai, travelled with her as Polly Lee, then had her lifted off the container ship to sail the last stretch."

"She was coming to Shotley. It was quite emotional for her."

"Which was how she took everyone by surprise. I can't help wondering what would have happened if she hadn't."

"Her different names confused them mainly. Flint didn't know that she was Polly Lee. Or that Palmer had been changed to Walker. Nor did I. Combination of Granny Edith and Gold Dragon certainly managed to brush over the family tracks."

"All the same, you're tackling some powerful illegal organisation here and I wouldn't be at all surprised if it doesn't also have a base in Holland. Rotterdam's the biggest container port in Europe and it's so close. I wish I'd thought of hiding her identity when I took her to the hospital. I think she may have been watched while she was there."

"It was amazing you turning up to rescue her at all."

"I've been looking for my sister all my life without knowing she existed. I think I earned a miracle."

Skye was steering *Strong Winds*, just as she'd done that night. She was confident and steady, her eagle eyes looking ahead for the next buoy.

"But if I'd known earlier that it was you," said Defoe sadly, "I could have followed you from the sky. *Pride of Macao* would never have dared attack and Ellen would still be well."

Another text arrived:

Back to club for lunch. No fattypuff here. Last seen lurking near Landguard. Sis sailing like a demon☺ I videoing for the greater good xxM

"Why does videoing Xanthe count towards the greater good?" Donny wondered aloud. He didn't understand why Xanthe had changed her mind so suddenly but he certainly didn't grudge her this outburst of racing – he'd silently promised *Lively Lady* that before the weekend was out he'd have her down from her davits and back into the water where she belonged. He just didn't see how winning the Laser area championships fitted into the bigger picture.

"I'll ask," said Anna, thumbs twitching.

They had passed the South Galloper and were once again approaching territorial waters and the Long Sand Head. Great Aunt Ellen had sat alone a long time in the bow of her ship then had gone peacefully below to sleep. Skye and Defoe had made lunch as if they'd been catering together since childhood and now there was nothing for anyone to do except keep the junk on course and enjoy the summer's day.

Except think. And worry.

There was no obvious way Flint could harass them. While Gold Dragon had been in hospital, Edward had returned from his fishing holiday. He and Defoe had made sure all *Strong Winds'* paperwork was up to date and her EU residency established. Even the VAT had been sorted out. All the same Donny knew they didn't want a confrontation.

Maggi texted back almost before Anna had finished.

"She's videoing Xanth because they want to ask the Port of

Felixstowe management if they'll sponsor *Spray*'s replacement. As long as Xanthe wins everything this weekend – which is pretty well a cert – they're going to make an appointment with the PR people at the docks and offer them a showing. It's their idea for getting past the gates. Then we can fill that unexplored space on our map and get another look at the container. They'll write the numbers down so I can trace where it came from and they'll use their phones to take a photo of the Mark."

"Brilliant," said Donny.

"She wants to know where we're headed and our ETA."

"Say we're not sure: you'll text her later."

Gold Dragon had appointed him skipper for this trip – where should he take them? Gallister Creek was too remote – what if his great-aunt needed a doctor? Shotley marina felt too public and he didn't know if anyone had any money. He'd been planning on a return to Pin Mill but not with Flint cruising the Orwell entrance.

"What about the River Deben?" suggested Anna. "You come in past Bawdsey – like we did last March – then you can go right up to Woodbridge. I've been there with Mum and the kids. We're going to school there in the autumn. You should check it out. If Skye and Gold Dragon like the town and you can get a mooring for *Strong Winds* maybe you could transfer as well?"

"Fees … exams … posh parents with big cars. Get real, Anna! They won't have me at your new school. You inherited three million pounds, remember? Skye's still on income support."

She put her mobile away and laughed as if this was the best thing that had happened all day.

"Sometimes you're so way off beam that you could hit an

iceberg on the equator. I'm not going to a private school. I never was. I only took their exams to prove that I could go if I wanted to. And I could. I got really good marks – even in Latin. They didn't have exams in my actual best subjects – like electronics and computer science. Luke and I are going to the local comp. I'd have told you ages ago if you'd bothered to ask. But you've been in such a sulk."

"Oh Anna!" he said and hugged her for the first time ever. "I'm such an idiot!"

"You are," she said and gave him a quick hug in return, before backing off, looking pink again and glancing quickly at Skye and Defoe.

"Saxon King Raedwald went up the River Deben," said Defoe, covering her embarrassment. "I believe we could sell the idea to our noble cargo."

"I'll check the tide times first," said Donny recovering his wits. "There's a shingle bar across the entrance. She won't want us going in on the ebb. But if it looks okay, I'll work out our new course."

He took the remains of his tea and headed for the cabin. Anna followed. His great-aunt seemed to be asleep.

"How could I have thought that all this time!" he asked her, "How could you have let me?"

"Mostly it was funny but some days I felt totally furious with you. Then I worked harder. So it was quite useful."

"Makes me shiver. Could you maybe direct that fury back towards Flint and Toxic?" He'd found a chartlet of the River Deben entrance but he wasn't looking at it. "They are so much worse than the Tiger because they've got no excuse. They're not from some poor island somewhere. They're arrogant and greedy and they're abusing a system that's meant to care for people. But I can't see how we're going to finish them off. I can't get the connections."

"No faith in your own map-making?"

"You said yourself that I could hit an iceberg on the equator!"

"This isn't navigation. It's a map to help us think. We've seen things happening. Definite things in actual places. So we put them all down and see if we can join the dots. If you spotted an iceberg on the equator, you'd put some sort of cross on your chart, wouldn't you? And then you'd probably start asking yourself how it got there. Winds and currents and stuff."

"Or whether maybe I'd miscalculated the equator?"

"But we're not doing calculations. We're only putting things that we're sure about, things that have actually happened."

"And what's about to happen if you dismiss calculation in that arty manner," said a sharp voice from the opposite bunk, "is that I'll take back my command. *Strong Winds* has got a GPS. If you've lost the use of compass and pencil you'll find the current Woodbridge Haven waypoint already entered. You can be as forensic as you like once we're back in port, but if you're planning to waft me to a grave mound up the Deben, I'd prefer that you did it without running us slap on the Cork sand."

They'd made that mistake again – they'd thought Gold Dragon was asleep or too far away mentally to understand what they were talking about.

"Um, I don't think we're quite as far as the Cork yet."

"No doubt that's what they thought on the *Titanic*."

Donny shut up and got busy with his plotter and dividers. When he'd finished and given Skye their new course, he sat down beside his great-aunt. Anna had gone back on deck.

"We've been trying to make a chart," he said. "We didn't do one on holiday so I couldn't answer your message. You asked whether we'd done war or exploration and Anna said to say 'forensics' because it felt like we'd been at a crime scene. We're marking stuff in. Things that have happened since I've been living down here."

He had the beginnings of their chart with him. He unrolled it on the saloon table.

"We saw Flint and the Tiger killing a budgie in Felixstowe dock. And we know that Bill was bribed and frightened there. Except he's still too scared to say. And we saw other birds fluttering round the *Hispaniola* (okay *Beckfoot*). And we know where Lottie lived in the town with some of the hidden workers and how she was trapped by her debts. Except she still doesn't want to say all that much because she doesn't want to get the others into trouble if Zhang's still in charge. Cage-birds is a word they use but she won't explain exactly what it means. There was that Chinese cleaner, I told you about her. She was nice. But Joshua's having a problem in the hospital because Pura-Lilly have been cleaning his ward and all his patients have been going sick. That's why he wants to leave. June wants him to stay and get evidence."

He was showing her his drawing as he spoke and she was nodding, her face tight as a skull. He wondered whether he should stop but she rapped her hook on the table to make him carry on.

"We're putting in all the places where we've seen Flint or Toxic and who we've seen them with. Like the kids who gave Skye the plastic bottles with the vodka to make her an addict. We saw them in the town with Toxic. The day Xanthe rescued that dog."

"The night I was trussed like a chicken in my own saloon. You're putting that in, I hope?"

"Would you be okay with testifying?"

"I'd be better seeing all three of them swinging from my yard-arm. But yes."

"Then you're the only adult we can rely on. Except for Mum and no-one ever listens to her."

Donny sat down on Gold Dragon's berth with a thump. Peered harder at the chart. Accepted that she was going to sit up and peer at it with him.

"Point Horror was an accident, no-one planned for that container to fall over board in that storm and then be washed up exactly there. So it's not going to tell us all that much. I mean obviously the police and the port authorities will be checking where it came from. But they don't know about the special mark. The Welcome Mark that Bill was paid to look for on the crooked containers. And they also don't know that I left the same Mark, by accident, on board the *Beckfoot*. That weekend we were attacked she went up the river as a schooner then out to sea as a gun-ship. Now she's back on her mooring as a schooner again and I want to find out why. She's my iceberg on the equator. What's she doing there?"

Her blue eyes had regained their sharp and steady focus.

"You're telling me this because …?"

"Because it helps me say it aloud. I'm still missing something, I know I am. Also I might need to go on board again. Zhang's sign says trespassers will be prosecuted but if she's sort of your ship really, and you say it's okay, then I'm not trespassing, am I?"

"And if I say no?"

"Then it'll probably be Xanthe who scrambles up the bobstay. She's desperate for action and she's not as hung up as she used to be about telling her parents things."

Gold Dragon smiled. But the smiling made her cough, and it was a while before she could catch enough breath to speak clearly again.

"I wouldn't want to prove ownership in an Admiralty Court. Speaking strictly as your great-aunt, I want you to promise that if you go on board again, you'll take an adult with you. Young Ned'll be keen enough. He seems a handy lad."

"Okay," said Donny. "I promise."

He hadn't forgotten the Tiger kicking him backwards into that cupboard, driving at him in his van and jumping him in the dark lane. Or the way he'd nearly killed Gold Dragon. He remembered his killer's knife too and the slashed flag. He was no schoolboy secret agent – he wouldn't have any problem inviting his uncle along.

From the deck above he could hear the shake of canvas and a rattle of battens. *Strong Winds* seemed to hesitate for a moment before she settled to her new course.

Donny stood up. He'd better go check all was well.

Great Aunt Ellen's breathing had speeded up while they'd been talking; she was sweating slightly and her hand trembled. He helped her back onto her cushions and asked whether he should fetch some of her medicines but she shook her head. She looked uncomfortable and all the wrong colours and he stood there wondering whether he should try to insist. He didn't suppose she'd take any notice.

They both felt *Strong Winds*' motion fell into a regular pattern again. He heard her sigh as her eyes closed. Then he went up into the cockpit to talk to Defoe.

Anna went into the cabin when they were closing the Woodbridge Haven buoy. She was going to ask Ellen whether she wanted to come on deck to pay her respects to Oboe, the man she'd loved, whose ashes she had scattered there. It looked as if she was sleeping so Anna turned and tiptoed back on deck without waking her. Said she'd looked okay, just really pale.

They had arrived at the River Deben entrance with a good couple of hours of spring flood under them. Crossed the bar without incident.

Strong Winds' speed was exhilarating as the tide caught her and whirled her through the shingle banks. A few miles further up river the wind died. The flood still carried them onwards while the sails hung flaccid and dull.

Then Skye found that Ellen too had gone. She wasn't sleeping any longer: she was dead.

At the moment of Skye's discovery the channel swung round into a wide and open reach. *Strong Winds*' sails filled and she heeled slightly offering them all just a few moments of the most perfect summer sailing. Then momentum slowed: the sails sagged: the bereaved vessel continued floating up the pretty river as if she were a log. *Strong Winds* had known Gold Dragon for so long: they had depended on each other, explored the world together. She should have stopped, quivered, spilled her last faint breath of wind in grief.

Angrily Donny pushed the tiller away from him, forcing the junk to luff. They should start the engine, drop anchor, take the sails down, row for help: do anything except continue to ghost placidly up the river with the tide

"No," said Defoe, returning *Strong Winds* to her original course. "She trusted her boat to you. You have to finish the voyage."

Tears were streaming down his uncle's cheeks and Anna's too. Donny forced himself to take the helm again and look ahead. Skye turned and went below and sat with Great Aunt Ellen as her body stiffened and her boat drifted onwards into the evening light.

Harwich Harbour, June 2007
Silence is my only refuge. I hate the poison queen but I do not fear her. When she takes my photograph I understand it is because she needs to prove I am alive.

I hate and fear the fat man because he hurts me. I understand that there are reasons why he cannot kill me – yet.

Because I do not answer them they think that I am stupid. Silence and understanding are my weapons as well as my defence.

CHAPTER TWENTY-FIVE

Dead Men Don't Move Boats

River Orwell, Sunday 1 July 2007
They didn't stay long in Woodbridge. Joshua knew two doctors who lived on the Tidemill quay so Donny and Defoe moored *Strong Winds* alongside while the death certificate was dealt with and the local undertaker contacted.

Polly Lee slept one more night aboard her ship while the kindly medics made space for her family in their flat and Anna went home with Maggi and Xanthe. Then, early on the Sunday morning, her body was taken away and Skye, Donny and Defoe cast off to return to the Orwell. It was a harsh, blustery day and they saw several of the racing dinghies in trouble. There was no sign of Flint. But, just for now, who cared about him anyway?

Erewhon Parva, Monday 9 July 2007
Great Aunt Ellen's funeral was quite different from her sister Edith's. The vicar knew the person she was talking about and the first few rows of the small crematorium chapel were comfortably filled with family and friends. Ai Qin from the Floating Lotus was there and Donny's tutor Mr McMullen. There were people from Shotley marina and the Pin Mill boatyard. Even Sandra, Donny's ex-social worker. He froze a bit when he saw her but she hurriedly explained that he'd finally been signed off the register at yet another of those meetings which no-one had told him

about. She had come because she'd wanted to say goodbye and wish him luck. Maybe this wasn't the place but otherwise she wasn't sure that she knew where he'd be?

Donny wasn't sure that he knew either: at school he supposed, until the end of term, but then?

The doctors who had helped them in Woodbridge came and sat unobtrusively at the back together with the Commodore from the Royal Orwell & Ancient and a man in a blazer and official tie who turned out to represent the Port of Felixstowe and Harwich Haven. Xanthe, whose mind kept working even when she was emotional, went and spoke to him as he was heading off to the car park afterwards and got herself an invitation to his office. He didn't look too shocked when she asked for sponsorship but gave her his card and said she should telephone when convenient and ask for Mr Hutchinson Bennett.

Rev. Wendy had dug out some good hymns and readings. There was one about a ship disappearing over the horizon with everyone waving goodbye, then arriving somewhere out of sight with a new set of people waving hello. There wasn't really a speech, but some of the adults said things, and Xanthe did a reading while Donny signed. He'd wanted to find something from Sailing, Great Uncle Greg's book, but there wasn't anything quite right. He'd seriously considered a section called 'Management of a Yacht in a Rough Sea', but in the end he chose the description of the hidden harbour from *Swallows and Amazons.*

When they were standing around afterwards, Defoe told him that that was one of the passages he'd read when his own parents had died, together with a section from *Hiawatha* about travelling to the Kingdom of the Hereafter.

"Mum would have liked that. When Granny Edith died Mum made a totem and burned it. She burned pretty well everything so old Nokomis could travel without burden to the Land of the Hereafter. I know she was right and we had to let go – but I don't want to burn everything that was Gold Dragon's."

Being at the crematorium had reminded Donny startlingly of all that had happened before he and Skye left Leeds.

His uncle nodded. "I burned my father's *Houdalinqua*. I knew I would not stay in Costa Rica and I couldn't take her with me. I wanted her to end going upwards in flames rather than subsiding into rot."

"You and my mum are so alike. But I'm not. And I don't think Gold Dragon was either. When her brothers had drowned and Eirene left and she'd quarrelled with Edith, she was miserable because she didn't have anything to help her grieve. That's how I feel. I don't want to burn *Strong Winds* and I don't even want to scatter Great Aunt Ellen's ashes out at sea like we did Oboe's. I want to keep something. More that just memories."

Defoe made that special sign of peace.

"*Strong Winds* is yours," he said. "We cannot burn her, even if we wanted to. When Edward visited Ellen in Rotterdam, he drew her up a Deed that gave the boat to you, with my sister and I as her keepers until you reach eighteen. That's why she insisted that you should be skipper when we brought her back. It's why I made you carry on."

He couldn't take it in.

"Did Gold Dragon know she was going to die? Before we even got here?"

Yet again Donny thought over his last conversation with his

great-aunt – the bit about the grave mound was definitely okay, because she'd said that, but should he have told her all that stuff about the map and Point Horror?

"She knew as much as we all do … and a bit more. She told Edward that she'd enjoyed this last gust of family life more than all her voyages but it had blown too many holes in her canvas. She said it more than once. She was very tired. You must have seen that."

Defoe looked tired too. Donny realised how sad it was for him. He'd only just met Gold Dragon: never seen her when she was properly in action.

"She was amazing, you know. Were you there when she sailed *Strong Winds* through that gorge? When it was inky black and there were whirlpools on every side "

"In our dreams I was."

Then it was back to the vicarage for sandwiches. The well-wishers stayed for a while, then said their goodbyes and left. Hawkins the canary flew free and the families sat down.

"Memories are all very well," announced Xanthe suddenly. "But revenge needs eating hot. We wouldn't have to be having a funeral today if the Tiger hadn't driven an ex-gunboat straight at Gold Dragon – and at Donny and Skye and my Beloved Mother. And *Strong Winds* wouldn't have been fleeing across the North Sea were it not for the unremitting persecution meted out by Flint and Toxic and their criminous associates."

"And Zhang would not have considered it safe to attack had not I, that very morning, confirmed to the hospital authorities that I had accepted the termination of my contract and would be withdrawing from the area, taking my family with me. Including the Beloved Mother of my troublesome daughters who had begun asking too many questions about the activities of the Pura-Lilly Cleaning Company – managed by that same Mr Zhang but owned, June is almost certain, by the fragrant Denise Tune." Joshua had stood up and moved to the centre of the room to say all this – almost as if he were making a forced confession in some dread House Meeting. "This was a cowardly action for which my family have been making me suffer ever since."

"Too right we have," muttered his oldest daughter.

"Under this domestic pressure I caved in yet again," Joshua continued. "I checked the small print of my contract and spent time talking to colleagues in other Trust Areas. I discovered that the hospital had a duty to afford me all reasonable support to carry out the advanced neuro-surgical operations for which I was engaged. So I went back to the management and told them that a clean ward was among the facilities I was entitled to expect and I was therefore withdrawing my resignation."

"Go DAD!" shrieked his daughters.

"They understood at once – they are decent people – and mounted an immediate enquiry into the allocation of cleaning contracts."

"So, have they got Zhang?" Xanthe wanted results.

"Mr Zhang is dead. After being admitted to hospital with injuries sustained in some form of … accident involving a collision flare, he caught MRSA. His ward was cleaned by his own company – and he never left it."

"And Toxic? Have they got her too?"

"Do you know who they're talking about, dear?" whispered

Gerald to Wendy. "I know about the cleaning company, but who is 'Toxic'?"

"I'm very much afraid, dear, that they may mean Denise Tune, our Welfare Supremo."

"Oh!" Gerald looked rather shocked but Rev. Wendy, Donny was surprised to see, appeared to be taking this in her stride. In fact, with her eyes narrowed and jaw set like that, she looked tougher than he'd seen her for ages.

"Not yet. But with the close attention now being paid to everything connected with Pura-Lilly, I am certain that it is only a matter of time."

"Especially if someone like me comes forward and explains how I was pressurised into working for the company when I was desperate. And how I was paid and how I was treated." Lottie spoke out eagerly. "If the Tiger Zhang is dead there'll be no retaliation on my work-mates. So I'm not frightened any more."

"No more am I," said a new voice and Bill Whiting came out from Rev. Wendy's study. "We got your news, Anna, when we was at the festival. Lottie and I came to a decision that if an old lady like Miss Walker could take 'em on – and lose her life as a result – then it didn't suit very well that I should be on the run."

The prison grey had gone from Bill's cheeks and his body looked broad and strong again. Ready to haul in a net or hold the wheel in a freezing sea. Now that he'd taken off the black woolly hat, you could see that his hair was as springy and abundant as Luke's blond mop but as carroty red as little Vicky's.

"What did you say, son, when we was talking?"

"I said let's not dodge 'em any more, Dad, let's fight 'em," repeated Luke.

"And I agreed. I'm ready to tell my tale as and when required. Meanwhile, so we has the advantage of surprise – and for no other reason – I've chose to park the van up at Swallow's End, Mrs Everson's place. I'll be handy there when called upon."

Now they might, just might, get Flint.

"I wish Edward had stayed to hear this," said Anna.

"I'll call him tomorrow," promised Lottie. "And arrange a meeting with the defence team next week."

"I've filed a request for a large amount of paperwork from Companies House," said June. "That should give us final proof of the ownership of Pura-Lilly."

"And we'll go see Mr Hutchinson Bennett and get a photo of the container with its serial number as well as the Mark," said Maggi.

"Actually," said Anna, "Liam remembered the number. He worked it into a football routine. Turns out that's what he does. He makes a pattern with his moves. So I tracked it on the Internet. That container was loaded in Rotterdam."

They didn't need him or his map, thought Donny. Everything was going really well. He'd even realised that it must have been the Tiger, or one of his associates, who had stolen Granny Edith's diary from the bungalow – way back when the campfire kettle was still the place they kept their front door key.

"This may not be the right moment to make our own small announcement." Rev. Wendy was looking pink and … fluttery. Was this the woman who was managing six parishes and had been recommended for Rural Dean? "But my husband and I," Gerald had moved closer and was holding her hand. She began to gabble. "Have decided to tell you that we're going to have a baby and because I'm so … elderly … I've had to go for all sorts of extra tests and we have discovered that the … baby I'm expecting is a little girl. If it, I mean he, had been a boy we would have called him John – because of Zacharias and Elizabeth in the Bible being so … elderly and getting such an unexpected … surprise. But she isn't. A boy I mean, not a surprise. She was certainly that!" She'd utterly lost her grip on whatever it was she was trying to say.

"So, if no-one has any objection, we're planning to call her Ellen," finished Gerald.

Donny's hands fell over one another as he signed this news to Skye.

"I saw. She has been feeling her body change for many weeks."

Although Skye had noticed, no-one else had. After the immediate silence there was a hubbub of question, exclamation and congratulation. Liam was clearly heard insisting to Luke that vicars don't have babies and Gerald wasn't God.

Fortunately Gerald missed that bit because he'd disappeared into the kitchen to fetch a bottle of pink frizzante which he had ready-chilled and which was served to all the adults, except Wendy, with much flourish and hilarity.

In the bursting pride of fatherhood he forgot that he shouldn't give any to Skye but it was okay, she gave it back.

A little Ellen, child of Wendy and Gerald. That was an idea that would take a bit of getting used to. Which of Gold Dragon's fine qualities might she inherit? How would her parents cope?

Donny grinned to himself and then he felt that lump in his throat again and the tears pricking the backs of his eyes. He urgently needed a sail.

"Vicars don't have babies!" he repeated to himself, as he and his dinghy blew gratefully away from the land out into the broad expanse of river.

"And dead men don't move boats."

He was looking towards the field where they'd camped. That was the night the fake *Hispaniola* had come stealthily up the river, preparing to reveal herself in her true colours and begin the sequence of events that would lead to Gold Dragon's death.

The Tiger had died too. He'd been taken straight to hospital in England and hadn't left it.

So it hadn't been him who'd transformed the *Pride of Macao* back into a three-masted schooner and returned her to her mooring. It had been one of the others. And then they had seen the shark-boat at Point Horror. Why hadn't they made the connection?

Lively Lady's lee chine was skidding across the river surface as if she was a one-man bobsleigh instead of a boat. Donny was on her windward gunwale, leaning out as far as his body would stretch, driving her mercilessly into the freshening breeze. He had guessed who was being kept on the schooner.

This was already the windiest summer on record and last week-end's idyllic North Sea saunter had vanished into memory like something from a different era. Big clouds were piling from the south-west, not majestic but urgent and continuous: not warning of grim weather to come but stating that it was already here.

He was sailing the dinghy to her limits, one shift of his weight, one moment's inattention and she'd be over. All those months dangling from *Strong Winds*' stern davits, unused, uncared for in Oostende – would her tackle hold? He whirled *Lively Lady* up into the wind, let fly his sheets and stopped her in the lee of the *Beckfoot* as effectively as if he'd fitted her with brakes. That same rope was dangling, apparently accidentally, from her repainted deck. Except he knew now that it wasn't accidental.

Donny apologised mentally to his great-aunt for breaking the only promise she'd ever asked him to make and to his uncle for not giving him the chance to share this adventure. He dropped *Lively Lady*'s mainsail and hauled up her centre-plate; allowed himself a few extra seconds to attach a stern line so she couldn't swing round. Then he took the painter with him and left the jib flapping. Scrambled onto the schooner's high deck as if he was completing the final stages of a timed assault course.

Donny didn't get down on his stomach and wriggle along the deck. He ran towards the wheelhouse.

It was good to see that whoever had been ordered to repaint the vessel hadn't managed to obliterate the scorch mark where Gold Dragon's first flare had struck. It had been glossed over with a couple of coats of cheap brilliant white, but the ridged marks where the paint had bubbled had not been sanded out and a sooty blackening showed obstinately through.

"Good," he muttered to himself, "that's evidence."

The wheelhouse door was as aggressively padlocked as it had previously been but Zhang's daubed warning sign had been replaced with a more official-looking notice, correctly spelled and including references to some specific section of the Private Property Code. Surely that was evidence as well?

Donny paused and scanned the surrounding harbour thoroughly for any glimpse of the shark-boat. All clear. And Flint couldn't be on board already because he couldn't have got here without transport. There was no sign of the black sharklet speedboat either.

The small, utilitarian foot-ferry that ran between Felixstowe, Harwich and Shotley was completing its last time-tabled stage of the day. Only one passenger.

Donny turned his attention back to the bar across the door. As usual all that he had with him was Xanthe's old rigging knife with its marlinspike. It wasn't going to make much impression on these heavy-duty security devices.

One important alteration had been made since from his previous visit. Then, all the windows, portholes, deck-lights had been blacked out from the inside but you couldn't go out to sea with your wheelhouse windows black. You couldn't even move a vessel up and down the River Orwell if your helmsperson hadn't at least the possibility of 360 degree vision. So now there were blackout curtains but the paint had been cleaned from the glass.

Great Aunt Ellen had given her hand for this ship and its crew.

Donny hurried for'ard to the anchor winch, grabbed its manual handle and returned. Then he smashed the starboard-side wheelhouse window as thoroughly as he could. He chose the side away from the Shotley shore. The summer sailors had headed for shelter as the weather was worsening fast: it was unlikely there'd be anyone looking this way.

The glass was so tough. Impossible to knock out every last spike. He took off his buoyancy aid and draped it over the bottom of the frame so its foam rubber protected him as he gripped the sides with his sailing gloves and climbed in. The buoyancy aid was getting a bit wrecked but Donny didn't care.

The *Beckfoot* had periscopes concealed inside her ventilation cowls. That was interesting. It meant that, even when all her windows had been obscured, someone would have been able to keep watch across the harbour, unseen.

He'd guessed that already so he didn't spend long peering through them. Not long enough.

Donny went on down the metal companionway that led into the hull of the ship. There hadn't been any re-decorating here. The old cream paint was flaky and discoloured, rust stains were showing through and there was a bad smell of stale air – and worse.

He shouted out but there was no reply.

The first door he tried led into the engine room: two big engines, obviously in good working order, large diesel tanks, wiring ducted through new-looking plastic tubes and a smell of grease and oil. Batteries, spares and maintenance equipment. All modern, practical stuff.

Then there were two aft cabins: one obviously lived in. The Tiger's liar? Scraps of girls' stuff in the other. Hurriedly he shut both doors.

The main saloon and crew's quarters had been converted to an aviary. No living birds remained but there were cages, feathers, droppings, empty plastic bags of seed and one small, bedraggled corpse. Donny shuddered. This boat was horrible.

That wasn't fair. It wasn't the boat that was foul: it was the people.

The worst of the stink was coming from the fo'csle end. The heads must be overflowing: did he really want to look?

"Hello?" he called out again.

There was no answer. The certainty that had brought him here was weakening. Best be thorough. Then he could leave.

He wouldn't mind being wrong about this.

But he wasn't.

A space and a cage. That was all there was. Not a bird cage or a chinchilla cage but a human-sized cage with a live human in it. A toilet. And a belt.

"Don't touch that!" Donny yelled and flung himself towards the coiled belt just as the boy in the cage grabbed out for it. "That's evidence!"

He knew whose big belly had strained against that piece of leather; he knew that at last he had something tangible to prove that Flint had been here, something that would be impossible for the fat policeman to explain away. He had to keep it safe, make sure that any fingerprints or DNA or whatever clever stuff prosecuting lawyers could flourish in court, was delivered to them, immaculate.

Donny thought for a moment, staring hard at the other boy.

"Please," he said. "Don't touch it."

Min tried to answer. Couldn't.

Donny didn't have time to wonder why. Wrong language, he assumed. No time to lose. He dashed back into the aviary, grabbed an empty feedbag, scooped the belt into it without touching, then shoved it safe inside his sweatshirt.

"Okay," he said to the other boy, "I know who you are. You're the survivor who everyone forgot. I'm really truly sorry. But how are we going to get you out of here?"

Min clutched at the bars with both hands pulling himself against them. His knuckles were white, every muscle taut. He crammed his head against the metal. It hurt. His mouth kept opening and closing but he couldn't make any words.

Donny gave him a thumbs-up.

"I've got an idea," he told him, "Wait here."

That was a stupid thing to say he scolded himself as he ran the length of the ship back to that well-maintained engine room. Wait here!

But his main idea wasn't stupid. There was a good set of tools in the engine room including a really powerful, battery-operated implement for taking nuts off. The cage wasn't a part of HMS *Beckfoot*; it had been added recently. A large section of its bars could therefore be removed with this juddering noisy tool.

"Don't worry," he reassured the other boy. "There's no-one to hear us."

He said that because he hadn't heard them.

Min didn't know how his tormentors arrived at his prison and now he couldn't speak to warn Donny. He'd been silent for too long. He'd seen too much. Now he was mute.

When the bars were down and the boys had made it back up to the wheelhouse, they were just in time to see the cross-harbour foot-ferry returning once again to the Shotley landing stage. This time it had a small Mirror dinghy secured alongside.

Hey! Donny started to climb back out of the window. He'd wave and shout so that the ferrymen would see him, realise their mistake and bring *Lively Lady* back.

Then he saw their passenger: a petite figure with her gold locks coiled inside a stylish Gucci cap to save them from the wind. She directed the ferrymen to secure the dinghy to the far side of the marina waiting-pontoon, paid them from her crocodile-skin handbag and stepped briskly away in her high-heeled boots, a mobile phone pressed to her ear. The Welfare Officer wasn't going to waste her time dealing with a couple of maladjusted teenagers. She'd removed their means of escape and now she was calling her colleague, Inspector Flint. She was sure he'd relish the assignment.

And if they drowned meanwhile? Research suggested that adolescent males from dysfunctional families frequently failed to develop adequate risk-assessment strategies. It would be death by misadventure.

CHAPTER TWENTY-SIX

Sanctuary

River Orwell, Monday 9 July 2007

Donny had to clear a lot more jagged glass before they could climb out of the window without cutting themselves. Toxic had taken the buoyancy aid.

He wondered, briefly, what lies she'd told the ferrymen. She was probably a regular customer now that her sidekick, Zhang, was gone. He remembered, now, that the Tiger had stolen the cross-harbour ferry on the night he'd attacked *Strong Winds*. Even before that, Donny had watched the ferry when he'd lain hidden in *Lively Lady*. It had been Zhang again, pushing something in a wheelbarrow, crossing from Felixstowe.

The schooner lay at one side of the harbour; the newly arrived containers at the other. If he'd included the ferry's track on his forensic chart he would surely have spotted the link.

He and the survivor had to get away. The *Hispaniola* had no sails; her masts and spars were bare. Neither did Donny have any idea how he would go about starting those engines. If only he'd done as he'd been told and brought Defoe.

He looked towards the shore then tapped the other boy gently on the shoulder and made swimming motions.

Min couldn't. He ran clasped his arms round the base of the mizzenmast and shook his head violently.

Donny didn't feel that keen either. He'd rather given up

jumping off ships.

The rising gale was coming straight in off the sea. Spindrift was blowing off the tops of the waves and the big clouds had been slashed into tatters. The *Beckfoot* began lurching and veering on her mooring. Then she swung ninety degrees and steadied, lying to the wind with her stern towards the Shotley shore.

It was this that gave Donny his only possible idea. They should cast her off and let her blow onto the end of the peninsula – Bloody Point, it was called. Surely he would be able to persuade his companion to splash or swim whatever reduced distance was left? There must be flotation gear on board somewhere. Then they could head for the safety of Erewhon Parva by way of the seawall.

He could see that the other boy had very little strength but anything was preferable to an encounter out here with Flint. That was surely who Toxic had been calling.

He tried to explain what they were going to do but the sight of the tossing grey- brown waters all round him appeared to instil terror in his companion and he carried on clinging to the base of the mizzenmast. Wasn't surprising really. He'd been in that container when all those people drowned.

If Donny did manage to cast off the *Beckfoot*, it would get scarier once they began to drift out of control onto the shore. Best get him back in the wheelhouse. Give him a job.

Min wasn't keen to climb back through the window but Donny persuaded him. Then he stood him at the wheel. He showed him how to turn it and hold it in position. Having the rudder hard over would possibly help anyway.

Then he climbed out yet again and went forward to battle

with the heavy mooring lines. Had to fetch a hacksaw in the end. Grateful once again for the Tiger's well-stocked engineroom.

They were free, adrift in the turbulent harbour.

The *Beckfoot*'s bows swung away from the wind and Min instinctively straightened his steering as he felt her come round. Donny stood still beside the broken window wondering what was going to happen next.

Now the wind was pressing on her aft quarter and the corner of her wheelhouse and those three tall masts. Instead of drifting sluggishly sideways onto the lee shore, she began to move diagonally forward. She must have been cleaned underneath, for speed at sea.

"Wow!" said Donny. "Unbelievable! Come on, you old beauty!"

He shinned back through the window, lifted Min's hands from the spokes and shifted him aside. If ever he needed Great Uncle Greg's spirit to take him over, it was now.

All those years of Navy service!

Donny watched the direction of every wave rolling up on the schooner's quarter. He needed to judge the precise angle of the wind on her superstructure then play gently with his steering to keep the sum of those forces pushing her forwards, not sideways. He began to feel the old ship coming alive under his hands and he knew that he was doing this by himself, with his ship. He didn't need ancestral extras.

He and HMS *Beckfoot* were edging past the shallows. They were crabbing round Bloody Point to reach the deeper water. They were going to find the last of a favouring tide and a clear course up the Orwell. They were sailing up the river together without a scrap of canvas on those three tall masts.

Donny hoped they wouldn't meet anything big coming down from Ipswich. He guessed the *Beckfoot* didn't draw much more than a couple of metres but he wanted to stay in the centre of the channel for as long as he could. It was getting dark early and there were moored yachts to avoid. He didn't have time to search for nav lights.

Min stood beside him, looking out intently. He still didn't speak but Donny sensed he wasn't panicking any more. They were together in this adventure.

They rounded Collimer Point and the wind began pressing more strongly onto the schooner's beam than her stern. Donny struggled to keep her angled so she was not pushed over to the far shore. There wasn't much further to go. He'd never get through Pin Mill anchorage without hitting someone so he had to run her aground soon. Infuriating to finish on the wrong side of the river.

Min touched his arm and pointed.

Searchlights coming towards them. Searchlights coming down river, leaping skywards then nose-down. Swinging fantastically from side to side.

It was the shark-boat. Using every hp of its expensive engines to push it up and over the waves.

Initially they were dazzled by its lights. Trapped and frightened, like rabbits. Then, as it got nearer and they could hear it roaring into the wind, they realised what a rough time Flint was having. Every time the boat reared up they could see the expanse of its white underbelly and every time it crashed down in a shower of spray they knew Flint's blubber would be plummeting.

Donny had glimpsed Swallow's End. He needed every scrap

of momentum to swing the schooner to port and run her ashore before they reached the first of the moorings. The tide was on the turn: the *Beckfoot* began to lose her steerage way. He couldn't be distracted by Flint now.

He spun the wheel. The shark-boat was metres away from them. Its lights were blinding. Surely Flint wasn't trying to board them in this?

A rendering, shattering, splintering impact. The shark-boat smashed into their starboard bow at an acute angle, howled its way half the length of the *Beckfoot*'s side.

It was exactly what was needed to push the schooner round.

Did Flint shout? If he did, they couldn't hear him. As the shark-boat sheered away Donny and his companion had a perfect view of the fat policeman hanging sideways out of his padded driver's seat. He looked semi-conscious.

There was a jagged tear in the power-boat's side. They saw it begin to list as the first of waves came flooding in.

Donny had to watch ahead now. That crucial last push towards the shore. Had it been enough to get them into shallow water? The wave shapes changed as the ebb began to run. Wind against tide: the *Beckfoot* was caught between two conflicting forces.

She stopped. In a moment she would begin drifting backwards.

If he was in *Strong Winds* …

He had to treat the *Beckfoot* as a boat.

"Come on!" he yelled.

He was out of the window and running forward. Min was close behind him. He'd armed himself with a hefty spanner. Donny grabbed the winch handle as they went. Within seconds they were knocking out chocks from the heavy chain and listening to the blessed sound as the ship's anchor fell with a muffled splash and the chain rattled out through the hawser to hold her fast on the windward shore.

"Woo-hoo!" shouted Donny and Min's face lit up. They did high-fives. Then they both ran aft.

The shark-boat was barely visible. Lying on its side, wallowing to every buffeting wave like a punch-drunk boxer. Or a semi-submerged container. It was probably amazing that it hadn't sunk yet. Must have some seriously good in-built buoyancy.

The wreck would soon begin to drift. Donny thought he could make out the large heap of Flint sprawled on top of the hull. There couldn't be much to grip on to. He surely wouldn't last the down-river journey. If he did, and if the hulk didn't run aground or snag something, he would be carried out to sea.

They should probably try to help. Where on a ship like this would you keep warps? There'd be a locker on deck, wouldn't there? Unobtrusive, handy?

Donny couldn't work up much enthusiasm. Min did nothing at all.

If he found a rope, how would he get it out there? Gold Dragon would have flung a heaving line.

Or would she have left Flint to down?

Laws of the Sea. He could maybe float a warp. Needed to find a life-belt or a fender or something. Donny forced himself to try to act. It felt like he was wading through liquid mud.

Then Bill arrived. He had been watching from the camper van parked near Mrs Everson's cottage and now here he was with *Vexilla* nicely balanced and her outboard ticking over. He'd guessed it would be Donny and had come to help. Bill was about the last person who'd feel any duty of care towards Flint.

The wreck had begun to drift. Donny showed Bill the warp and the life belts he'd discovered.

"Mmmm," said the former fisherman. "I smell a salvage deal. Might need witnessing."

A white shape battling though the gloom. Mrs Everson's sturdy daughter rowing the *Margery*. Ben Gunn, the black terrier, was in there with her, his front paws braced against the motion.

"If it's salvage," she shouted, "you have to make him agree to leave his vessel. Then you get a percentage of her value."

"That'll be worth a tidy sum," said Bill. "Reckon I don't mind putting meself out for that. I'll be paying me own lawyers soon. Suing for compensation."

He looked determined and sort of grimly cheerful. There was no-one else in sight on the wild river. Flint had no other options. Except to drift away into the gloom, soaked and frozen, struggling to cling to the plastic hull of his sinking ship.

"We may as well wait here," said Donny. "I've got one end of a line made fast but I'll only winch in if you give the word. And if Flint says please."

Min was beyond exhaustion by the time they got him to the vicarage. Their journey to the shore in the rowing dinghy was rough but it was the sight of Flint in *Vexilla* that had sent him back into trauma. Donny wished now that they'd pushed the bully under the waves and held him there.

Mrs Everson's daughter drove the two boys in her farm truck while Bill returned to the boats and Flint sat in the Swallow's End scullery, wrapped in horse blankets and guarded by Ben Gunn. The shark-boat's pounding had left the police-man dizzy and with blurred vision – as well as soaking wet and stinking of vomit. He had accepted Bill's help abjectly and had agreed without a quibble that the rescue was salvage. He was probably concussed.

Donny couldn't be sure that their troubles were over for the night. There was still Toxic and the SS and possible deportation orders. They'd have someone on duty 24/7.

Anna's first phone call was to Ai Qin who'd returned to the Floating Lotus after the funeral. The Chinese boy needed to try to speak to someone in his own language even though they weren't sure exactly which this would be. Ai Qin said that she would leave the restaurant at once and would hurry back to Erewhon Parva. It would be an hour before she could arrive from Lowestoft.

Anna wanted to ring Edward next.

"If anyone needs Witness Protection it must be this boy," she said. "He knows first hand how the smuggling system works. He's been in it. We can't let anyone scare him any more."

"This boy," said Rev. Wendy, "needs Sanctuary. For tonight I intend to fortify the house. Tomorrow, if we must, we will camp out in one of the churches. I defy Denise Tune, Inspector Flint – or the bishop himself – to take him from us there."

Having a baby Ellen in her womb had certainly gingered up Rev. Wendy. The Ribieros had gone home but Skye and Defoe were still there with Lottie and her family. Wendy marched around the vicarage directing Defoe and the boys to barricade all doors and ground-floor windows.

"And if you should have a basin or bucket of some

soapy solution balanced near the upper windows and they should happen to tumble when the forces of evil are seeking entrance, I would consider it only as a regrettable accident. Even if dear Vicky's soiled nappies had been soaking inside the bucket … well, such misadventures happen."

Did they indeed? What planet was that on? Donny, Luke and Liam looked at one another in amazement but didn't presume to query Wendy's militant instructions. Gerald had retreated to the kitchen where he could be heard ransacking his store cupboards for anything that might make a nutritious meal for a fugitive – rather as he had done on Hawkins's first evening, Donny recalled.

Anna was setting up her web cam to cover the front door but Lottie had shut herself in the study to make more phone calls. She asked Donny if he had Mr McMullen's number. He suggested that she look it up via the sub-aqua club.

Min huddled against one end of the sofa with a duvet tucked around him. He was shaky, confused and speechless. Donny wondered how long he'd been in that cage. On the news bulletins that they'd watched after the accident it had said that the single survivor had been taken to a secure location where he would be interviewed by police. Donny could imagine only too well what that could have meant.

Skye had seated herself at the other end of the sofa. She had Vicky on her lap and was playing finger games. Min watched without moving.

A knock at the front door. A crackle of cap-gun fire from an upper window. Luke and Liam had disinterred their secret cowboy kits. Would the contents of a nappy bucket follow?

Sandra the social worker, who had been with them at Great Aunt Ellen's funeral earlier, held up a piece of white paper with a red cross on it.

"Humanitarian aid," she called. "I'm one of tonight's duty workers and was ordered here by my line manager."

"Creepy Tony?"

"Well … er … yes … But I swear I come in friendship. You have a youngster with you who may be in deep shock. I have bought a full crisis emergency pack and my own sleeping bag. I have had enough of inter-agency initiatives. I have been a social worker for twenty years. I have training and expertise. I am not going to be pushed around any longer by any other service provider. I am here to protect the child. I will not allow anyone else to interfere."

"Has Tony agreed?"

"Er … yes."

"Sandra," Donny called down to her. "Come clean. Did you threaten him?"

"We had a full and frank exchange of views. In the course of our discussion I mentioned certain actions that I would feel obliged to take if … IF DENISE TUNE OR INSPECTOR FLINT WERE ALLOWED TO HAVE ANYTHING TO DO WITH ANY OF MY CASES EVER AGAIN!"

Rev. Wendy flung the front door open. "Come in and join the turning worms."

"I also informed him that there were to be no further intrusions tonight under any pretext whatsoever."

Whatever she had said to Creepy Tony worked. No-one came. Luke and Liam were most disappointed.

Anna was a bit miffed too. As she explained to Donny later, she'd been hoping to get some really good footage of the bad'uns being pelted by the kids.

"Then I was going to post them on Skoo-tube."

"What's that?"

"Local website for kids. So that all the children who Flint and Toxic have ever intimidated could get a good laugh. Every time Toxic's been round lately I've been setting up the camera in case Luke could get Hawkins to try picking up her hair. I'm sure that it's a wig."

"Has she been round?" This was news to Donny.

"Certainly has. I couldn't guess why but she's been all chummy with Rev. Wendy. She makes out it's to do with the Diocesan Mission Lift – which is totally none of her business – then she keeps asking Wendy if she's Coping and offering her Individual Counselling and the Right of Choice. It's been driving Wendy completely bonkers. Until today I didn't get what it was all about. I've been unbelievably slow."

"It does take a bit of getting used to."

"Wendy and Gerald as a mum and dad. I pity their kid."

"Oh, I dunno. If it's going to be a baby Gold Dragon we might find ourselves pitying them!"

Anna laughed. "We'd best keep in contact, then. And I never thought I'd hear myself say that."

"Could you take a photo of this?" Donny asked, pulling out the bag with Flint's belt in it. "Then I'll give it to Sandra to keep safe. I found it next to the cage."

Anna looked sick. "Cage? That's foul."

"I'll tell you later."

Ai Qin arrived just as Lottie had finally finished her phone calls.

"Is he the boy from Fujian province?"

"I think so. I remembered his mother from my time with Pura-Lilly. Donny's teacher is out seeking her now. He's gone to Ipswich, to the containers where we lived."

"How does he know who she is?"

"Because he likes to keep his department open late into the evening. Most people don't talk to us agency cleaners but he did. We were instructed that we shouldn't reply but he was persistent. Also Karen was involved when Donny was attacked in the DT room."

"Karen?"

"Sorry. That's what we called her. I can't remember her Chinese name. She was the one who released Donny from the cupboard. The Tiger was angry because she let him out too soon. He sent her to the cage-birds for a week. Only brought her back because she owed him so much money. He needed to keep her earning. She told me that she had done it because she had a boy herself in Fujian. She thought they would be about the same age. So I took a guess this evening when I saw him."

"I hope you're right. The woman I am looking for is called Chen Xiao Ling."

"I think I am. Family resemblance is a wonderful thing."

I suppose it is, thought Donny, happening to look at his uncle and his mum as they sat together, playing with Vicky and talking to each other through hands and pictures. And somewhere in the world is a man who looks like me – no, a man who I look like. But he won't ever know.

It was always going to feel sad but he could live with it. The anger and the fear had gone. He was his own person. He'd brought the *Beckfoot* up the river and Great Aunt Ellen had trusted him to be the next owner of *Strong Winds*. He hadn't even told Anna yet.

CHAPTER TWENTY-SEVEN

Return of the Campfire Kettle

Erewhon Parva Vicarage, Tuesday 10 July 2007

Min put his head in his mother's lap and fell asleep on the sofa. He was still mute. The old house settled peacefully around them. The younger children had been persuaded into bed even before Mr McMullen and Karen arrived and it wasn't long before Rev. Wendy followed them upstairs.

Ai Qin and Mr McMullen left as soon as they knew that their identifications had been correct. It was past midnight when Defoe and Skye set out through the darkness, walking to the river and *Strong Winds*.

"Do you mind if I stay here for the night?" Donny asked them, "I want to be near Min and his mother. We're going to have to talk to the police about the *Beckfoot* and I need to ask Sandra for advice."

"Mrs Everson's daughter has already reported the wrecked power-boat. The insurance company will either move it in the morning or buoy it. You winched it well out of the channel and Bill's fitted an anchor light on the *Beckfoot*. And in case you're anxious, Mrs Everson herself says that she can confirm all the movements of the *Hispaniola | Pride of Macao*. She noticed every time the identity was changed. Mrs Everson's a light sleeper and she likes to watch the river from her bedroom window. She'll make a statement as soon as anyone asks."

"It's not that. I mean, thanks – that's great news. But it's the *Beckfoot* herself; she's a crime scene. I shouldn't have let Bill go on board. He'll have left prints everywhere."

One of the best things about his uncle was the way he took things without fuss.

"Then we must call Edward and take his advice. First thing tomorrow. And June Ribiero too. You've done so well, Donny. Stay by all means but please, get some sleep."

"Only good dreams," signed Skye.

Gerald had made a bed in the study for Sandra. Anna and Lottie were in there with their coffee mugs. Anna had her MacBook open.

"There's some fruit cake left over from the funeral," Gerald said wearily. "And plenty of milk. If you want anything else you'll have to fetch it yourselves. I'm going to bed."

"Gold Dragon's funeral! Was that today?"

"Technically," said Anna, "it was yesterday. You need to tell us what you saw. Why you pushed that belt at Sandra. Then we can maybe all go to bed. Some of us have school tomorrow."

"Not me," said Donny. "Whether or not I'm allowed. "That belt belongs to Flint. I've seen him wearing it. I gave it to Sandra because it needs to be tested. She's the only official I trust and it's got to be done totally properly. That belt was beside Min's cage. It proves that Flint was there. There's other stuff on board but they might all be Zhang's. Except for the women's things."

"Clothes belonging to Toxic?"

"Don't think so. I mean I know she's been on board but she wouldn't leave stuff like that. Cheap stuff."

"I think," said Lottie, "that the ship was where the Tiger kept his cage-birds."

"Oh yeah. There was definitely bird seed."

"His cage-birds didn't all have wings."

"Oh."

"I never went. It was the worst punishment."

" … Karen?"

"May be able to say more. When she is convinced that she and her child are safe."

"I'm sorry," said Sandra heavily. "I promised no more interference. I told you I've been a social worker for twenty years. I think this might be the worst case I've come across. It's almost one in the morning. I'm going to have to call the head of children's services."

"Do you need to get her phone number?" Anna pushed the computer across. "I'm already on the council website but you'll want to access the private area."

"Oh, okay," said Sandra. She sounded surprised. Maybe because they hadn't argued with her. "I mean, I've got it on my mobile somewhere."

She was typing her password into the computer.

"This'll be much quicker," said Anna. "Mobile phone reception's not very good here. Rev. Wendy won't mind you using the landline."

She smiled helpfully and took the laptop back as soon as Sandra had the details she needed.

"Would you like us to leave the room?"

Huh?

"No, of course not." Sandra seemed preoccupied. "I'm not

going to say anything that I wouldn't want you to hear. I'm only passing on what Donny's told us. Plus what Lottie said. I have no choice. I'm ringing our service head because it's so serious – and I simply don't want to report via Tony."

"Quite right." Anna's fingers were flying over the keys. Donny'd never seen her when she wasn't searching for something: checking, scrolling down, making notes, refining her search terms. Why couldn't she play Runescape or Second Life like everybody else?

He was exhausted. Hoped Sandra wouldn't talk for long. He knew it had to be official now.

Had known it ever since he'd seen how Min was being kept. Sandra seemed to be taking her time, repeating herself. The person the other end must have been asleep. Maybe he could rest his head on his arms for a moment.

"Donny," hissed Anna.

She was shaking him. Why?

"Do you want to come with us? You don't have to."

His head was pounding. He wasn't on board *Strong Winds*.

"Mum said I had to ask you. We're going after Toxic but we're completely cool if you'd rather stay here. You could go to bed even."

"Where?"

"Wherever. I don't care. You've got your old room upstairs or you can carry on kipping in that chair. Like you have been for the past two hours."

"Don't get stressy, I meant where's Toxic? You said you're going after her?"

"If you don't keep your voice down you'll wake Sandra too. If you're coming, come. I'll tell you in the car. Mum's there already."

"Okay. Long as I can have a pee first."

"Boys!"

Lottie's Toyota slid stealthily out of the drive. First streaks of morning already in the sky. Donny stuck his head out of the window for a few moments to wake himself up. Then he turned to Anna.

"Okay," he said, "where and why?"

"I got Toxic's address off the private area of the county council website. The one Sandra logged into. Then, while Sandra was talking, I got loads of other social worker links. And education. Norfolk and Essex as well as Suffolk. The top lady's coming to see you in the morning, by the way. She's called Kathryn. Then, when Sandra had dozed off, I did a proper search on Toxic."

"And?"

"It's all phoney. Nothing goes back more than two or three years. Her CV is just a paper trail and her qualifications … well, they look impressive but when you check the dates and places, they're completely fake."

"This is in your professional opinion?"

"Research suggests …"

"That Denise Tune's a fraud and a clever one," said Lottie. The morning light was getting stronger, the roads were empty. She was driving fast.

"I had time for a quick snoop into Pura-Lilly as well. Its registered office is in the Bahamas. That's where her money will be waiting for her."

"Or in Singapore," said Lottie. "Where most of the foreign workers had to send their giros. Then wondered why their families said the money never reached them"

"And no extradition treaties from either place."

"She could have a twelve-hour start on us," said Donny. "If she didn't wait for Flint. If she realised as soon as she saw that I'd gone on board the *Beckfoot* that I was sure to discover Min. She hijacked *Lively Lady* to slow me up but she wouldn't have been able to fool the ferrymen for much longer. Not when people really started asking questions."

Toxic's house was a sugar-pink ranch-style bungalow behind high gates. They were electronically locked of course and there was no response to the entry phone or any of the numbers Anna had copied from the private area of the SS site.

"We could try climbing in but she'll have left everything alarmed and it'll be another way of holding us up," said Anna. "Mum, how do you feel about a drive to Stansted Airport? It might be a waste of time but I can be calling other people as we go. I could start with June, for instance. She's almost there with her investigation."

"Tell me why we're going to Stansted once you've made your calls," said Lottie. She'd swung the car round and was re-programming her sat nav. "As long as we get Donny back in time to talk to Kathryn. I'm fairly sure she wouldn't be able to fly direct to the Bahamas or to Singapore from Stansted, if that's what you're thinking. She'd need Heathrow or Gatwick and if we're trying to catch her boarding a plane somewhere it'd be more effective to ask the police."

"It's not exactly that. But yes, if you're okay to drive I'll ring June and see if I can get her on the case. Get flight departures watched. I wish you'd said a bit more earlier," she grumbled at Donny.

"Sorry." He'd been so obsessed with getting Flint. He hadn't given a thought to Toxic from the moment he saw her mincing away towards the ferry steps, talking into her BlackBerry.

"You might decide to turn around and go straight back," said Anna to her mother a half an hour later when she'd finished a string of calls and they were heading south-west along the almost-deserted A12. "But I'll tell you now. That last call was to Wendy. She confirmed that the Diocesan Mission Lift is due to leave Stansted Airport on a chartered cargo plane sometime later this morning."

"Going to?"

"Victims of the Indonesian floods. Via a depot in Singapore."

"Your point being …?" Donny didn't entirely get it.

"That the only things about Toxic which are real are her clothes and shoes. None of them are fake, you know – all those Jimmy Choos and Gucci bags. The Hermès scarves and Christian Louboutin boots. I've seen the way she looks at herself wearing them. And never the same outfit twice. She must have rooms-full of them. They'd need a lot of transport."

"So? Why would she bother taking them with her? I mean she can always buy more. I thought that was part of the point – shopping, I mean. It's what girls do."

Anna would probably have killed him then, if Lottie hadn't responded.

"I heard Wendy ask if she'd anything she'd like to donate to the appeal. If it had been something good the Mothers' Union were going to raffle it to raise funds. 'Ai don't think so,' she said. 'It would hev to be something Ai'd worn. Ai wouldn't want other people touching it.'"

"Don't break the speed limit Mum. We'd look so stupid if we got stopped now."

"I hate Denise Tune. I really really HATE her."

Lottie was a fierce hater but she was also charming and persuasive. She got them to the freight sheds at Stansted in record time and demanded to see someone from Customs and Excise. She explained that she was a charity worker from the Suffolk Diocesan Mission and represented the Rural Dean. They were very much afraid, said Lottie, that their shipment to the flood victims was being misused to transport stolen goods. Had there been any last-minute additions to the consignment or any request for label changes?

"Nothing like that at all. No irregularities. Sorry, Miss, but we're very careful about these things. Plenty of people might think an aid convoy is a soft touch but they'd be making a mistake. We check every package individually against its manifest – using sniffer dogs and the full range of technology – and then we seal them. Once they're sealed they're treated as bonded stores and locked into our forwarding depot until they're loaded."

"And how long have … our Mission gifts been sealed?"

He checked his papers. "Three weeks."

"She could have planned it," Donny encouraged Lottie. "After Zhang died."

"An exit strategy."

"But it's her we want. Not her shoes."

The Customs Officer began to look impatient.

"The Suffolk Mission Lift is already being loaded. The plane's due for take-off within the hour. Direct to Singapore. And, if you'll excuse me saying so, I'd expect queries about stolen property to come through more conventional channels."

Lottie looked dejected. Anna took her hand and stroked it. They looked more like sisters than mother and daughter with their fragile prettiness and devious ways.

"Mum got into trouble with the Committee. She'd been out collecting for those poor people – you must have seen them on TV – and she went to a local couture shop, to see if they'd like to donate and they weren't sympathetic at all. Then there was a break-in at the shop – except nobody thought it was really. The business wasn't doing well so people assumed the owners were collecting on the insurance. And then we got all these boxes which were full of goods that looked awfully like stock from the shop. All beautifully packed, which were going to an address in Singapore, and the shop owners said if their boxes could travel with our consignment they'd donate towards the freight cost. And the Committee agreed because they hadn't really collected as much as they'd hoped so there was some space in the container and a gift of money seemed heaven sent. But Mum thought it was wrong."

"I thought it was stolen goods and they might be going to those factories to be copied. You know, like they do out there and then they send them back here without any proper standards."

Lottie sniffed and wiped her eyes. Anna passed her a Kleenex.

"Mum had a bad experience," she explained to the Customs officer.

"Sorry to hear it. Er, what exactly were these items? Can you describe any of them"

"They were clothes and shoes."

"The whole consignment's clothes and shoes!" He sounded completely exasperated. As if he'd been on duty all night and simply wanted them to go away so he could get home for his breakfast.

"Oh, but those crates had a special mark," said Donny. He might as well add his scrap to Anna's crazy story. "I could show you if you've got a bit of paper."

"And I could write down our mobile number for you."

The Customs officer took Donny's sketch and Anna's number then sent them away. They got back into the car and began the journey home, deflated by their failure.

"I suppose I hoped she'd be hanging around there somewhere but it was never going to be that simple," said Anna. "What's the point of managing a snakehead if you can't get yourself out of the country when you need to?"

"Rotterdam," said Donny.

"Huh?"

"That's where Defoe thinks they've got their nearest link. That's where you said the container came from. She could get there easily."

Anna had mobile Internet. She began searching.

"Not from Stansted she couldn't, not directly anyway. But there's an overnight ferry from Harwich. Leaves soon after eleven pm and connects with a train to arrive at Rotterdam Central for breakfast. She'll want comfort – you won't find her squashed up in the dark in a container lorry. Or even on a cargo plane."

"We don't have any proof that she's gone anywhere at all," said Lottie. "Why don't you two put your busy brains to sleep and let me concentrate on driving?"

They'd hardly got back onto the A12 when the mobile phone went off. It was their new friend from Customs.

"Fifty-eight crates!" He was shouting so loudly that Anna had to hold the phone away from her ear. "Amazing collection. They must have raided a dozen shops. We're going to need some guidance from Suffolk police on this. But your mother can tell her Mission Committee that they almost looked very silly. Very silly indeed. Accepting designer goods onto an aid consignment. We've sent the rest of it on. Plane's half empty now!"

It was hard to know what to think.

"One belt from Flint and fifty-eight crates of gear from Toxic. But what does it prove?"

"My brain hurts."

"It proves she meant to leave."

"I bet they don't catch her. She's got such a nerve."

"I'm going to ring June again. She knows how to talk to people. She'd already got onto the fraud office. I'm going to tell her what you said about the snakehead having a base in Rotterdam and I'm going to ask her to ask the police to meet that Harwich ferry."

Sandra's boss, Kathryn, was an American in a tweed business suit. She was married to an English academic and lived in

Cambridge. She hadn't been Head of Children's Services for long.

"Thank you for allowing me to make this a breakfast meeting," she said, once she'd introduced herself to everyone. "I'd sure love some coffee if it isn't too much trouble. I called at the patisserie before I left town."

Gerald had cleared the large table in the middle of the sitting room and arranged ten chairs around it. He'd set out a water jug and glasses but was soon bustling around fetching a cafetière and mugs and a pot of tea for those who'd rather. Perhaps Wendy could risk something decaffeinated now she was past her first three months? He patted her shoulder as he passed.

Kathryn reached into her carrier bag and produced an enormous yellow and white striped cardboard box tied with curled ribbons. It was loaded with freshly baked croissants, muffins and Danish pastries.

"I wasn't certain that I fully understood what my colleague told me over the telephone so I thought I'd come and listen for myself. I want all of us to be as informal and as comfortable as we can but I do have to tell you that if I hear anything that makes me think there is a child or some other person at risk then I will have to take official action. I will try to be as open as I can about the actions I decide to take. If I believe that you should be making an official accusation against a named person I will advise you of the route you need to take and, similarly, if you find that you wish to make a complaint against my organisation I will explain the procedures. If you are not happy with the way I am approaching this you have the right to complain to an independent adjudicator. How are we doing so far?"

No-one answered. Skye was there and Donny was signing. Min and Karen were sitting close to one another looking anxious. Anna had been given permission not to go to school. June had already arrived and Edward was expected later. He'd made a detour via Swallow's End to have a chat with Bill.

"Okay, then," said Kathryn. "I suggest we all pitch in. We'll start by going round the table and each person can introduce themselves and say which of the pastries they choose. I'm Kathryn, as you know, and I'm a blueberry muffin."

It was a good technique for relaxing people. Only Min did not seem to respond. His mother said that she would choose for him. They would both have cinnamon swirls and she would interpret.

"Now, Donny – none of us are going to mind you pausing every once in a while to take a bite of that handsome double choc chip – what I want you to do is take me carefully through what happened yesterday from the moment that you left your great-aunt's funeral. I'm going to try hard to keep my questions to the end so that I don't interrupt your story. Can you sign as well as talk and eat? I think your mother needs to hear what you are saying. And if Mrs Chen asks you to stop at any point I expect that you will do so."

Kathryn sipped her coffee while Donny talked but she didn't actually touch the muffin. When she saw that he had finished she thanked him.

"There is a question that I have to ask. When Sandra rang me last night she said that you had given her a belt. Can you tell me why you did that?"

"Because I thought I recognised it and I wanted it to be kept safe until it could be tested to see if I was right."

"You thought it belonged to Inspector Flint, a named person. What did you think Inspector Flint's belt might have been doing on board that boat?"

"I didn't know … I didn't really have time to think. Mainly it just proved he'd been there,"

"Not necessarily …"

Kathryn was approachable, she was fair-minded, she was determined – but like anybody else she didn't want to believe a complaint against a fellow professional unless she had to.

"Inspector Flint is the fat policeman? He liked to hit me with his belt. He left it there so that I would always know that he would be back again. I think he also hoped that I might use the belt to hang myself one day."

Min's spoken English was quiet and exact and clear. His mother looked more shocked than anyone. Min did not look at anyone except directly at Kathryn.

"Inspector Flint is a bully. He is also stupid. He and the poison-queen did not think that I could understand what they said. If they had treated me kindly for even a few moments when they took me away from the place of death, I would have told them all that had happened on the journey. Once I understood what they were like I said nothing in any language. Even the language of pain."

"You speak so beautifully," said his mother.

"I have studied hard ever since I went to school. I wished to deserve all that you have done for me. It is seven years since you left."

"Chen Min," said Kathryn. She wasn't bothering about coffee and cakes anymore. It was obvious that she was completely convinced. "I am so deeply sorry for all that you have been through. I am going to have to ask you to testify against the people who have made you suffer. I cannot pretend that this will be easy or a pleasant. It will also take a long time. I hope that you will be willing to do this and I will promise you and your mother all the support that it is in my power to give. There will be full-time education and somewhere safe for you both to live. It may take years. After that I cannot even promise you the right to remain in this country. I am sorry. All I can say is that I will help you in every way that I can."

"I don't want to stay here for ever. I want to go back to Xiamen and live on the right side of the river. I want to pass my exams and go to university. But my mother has debts that she must repay and we will need to earn the money for our journey."

"We can help," said Anna.

"There's a fund," said Lottie.

"No," said June, angrily. "He has been criminally injured. There must be official recompense."

But everyone knew it was too soon to think of that and anyway it would probably never happen.

Kathryn had one more important question. "I would like you, if you can, to name the other person who made you suffer. The one you call the poison-queen."

"The policeman called her Denise. I noticed however that he was afraid of her. When I was in Rotterdam I heard talk of a *gweilao* woman who commanded Tiger Zhang. I think that it was she."

And at that moment June's phone began to ring. The connecting train from the Harwich overnight ferry had arrived. The Dutch police were waiting and they'd got her. A moment later a text came through for Kathryn. The Head of Children's Services was needed urgently back in her office at County HQ.

No-one said anything immediately. There was a feeling of waking from a nightmare, of a dark cloud lifting away. The enormous yellow and white striped cardboard box stayed open in the middle of the table, its curled bright ribbons trailing across the clean formica. Fluted paper cases, scattered crumbs and empty mugs gave the impression that there might have been a party but the box remained three-quarters full. There would be plenty left for everyone else.

Min was the first to break the silence. "I was advised to find Jin Lóng when I arrived in Suffolk. Her name in English is Gold Dragon. Hoi Fung the sea cook sent me."

"I'm sorry, Min, Gold Dragon's dead. Her funeral was yesterday."

"I hope that her spirit walks in peace. I think Hoi Fung may be dead also."

"Donny," said his uncle, later, when they were sitting, just the three of them, in *Strong Winds*' cabin, "My sister and I have been dreaming. When everything else that must happen has happened – however long that takes – shall we sail northwards? Shall we explore the Baltic Sea?"

The junk was pulling against her mooring as the ebb tide hurried past. Donny could sense the restless breeze tugging at her three furled sails. Gold Dragon's spirit would never walk in peace for long. They'd carried her body ghosting up the River Deben on that last, long, tranquil evening but her spirit would be strongest when they were out of sight of land: when they were lifting and falling to the rhythm of the waves and the wind had run free for miles before it buffeted past them and on.

Wherever they went Granny Edith would be coming too. He'd walked to the van at Swallow's End that afternoon and collected all the letters she'd written and the files she'd organised. He'd also brought home her campfire kettle.

They could go anywhere now.

From the Chart Table

Much of my thinking about the *Strong Winds* Trilogy has happened on board our boat, *Peter Duck*. *Peter Duck's* logbook from the summer of 2007 reminds me that was the summer that we failed to go to sea. Certainly we intended to. I'd done a string of RYA refresher courses, mainly with the legendary George Jepps (a character waiting to happen). We'd planned our passage, checked the Ship's Papers and freighted up the GPS with every conceivably useful waypoint. We'd even installed a small radar transmitter and learned to love it.

The holiday week arrived and we began with a trip up the Orwell to Ipswich to buy copies of the final instalment of *Harry Potter*. The wind was force 6, a yachtsman's gale, and as we went scorching through Pin Mill anchorage we noticed that *Nancy Blackett* (Arthur Ransome's *Goblin*) had decided against joining the Old Gaffers' Association passage race across the North Sea. Later I was sad to learn that Jon Wainwright, author of *Only So Many Tides*, had died of a heart attack while taking part. He was so kind as well as enthusiastic and had done his best to encourage us to participate. There'd been another sad loss earlier that year when flags in the Woodbridge boatyards were flown at half-mast to mark the death of Christine Knights. I'd known Christine all my life and will always be grateful to her for telephoning us when *Peter Duck* returned to the River Deben from Russia.

But there was no sadness on board when we left the Orwell the following morning with Oostende, Zeebrugge or Calais in our sights. The forecast was ominous but the day started bright and fresh, the colour of the water between the deeps was especially beautiful and we watched gannets fishing with the sun on their wings. By teatime the weather had worsened so dramatically that we abandoned all our foreign plans and fled back to Ramsgate with the propeller rolling out of the water.

And that was it. Late the following day we took advantage of a quieter evening, ignored the strong winds warning and sailed for Dover where we spent the rest of our holiday week trapped by gales and eating Chinese takeaways. We weren't alone. "Even the Dutch won't go in this," said the marina manager comfortingly as we traipsed up to his office for yet another version of the same impossible weather report. The sail home to the Deben on our final day was one of the loveliest I can remember, marred only by distant glimpses of the unreachable white cliffs of France.

I wrote the first version of *Ghosting Home* over that summer and autumn then put it away for some years. The logbook reminds me of other events that may have fed into its story – my brother Ned presenting *Peter Duck* with a new kettle, some happy days at Stone Point, the birth of my first grandchild – but it is all fiction.

Richard Woodman, author (among many other volumes) of the Nathaniel Drinkwater adventure series, was the person who told me that the red-and-white schooner moored off Shotley had been built in the 1950s as a naval patrol boat. Her name was HMS *Beckford*. She never served in the South China Sea, however. That was her sister ship, HMS *Ickford*, who operated out of Singapore during the Confrontation with Indonesia in the mid 1960s. Anyone who is any good at geography will have noticed that my fictional HMS *Beckfoot* is patrolling far too far south to be playing any effective part in the defence of Malaysia at that time. That's because she has strayed into Ransome-land.

My friend Andrew Craig-Bennett helpfully made the link between Ransome's fictional *Missee Lee* and the real 1920s pirate Lai Choi San who terrorised shipping around Macao. In *I sailed with Chinese Pirates*, the American adventurer Alecko E Lilius described Lai Choi San as the Queen of the Macao pirates. "So many stories centre about her that it is almost impossible to tell where truth ends and legend begins […] She is said to be both ruthless and cruel. When her ships are merely doing patrol duty she does not bother to accompany them, but when she goes out 'on business' she attends to it personally. When she climbs aboard any of her ships there is an ill-wind blowing for someone." My Li Choi San has also moved much further south, closer to *Missee Lee*'s un-mapped Three Islands.

Neither *Peter Duck* nor I have ventured so far east. I learned a great deal about modern China from Leslie Chang's book *Factory Girls* and Deborah Fallows' *Dreaming in Chinese* as well as additional details from my Cantonese friend Karen Lee. I am particularly grateful to Neville Lam, who lives in Shanghai but is a native of Xiamen, for allowing himself to be volunteered into reading an early draft of the manuscript. Any mistakes that have crept in since are all mine.

I'm also grateful to Dr Jane Mounty for telling me about her work for the asylum seeker charity, Medical Justice, which seeks basic rights for detainees.

The logbook tells me that 2007 was the year I met Claudia Myatt. I'd like to thank Claudia for being such a supportive reader as well as the perfect illustrator. My son Frank Thorogood is also wonderfully perceptive and helpful. I'm lucky that David Smith agreed to act as editor once again and that Megan Trudell took on the typesetting and design. It is a pleasure to work with Matti Gardner, John Skermer, Signature Books and Biddles printers. My friends Peter Dowden, Ros Elias Jones and Peter Willis are brilliant confidence-givers in the final stages and I'd particularly like to thank Amanda Craig, Christina Hardyment, Heidi Carhart and Jan Needle for their consistent encouragement. Love and gratitude to all my family, especially Francis.

This is the end of the *Strong Winds* Trilogy. I know as little as Donny about what, if anything, happens next. Like him I've discovered my private passion – for Donny it's sailing, for me it's writing stories. Also like him I've made some marvellous friends: members of the Nancy Blackett Trust and the Arthur Ransome Society, fellow writers at Authors Electric, children at Kessingland C of E Primary School and all the readers who have taken the trouble either to write to me or post reviews.

And, finally, without *Peter Duck*'s kind and expert friends at the Woodbridge Boatyard (Everson's) there would be no nautical adventuring at all. So, special thanks to them.

Julia Jones, April 2012

Maps

Donny's adventures have taken him a little further in each book. Here are the maps he's been drawing.

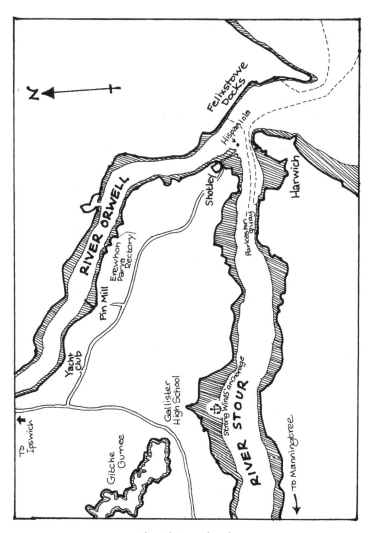

The Salt-Stained Book

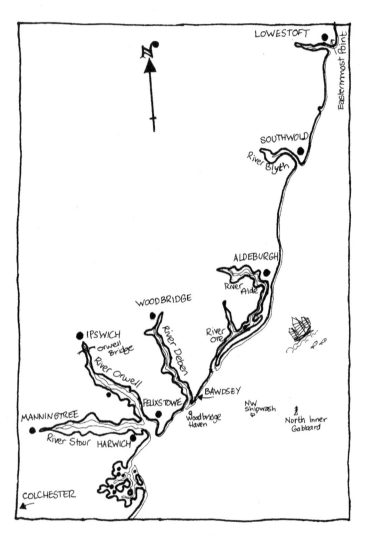

A Ravelled Flag

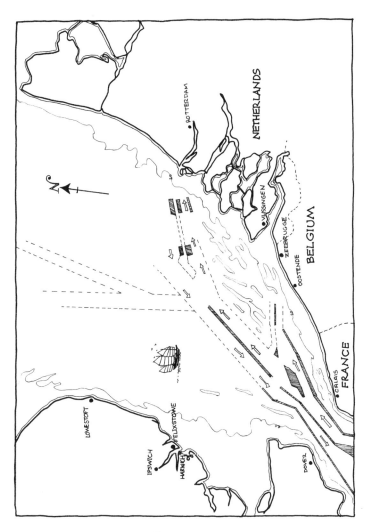

Ghosting Home

Books by Julia Jones

The Strong Winds Trilogy:
Volume I *The Salt-Stained Book*
Volume II *A Ravelled Flag*
Volume III *Ghosting Home*

The Allingham Biography series:

The Adventures of Margery Allingham

Cheapjack by Philip Allingham
(edited with Francis Wheen)

*The Oaken Heart: the story of an
English village at war* by Margery Allingham
(edited with Lesley Simpson)

*Fifty Years in the Fiction Factory: the working life
of Herbert Allingham* (forthcoming 2012)

Julia has ideas for a new series of stories but
no titles yet. Please keep in touch via Golden
Duck — either using the website www.
golden-duck.co.uk, the facebook page or our
Essex address.

Books by Claudia Myatt

RYA Go Sailing: a practical guide for young people

RYA Go Sailing Activity Book

RYA Go Cruising: a young crew's guide to sailing and motor cruisers

RYA Go Cruising Activity Book

RYA Go Inland: a young person's guide to Inland Waterways

RYA Go Green: a young person's guide to the blue planet

RYA Go Windsurfing (forthcoming)

Log Book for Children (new edition)

Buttercup's Diary and other tales

Claudia is an illustrator, an author and an artist. Visit her website www.claudiamyatt. co.uk to discover more about her work.